The little black dress team

Five interesting things about A. M. Goldsher:

1. If you laid all of A. M. Goldsher's CDs on the ground in one single row, it would run from the Tower of London to somewhere around Windsor Castle.

2. Favorite food: sushi. Favorite dessert: sushi. Favorite snack: sushi. Favorite position: sushi.

3. According to the author's mother, A. M. began reading aloud at the age of two. First book? *Valley of the Dolls*.

4. Goldsher hasn't paid for a haircut since 1995.

5. A former sportswriter, the author has seen far too many professional basketball players wearing not nearly enough clothes.

The True Naomi Story

A. M. Goldsher

First published in 2007
by LITTLE BLACK DRESS
An imprint of HEADLINE PUBLISHING GROUP

First published in paperback in 2008
by LITTLE BLACK DRESS
An imprint of HEADLINE PUBLISHING GROUP

A LITTLE BLACK DRESS paperback

2

ISBN 978 0 7553 3992 1

Typeset in Transit511BT by Avon DataSet Ltd, Bidford-on-Avon, Warwickshire

Printed and bound in Great Britain by Clays Ltd, St Ives plc

Headline's ... recyclable products ar... ogging and manufac... nmental

Prologue

These days, I get a little weirded out whenever I wander through one of those big national chain bookstores, not because I have issues with the stores themselves – any place that sells books, CDs and coffee is A-okay with me – but because it feels like their shelves are clogged with shoddily written biographies of yours truly.

I mean, check out some of these goofy titles: there's Naomi: A Woman, a Singer and an Artist. *Totally cheesy, right? Then there's* Diving Inside Naomi's Head. *I bet some people think that one's pornographic, and despite what a certain UK-based tell-all magazine claimed, I am far from pornographic. Then there's* Songbird: Naomi For Real, *which, according to my friend Marnie – who, for some reason, actually read the thing – is anything* but *real.*

There're almost a dozen more of these books, but I've purged their goofy titles from my memory. Then again, the title I came up with for the book that you're holding in your hot little hands isn't the best title in the world either. But when your name is Naomi and the folks at your publishing house are looking for the biggest and bestest name recognition possible in order to sell a bajillion copies of your book, well, your options are sort of limited.

All of those books are unauthorized, but not this one. This is the real deal. And since it's the real deal, it has to be accurate. So, my friends, let the accuracy begin . . .

Part One

Trouble at Tweeter

When Jenn quit the band, she quit *loudly*. So loudly, in fact, that you might want to cover your ears.

'I am totally outta here.'

'What?'

'I quit.'

'Hunh?'

'I quit. You heard me.'

Of course I heard her. The entire state of Illinois heard her.

'I'm quitting,' Jenn yelled, 'because you act like everything is all Naomi, all the time, and yeah, you're the one that the people see and hear first and foremost, fine, I accept that, you've been out front since day one, but it seems like you've conveniently forgotten there're three other people on stage with you, and one of them – namely me – is pretty much the person who makes this band sound the way it sounds, and if we don't sound the way we sound, we're still stuck at Beaned playing for, like, sixty people, and people are gonna realize that when they hear my solo stuff – and they *will* hear my solo stuff, trust me on that one, Naomi – and I'm also outta here because of what you've done to my brother, and I don't care that you didn't mean to, you did it, it's done, it can't be undone, and you know what else, well, I'm almost embarrassed to admit this in front of the entire tour bus, but I will because I'm on a roll here, but part of the reason I'm outta here is because I wanted this guy, and you took him, and he macked on me, and I didn't go for it, and I didn't tell you, and I don't know why, and whether you know it or not, honey, these are the kinds of things that tear bands apart, and, for that matter, tear friendships apart!'

It was the kind of harsh run-on sentence that makes you want to find safety under a fort of down-filled, satin-covered, perfume-scented pillows. The kind of harsh run-on sentence that makes you want to jump out of a tour-bus window. The kind of harsh run-on sentence that makes you want to throw somebody out of a tour-bus window.

The kind of harsh run-on sentence that makes you want to give up Double Stuf Oreos as atonement for your sins.

Later on, I feebly joked to both Marnie and our tour manager Gib that we should've named this tour 'The Murphy's Law Tour'. That would've been kind of funny, actually; the record label could've made up a bunch of those high-school letterman tour jackets. You know which ones I'm talking about, the ones with the big letter on the front, and the faux-leather sleeves. They could've had a huge 'N' for Naomi pasted on the right breast, the phrase 'And Then' – which, as I'm sure you know, is the name of our biggest selling single – embroidered on the left, and, in big letters on the back, 'THE MURPHY'S LAW TOUR'.

Okay, I'm exaggerating a little bit. If you tell people you're living a Murphy's Law existence, it implies *everything* is going wrong, and that wasn't the case here – it was just that one big wrong accompanied by a handful of little wrongs. Even so, the letterman jackets would've been pretty hilarious.

Then again, I was selling enough records – or, as Mitch Busey and the fine folks at Éclat Records kept putting it, 'putting up mad numbers' – that they could've afforded to skip the letterman thingies and do up those jackets in leather. And I don't mean leather like motorcycle jacket leather, but rather leather like a light brown, Roberto Cavalli soft calf skin. Granted, those retail for as much as $3000, but I *was* 'putting up mad numbers', remember? (It's worth noting that in my pre-mad-number-putting-up days, I had no idea what soft calf-skin leather was, nor had I ever heard of Roberto Cavalli.)

In any event, it all came to a head in Chicago, which had become one of my favorite cities. Before our first tour, this born-and-bred Brooklyn girl had hardly been *anywhere*. But once my band and I hit the road, once I got a taste of life away from the East Coast, I fell in love with traveling, the freshness of setting foot in a new city, smelling the non-New York smells, walking on the relatively clean non-New York sidewalks, checking out the local boutiques. And by the time we pulled into Chicago for what was the third time, I'd seen enough of America to be able to discern just how wonderful the Windy City was. But if you're being accurate – and like I said, this book *has* to be accurate, if only so you awesome fans will stop buying any of those aforementioned cheesy bios – we weren't actually in Chicago, but rather in Tinley Park, a suburb about fifty miles south of the city.

Chicago had been great to me, but Tinley Park that night, not so much. I guess the good Chicago vibes got lost somewhere on Interstate 57, which was unfortunate, because the Tweeter Center is where the big boys and big girls play. Like Earth, Wind & Fire. Like Alanis Morrisette. Like Barry Manilow. And I don't want to hear a single nasty comment about Barry Manilow. The guy rocks.

The Tweeter is what Mitch Busey and those music

industry types refer to as a 'shed', which is loosely defined as 'a state-of-the-art outdoor concert arena with a bandshell that seats six thousand or so people, and a lawn area with room for another three thousand'. Do some quick addition, and you'll see that when those places were filled up – as was the case almost every night on this particular tour – that meant there were over ten thousand watching and listening to me sing. But by that time, I was used to performing for a *lot* of people.

Right before we hit the stage, I peered out from the wings at the crowd, and while it was great to see a multitude of people in the seats, it was even greater to see the lawn. Not the people seated on the lawn, but rather the lawn itself. I pictured myself on that lawn with some wine, some bread and brie, some grapes – and me cuddled up in Seymour's lap. Or *somebody's* lap. Seymour's lap, while truly comfortable, had been giving me grief. Well, not his lap, actually – more like the rest of him. What I *didn't* picture, especially in light of me and my band's crises, was giving those ten thousand people their money's worth.

I had another problem that night, and from my perspective, for a few minutes, that crisis seemed as bad, if not worse than the Jenn or Seymour issues.

That problem: my bra.

Marnie, my assistant/styling goddess/masseuse/jack-ette-of-all-trades, was out for a late dinner with one of her local friends, so I was left to my own devices that night, which, considering the complexity of the infamous brassiere was not a good thing. I'd gotten better at putting on the space-age undergarment without help, but, as I learned that night, if you're in a rush when you're jamming on the thing all by your lonesome, it's virtually impossible to do it right. (That's fine German engineering for ya.) Instead of suppleness, lift and separation, I got stagnancy and aureole. The aureole part would've thrilled Mitch Busey and the fine folks at Éclat Records no end – nothing would've made them happier than if I got all skanktafied like, say, [Allegedly Virginal Ho-Bag-Looking Blonde Diva], or [Pint-Sized Ho-Bag-Looking Sometimes Blonde Sometimes Brunette Diva], or [Has-Been Fake-Boobed Ho-Bag Diva Perpetually On the Verge of a Comeback]. These girls, the record label folks believed, were my competition. And one of the best ways to keep up with the competition, in their horny, chauvinistic minds, was to fight sex with sex.

Despite the fact that by then I'd more or less come to terms with how my body looks, I was less-than-proud of my less-than-boobs, and it would've been way too embarrassing to give the first few rows a peek at them. But it would've been way *more* embarrassing to ask Jenn or Travis or Frank for help, so I hit the stage in a state that would've made [Pint-Sized Ho-Bag-Looking Sometimes Blonde Sometimes Brunette Diva] proud.

So here's the official Murphy's Law scorecard: the bra was messed up. Jenn was mad at me – although I didn't know just how mad until after the show, when she relinquished her position as our band's keyboardist/chief composer/musical director/background vocalist. I was mad at Jenn, mostly because she was mad at me. Frank was annoyed with everybody, and justifiably so, because everybody was being annoying, myself included, and Frank didn't like it when his fellow musicians were being annoying, because Frank is all music, all the time, screw the drama. As for Travis, he was seemingly mad at . . . *nobody*. But considering what he'd been through, I was surprised our floppy-haired, sweet-natured, easygoing bass player hadn't developed an ulcer. But I had to sing, Murphy's Law notwithstanding, and I'm a trouper, always have been, and the show must go on, so the show went on. And what a show it was.

The Hoohah Johnson Experience opened up for us, and those guys almost stole our thunder. They always kicked ass, but that night, they cranked their energy level up a notch or four. Hoohah's first single had only been out for a week, but their worshipful fans, already well familiar with their new material via some in-concert bootlegs that a fan had illegally uploaded, sang along with that soon-to-be hit with as much gusto as our worshipful fans would later sing along with 'And Then'. We knew we had to throw it down hard just to save face.

Guess what? We threw it down hard. My band mates, always in fine form, were in *finer* than fine form that hot summer night. Travis and Frank were flying in bass-and-drum heaven. Our rented string section – they were only on the road with us for a couple weeks, so I don't remember any of their individual names, please forgive me – proved to be worth the money, laying down a bed of harmonic goodness that had me imagining Seymour and I doing dirty, dirty things out on the Tweeter Center's lawn. (Yeah, the guy had become a thorn in my side, but he was great at doing those dirty, dirty things.) And Jenn – my partner, my protector, my oldest friend in the world, and the best musician I've ever performed with – kicked the piano's ass.

So we played song after song after song and then, next thing I knew, it was our third encore, and we kicked into 'And Then', for the bajillionth time. I'm not complaining about how frequently we've performed 'And Then', mind you; no matter how often I sing it for an audience – and I sing it a *lot*, at every single one of our concerts, for that matter – it gives me chills, each time, without fail. I always feel a tangible love radiating from the crowd; a love for that sweet, sexy Jenn-penned ode to romance. But how could they not fall in love with it? The tune is so honest, and heartfelt, and sincere, and earnest, and straight-up *hot* that they can't *help* but fall in love. Not for nothin', but they also fall in love with me a little bit, because it's me who's doing the singing. But that love vibe shouldn't really be for me, in a way, because 'And Then' isn't really my song. It's Jenn's. I just borrowed it from her. And she never asked for it back, not once, not even when she was ready to strangle me with a mic cord.

We finished the song, and, with the Tweeter crowd's cheers still ringing in our ears, Gib hustled us offstage, past the dressing rooms, past our crew people, and on to our tour bus. Always precise and punctual – and I love punctuality – Gib didn't like us to dawdle. He constantly feared that some overzealous fan might find their way backstage and try to grope Jenn's top, or my bottom – or, as likely would've been the case that evening, my aureole – so night after night, the moment the curtain dropped, we were outta there.

I went into the back of the bus and tore off that stupid, German-engineered bra which, much to the chagrin of Mitch Busey and the fine folks at Éclat Records, I destroyed, costing them about $6,500. I threw on my favorite light blue flannel jammies, slinked into the middle section of the bus, and crawled into my bunk.

What seemed like three seconds later, Jenn screamed, 'BAND MEETING!'

I rolled out of my bunk, crashed on to the floor, skinned my knee, then crawled up to the front of the bus. Jenn glared at me and said, 'Naomi, get up off your knees. Save that for Ass Boy.'

Frank looked away, embarrassed beyond words. Travis looked away, both embarrassed and disheartened.

'That's really cold,' I told Jenn.

She shrugged. 'Just calling it like I see it, honey.' Travis and Frank looked like they'd be happy to jump out of the bus right then and there – especially Travis – even though we were cruising along at about eighty miles an hour.

'You've made your position on the Seymour matter abundantly clear,' I said.

'And you've made your position with Ass Boy abundantly clear, too. Or should I say *positions*?'

'Now you're just being mean.'

'Hey, if the kneepads fit,' Jenn said.

Frank mumbled, 'On that note, I'd like to point out that it's way past my bedtime, and I'd really like to be in my bunk right now.'

And on that note, I'm going to tell you about Jenn Bradford.

Jennifer Bradford: Friend Extraordinaire, Goddess of the Piano, Giver of Awesome Advice and Encouragement

'Can you imagine how that conversation would go?' I asked Jenn the morning she unilaterally decided we were going to become rock stars. ' "Mom, Dad, guess what, Jenn and I want to be professional musicians, so maybe you could just hand me my college fund, because it'll be impossible to be rock stars while at the same time going to classes and stuff." That'd go over great.'

'It *would* go over great,' Jenn said. 'Your parents are mad cool, and they'd totally tell you to go for it.' This kind of positivity is one of the many reasons I unconditionally love Jennifer Bradford. No, I don't just love her, I *lurve* her, always have, always will. She's the sister this only child always dreamed of.

She's also the other half of my musical heartbeat; something I realized back in high school, back when Jenn and I would sit up in her bedroom and jam for hours at a time. We jammed on her amazing original tunes, and Joni Mitchell tunes, and Ani DiFranco tunes, and Sleater-

Kinney tunes, and Suzanne Vega tunes, and – when we got tired of making estrogen music – Beatles tunes. All this jamming did wonders for my voice, and for Jenn's ability to compose, accompany, and harmonize. After we graduated high school, we decided to become a band. Or as much of a band as a singer and a keyboardist could be.

As it turned out, Jenn was right about my parents. Not only did they tell me to take a stab at rock stardom, but they demonstrated some serious awesomeness by giving me a chunk of my college fund without me even asking. Jenn's parents also gave her a chunk, and next thing you know, we're settled into a tiny, starving-artist apartment in the East Village. We knew our respective chunks wouldn't last long, so both of us got jobs at a cute but lamely named coffee shop in Chelsea called Beaned. Bonnie, the manager, adored us primarily because we were wonderful servers. Actually, Jenn was a wonderful server who always had the customers eating out of her hand. Me, I was a decent server who managed to only spill three vanilla caramel lattes a week.

Three months into our stint, Jenn suggested to Bonnie that it might be mutually advantageous if Beaned were to present live music, specifically, us. A hardcore music fan, Bonnie agreed, and soon we were playing there every Wednesday night. Our temporary band name was The Intrepid Duo – silly, I know, but like I said, it was temporary. After about eight Wednesdays, in spite of Beaned's limited capacity and low-tech sound system, we had some fans. That's right, ladies and gentleman: skinny, klutzy Naomi Braver had fans.

Sadly, having fans didn't help me in the kissable boys department. You see, at that point in my life, I longed to kiss a kissable boy, as my lips and tongue were virginal. No kisses for Naomi. I knew it would be tough to get the male division of our fan base to kiss me, because they were all in love with Jenn, so I didn't even bother trying. Jenn – who, at the time, was juggling three or four boys, and had no interest in adding another one to the pile – sensed correctly I was bumming about my lack of success in the dating department, and when I was bummed, she was bummed, so she constantly offered me advice and encouragement, all of which was awesome.

'Naomi, let's face facts: you are a stone hottie. I know you don't think so, but you totally are. And it's not just your face and your body. It's also your voice, your demeanor, and your heart. Your insides are great, and so are your outsides. But I have to tell you, honey, your outsides could use some tweaking.

'Now I know you're Miss Anti-Make-Up, so I'm not talking a Tammy Faye Baker makeover here. Nothing drastic or dramatic. Just some Lancôme foundation – Maquicontrole is my personal fave – and maybe some Stila demi-blush – rose amber would look *so* phenomenal on you. Also, maybe a just a touch of Victoria's Secret Bronze Goddess Mosaic Power, and maybe some L'Oreal Endlessly Kissable – Shamelessly Nude would be a great color, because it's almost like you're wearing nothing at all – and a little bit of Christian Dior Maximize Mascara, and I'm thinking a scooch of Bare Escentuals shadow, and some nice Vincent Longo eyeliner.

'Oh, quit making that face. I know you think that's a lot of make-up, but it's not, and we won't put it on all at once, obviously, but what we put on, we'll put on so artfully that you'll look one hundred per cent natural. Okay, maybe ninety-six per cent natural, but that's cool. I've been operating at ninety-two per cent for the last five years, and that seems to be working pretty okay.

'We'll also hit Seventh Street, and go to all those thrift stores, and find you some cute little outfits that'll show off your figure. Yeah, I know you think you have no figure, but you *totally* do. You have kind of a heroin chic model thing going on, except you look healthy. If you work it right, you could totally be Beaned's official long, lanky model girl. You are The Woman, with a capital T, and a capital W.

'And that voice of yours? Now I know that *you* know that you're the best singer in the world, even though you'd never say it out loud. And you talk so sexy. Deep. Throaty. God, imagine what you could do to boys with that voice if you put your mind to it. I mean, if this singing thing doesn't work out – which it will, so I shouldn't even have to say that – but if it doesn't, you could make a ton of money doing phone sex. Work it, girl. Work it *hard*.'

She was inspirational, no doubt. So the next Saturday at Beaned, after a rigorous make-up session, an excellent reason to 'work it hard' dropped right into my lap.

Walking on Sunshine

He was tall. Pierced. Buff. Baggy skater-boy shorts. Baggy button-down shirt unbuttoned to the third button. Shaved head. Big smile. Stubble. Alone. Headphones on. Bopping to his iPod. Reading the liner notes from an Ani DiFranco CD. I *love* Ani DiFranco. And he was eyeing me. Not Jenn, the hottest girl in the place. Not Bonnie – who was quite the beauty herself, albeit in a sort of hippie-ish way. No, it was me!

Nowadays, since I'm on TV all the time, I get eyed pretty much whenever I set foot outside the house, and it's been that way for a couple of years, and it's gotten to the point that I can't help but notice. But back then, I was oblivious to that sort of thing. Jenn, on the other hand, *always* notices, so she sidled over, elbowed me in the ribs, and said, 'I think that boy is giving you the once-over. And he's cute. You take that table.'

'But he's in your section. You need the money.'

'You do too. But you also need to get laid. This virgin thing isn't doing much for your disposition.'

I glared at her. She knew I hadn't found the right guy – no one had even come close – and she knew my sex life, or lack thereof, was a subject I wasn't comfortable discussing in the confines of our minuscule apartment, let alone at work on a crowded Saturday. 'Can it, Jenn.'

'Nay, trust me, you'll be a better singer when you start getting consistent sex, because the more life experience you have, the better artist you'll be. Not that your singing isn't gorgeous now, but—'

'I told you to can it.'

Bonnie wandered over and asked, 'What's going on?'

I glared at Jenn again and said, 'Nothing. Ms Bradford and I were discussing something that shouldn't be discussed during work hours, let alone at our place of employment.'

Bonnie grinned and rubbed her hands together. 'Sounds interesting. Must be about sex.'

Jenn nodded. 'Yes, Bonnie, we're discussing Ms Braver's love life, or lack thereof . . .'

'Can it!'

'. . . and how it would behoove her to take that shaved-headed gentleman's order, even though he's in my section.'

Bonnie craned her neck to check out the guy. 'Ooh, he's cute. Naomi, if you don't want his table, I'm all over it.'

'No way, Bonnie,' Jenn said. 'This one's Naomi's. He's been checking her out since he walked in.'

Bonnie nodded and gave me a gentle shove in the direction of his table. 'Cool. Go get him, girl.'

I wandered over, and he gave me a warm, inviting smile that set off a roller coaster ride in the pit of my stomach. I couldn't help but feel more comfortable, couldn't help but smile back. 'Hey. How are you today? What can I get you? We have a special vanilla caramel—'

'Naomi Braver.'

My mouth formed a perfect 'O'. 'Do I know you?'

'Yep. We went to high school together.'

'We did?'

'Yep. Don't you remember? Senior year? Chem class? Lab partners?'

'*Tony Esposito??!?*'

He gave me a lopsided grin. 'Yep. Small world, huh?'

The combination of Tony's lopsided grin, his smoky voice, and the memory of his deep, dark, shiny black hair transformed me from Naomi Braver, the singer/East Village resident/almost cool chick to Naomi Braver, the tongue-tied, brainiac dweeb. 'I . . . er . . . um . . . I didn't recognize . . . you know . . . hair . . . gone . . .'

Tony chuckled. 'I totally recognized you, even though you're definitely cuter than you were back in school. Not that you weren't cute back then, but, y'know.'

I plopped down on the chair opposite his. As another roller coaster ride loop-the-looped through my tummy, I said, 'Mjopwieqr.' Then I took a deep breath, pulled myself together, and managed to get out a lucid thought. 'So what're you up to now?'

He mirrored my deep breath. 'Getting ready to get back to Harvard. Can't wait for the semester to start. I also can't wait for it to finish. Where're you at? I'm guessing Yale or Brown.'

'Nope. East Village U.'

Another lopsided grin. ' 'Scuse me?'

'Remember Jenn Bradford?' I pointed to Jenn, who was doing a horrible job of pretending she wasn't watching us. 'We have a place together on Houston, right by the Bowery. We've been performing a lot for the last couple years.'

He craned his neck so he could see over my shoulder and gave Jenn a half-wave. Jenn returned it, then pointed at me and gave a thumbs up, as if to say, *Naomi rocks*. 'Performing?' Tony asked.

'Oh, yeah. I sing, and she plays piano and writes songs, and honestly, we're pretty damn good.' Get me talking about singing, and just like that, I'm Ms Confident – even around a crushable, kissable boy like Tony.

'That sounds really cool,' he said. 'But I can't believe you're not at, like, an Ivy League school, kicking academic ass. You're much smarter than I am. Or, I guess, you *were* much smarter than I *was*. But it's probably still the case. I was *so* intimidated by you in chem class.'

'*You*? Intimidated by *me*?'

'Yeah. I'm a pretty intelligent guy, I guess, but your brains were *mercurial*.'

Nobody had ever called my brains 'mercurial'. My dad said I had good head on my shoulders. Jenn claimed I was The Intrepid Duo's way smarter half. Travis once mumbled, 'I love your . . . I.Q.' But 'mercurial'? That particular adjective had never been used to describe any part of me. (Interestingly enough, there was an article in *Billboard* right after our first album came out that said my voice was mercurial. That was flattering, but I liked it better when Tony said it.)

And then there was his assertion that *I* intimidated *him*. That was such a bizarre concept I was unable to process it, let alone make a comment. Eventually I pulled myself together and said, ' "Mercurial", eh? Guess they're teaching you some pretty big words up in Cambridge.'

Tony shrugged. 'Osmosis, I guess. I feel like I haven't learned jack. Matter of fact, I blew off most of my classes last semester. *Borrrrrrring*.'

'So what're you doing up there?'

'Partying. Chilling. Writing. Designing websites. Working out.' He rubbed his scalp. 'Shaving my head.'

'Yeah, what's the deal with that? You had some pretty awesome hair.' It took massive restraint not to refer to his hair as 'beautiful' or 'rich' or 'breath-taking' or 'the mane that made me walk into walls'.

'I joined the swim team after first semester. I shaved my head, and waxed my legs, and my chest, and, um, my entire body. Kind of started liking it, so I've been doing it ever since.'

Jenn, tray topped with three mocha lattes in hand, chose that moment to come over and say hi. She kicked my chair, which I assumed was a signal telling me that I was doing well. 'What's happening over here, you wacky kids? Looks like you're having a good old time.'

'Jenn, you remember Tony Esposito, don't you?'

'Tony. Do remember you. Didn't recognize you at first, though. What's the deal with the shaved head?'

'Hey, Jenn,' he chuckled. 'You guys both look great. Especially you, Naomi.'

She kicked my chair twice, then said, 'Well, that's my exit cue. I'll leave you two wacky kids alone.'

'Good seeing you, Jenn,' Tony said. 'Maybe all three of us could hang out together before I head back up north. I've fallen out of touch with more or less everybody, so I have plenty of free time.'

After Jenn wandered off, I told Tony about The Intrepid Duo's Wednesday-night concerts, and he promised he'd come and hear us perform at some point in the very near future. Just then, I noticed that two people had sat down at a table in my section; Bonnie also noticed, and gave me a loud *ahem*. So I took Tony's order (large decaf with sugar and a lemon poppy-seed muffin – yes, I still remember) and went back to work, walking on sunshine. And it felt good.

A Flashback From High School, Starring a Certain Kissable Boy Who Had the Blackest Hair Ever

I used to have a thing for boys with deep, dark, shiny black hair, so it would only stand to reason that I spent a solid chunk of my high-school years gawking at Tony Esposito. I mooned over Tony in freshman year English, sophomore year trig, and junior year African history. I gawked at Tony when I was lucky or unlucky enough to share a hallway with him – and I say 'unlucky' because more than once, my gawking led to minor-but-embarrassing collisions with walls, and/or lockers, and/or my fellow students. Even at packed student-body assemblies, I usually managed to pick him out of the throng, thanks to that hair, that hair, that glorious hair.

Back then, I was tragically lacking in talking-to-boys skills – especially boys with deep, dark, shiny black hair – and I was never able to muster up the courage to introduce myself to Tony Esposito, so it was quite possible that, despite our numerous shared classes, he had no idea who I was. (We were in so many classes together because he was a brainiac, and I was a brainiac, and our school kept the brainiacs separated from the great unwashed.) Tony was super popular, easily the most popular non-jock in school, one of the many reasons I wasn't keen to put the moves on him.

Jenn knew about my crush, and Jenn being Jenn, she did everything she could to boost my confidence to the point that I'd feel comfortable macking on Tony. She'd come up to me at my locker and say, 'Renée Miller told me that as of yesterday, Tony is officially *sans* girlfriend. Make a move, Nay Nay.' (I didn't mind when Jenn called me 'Nay'. But 'Nay Nay'? Not so much.) Or at the end of one of our rehearsals, she'd note, 'Tony looked really cute today. If you don't jump him at lunch tomorrow, I might have to step in.' Her saying that didn't bother me, because she'd never do anything like that. Besides, she had five boyfriends at that point, and taking on another one would've been a logistical nightmare.

One day she got totally fed up with my whining, and said, 'Quit being such a wuss, Naomi. He's just a boy. *Jeez*.' But shedding my wussiness was easier said than done. I mean, if Tony was untouchable by the likes of me from freshman to junior year, then come senior year, he was *un*-untouchable. I don't know what he did during the summer before his final year of high school, but when I saw him in chemistry class the first day of first semester, he looked the hottest he'd *ever* looked – and that was pretty damn hot. Maybe it was his subtle-but-still-noticeable tan. Maybe it was his Hollywood-sexy stubble. Maybe it was his newly classy wardrobe; during the years previous, he'd been a T-shirt and jeans guy, but that year, we were looking at form-fitting button-down tops and perfectly ironed slacks. His cool, masculine beauty was intimidating, but what ultimately made him *him* was his newfound sense of self-possession. He exuded a seemingly unattainable grown-up-ness.

Summing up, Tony Esposito was an Italian preppy God whose hair I wanted to touch only once, even just with the tip of my pinky.

This was why I was a tad disconcerted when he was assigned to be my chem lab partner. No way did I want Tony Esposito as my lab partner. Minor-but-embarrassing accidents notwithstanding, it was safe enough to gaze at him longingly from a distance, but having to sit only inches away from him for fifty minutes a day would have been torture. That said, I knew that, in those close confines, we'd inevitably become pals, because our high school's version of senior chem was incredibly difficult; a class in which you can't help but become pals with your lab partner, if only to hold on for dear life – all of which meant my level of infatuation would inflate to the nth degree.

Jenn was optimistic. Of course she was. If she decided she wanted to date her lab partner, they'd have plans for that evening before they even cracked their textbooks, so it made sense that she thought the lab-partner development was positively serendipitous. 'This is destiny,' she said during one of our many rehearsals up in her bedroom. 'It's like a signal from the heavens above. This is the boy you've been crushing on for the past three years, and he's literally fallen into your lap.'

'What's the point of even discussing it? We both know he won't go out with me.' I looked at her door, and whispered, 'And could we not talk about this now? Your little brother is probably sitting out there.'

Jenn nodded then tiptoed over to the door, her index finger touching her lips and shushing me. She smacked the door with the heel of her hand, then threw it open. Her little brother Travis was laying on the floor, grimacing, and holding his ear, clearly in pain, clearly itching to sprint away. Jenn grabbed his collar and said, 'Travis, I swear to God, if I find you eavesdropping again, I'm gonna break your skateboard over your head.'

He looked like he was ready to burst into tears. 'I was just waiting for you to start playing another song. I swear.'

Jenn said, 'As you heard, little brother, we haven't played a note in, like, twenty minutes. And as you *also* heard, we were talking, and not about music. At some point, you had to realize we weren't gonna be playing anything for a while, right?'

He shrugged. 'I guess.'

'Travis,' Jenn said, 'Naomi and I love that you love our music, but if I catch you at the door listening to us do anything other than play music, well, I wasn't kidding about the skateboard.'

After Jenn slammed the door on him, she turned to me and asked, 'Now what were you saying?'

'I was saying we're done discussing this.'

Jenn shook her head. 'No, we're not. Here's what you're gonna do: you're gonna confirm it.'

'Confirm what?'

'Confirm that he doesn't like you.'

'And how am I supposed to do that?'

'You ask him out.'

I shook my head in a big way. 'No way. Not gonna happen.'

'Yes, it *is* gonna happen. Here's the deal: by the end of this week, you are going to ask Tony Esposito to hang out with you. Not necessarily a date – just a hang-out.' She even offered to put together a group outing with her boyfriend, and some of her boyfriend's friends, and some of her boyfriend's friends' girlfriends.

'But if I do ask him out and he says no – which we both

know is exactly what'll happen – that "no" is gonna be hanging over our lab table for the next two months.'

'So what? After graduation, when he's off at Yale or Brown or wherever, you'll never see him again. Besides, while he's off at Yale or Brown or wherever, you'll be living in a funky apartment in Manhattan, singing night after night after night at some funky club, and you'll have boys falling at your feet, and Tony Esposito will be a distant memory.'

'Jennnnnn,' I whined.

'Nayyyyyyy,' she whined right back, 'here's the other deal: if you don't ask him out, you're not allowed to say the name "Tony Esposito" in my presence ever again. As a matter of fact, you're not even allowed to say the name "Tony", or even "Anthony". But if you do ask him out, and he says no, I promise you can cry on my shoulder about him whenever you want to for the rest of your life.'

She shamed me into it, but it still took a good three weeks for me to work up the nerve to do the actual deed. The fact that Tony and I had developed a solid working relationship made me feel a bit less stressed about the whole thing. Even so, on the big day, I was a mess.

It was a Thursday. I was wearing what I thought was my cutest outfit: a black T-shirt that was small enough to be baby-dollish, but big enough so that it didn't show off too much of my non-existent tummy; black jeans; and my black Chuck Taylor All-Stars. I'd straightened my normally cowlicky hair, so it hung down just below my shoulders. That afternoon's fifty-minute chemistry class seemed to take fifty hours.

A few seconds after the period-ending bell rang, I turned to Tony and spewed out the mini-monologue I'd rehearsed the previous night as I lay in bed not sleeping: 'HeyTony OnSaturdayJennBradfordAndMeAndABunchOfOther PeopleAreGoingOutToDoSomethingIDon'tKnowWhat

We'reDoingButItShouldBeFunAndItMightInvolvePizza AndIWasWonderingIfYou'dLikeToJoinUs.' When I get nervous, I have a tendency to speak in run-on sentences, but that was beyond a run-on sentence. It was a run-on word.

Tony's facial expression gave away nothing. 'I'm not sure, Naomi. Let me let you know tomorrow.'

I was shocked he didn't say no right off the bat, so shocked that all I could say was, 'Mjopwieqr.'

'Okay. Catch you tomorrow,' he said, then he took off.

That afternoon during rehearsal, I casually said to Jenn, 'So I asked Tony out today.'

'Really?!??! *Awesome*!' She looked at the door and yelled, 'Travis! Take a hike!' We then heard the pitter-patter of little feet running away. 'What'd he say?'

'Nothing definitive. He's getting back to me tomorrow.'

'I knew it,' she said, smiling hugely.

'Knew what?'

'That he's looking for a pre-graduation fling. And you're it.'

I sighed. 'I seriously doubt that, Jenn. He's probably on the phone right now with one of his buddies saying, "My skinny little lab partner asked me out today. I should probably blow off chem class for the rest of the year." '

I didn't fall asleep that night until well past 4.00 a.m. That was the second night in a row I'd gotten less than five hours of sleep, so that day I wasn't looking my best. I wandered through the hallways in a sleep-deprived daze, willing myself to be alert for seventh period. I had study hall before chem, which was easy enough to blow off, so I arrived to the empty lab a full ten minutes early, plopped down at my and Tony's workstation, and waited.

Tony walked into the room right before the bell rang. 'Hey, Naomi,' he said.

'Hey, Tony.' And then, after what seemed like a bajillion hours, I asked, 'So, um, y'know, er, um, Saturday –'

He fiddled with his notes, then, never raising his eyes to meet mine, he said, 'I'm working on Saturday night, so I'm not gonna be able to get together. Sorry.'

That sounded mildly promising, so I said, 'Jenn and I hang out almost every Saturday night.' That was a lie – she was usually out with her boyfriends, and I was usually in with my parents – but desperate times called for desperate measures and I knew she'd back me up anyhow. 'You're welcome to join us any time. Like next Saturday.'

'I'm working then, too.'

'The Saturday after?'

'Working.'

'After that?'

'Not sure yet, but most likely working.'

'The Saturday after?'

Tony Esposito finally looked at me and sighed, 'I work a lot, Naomi. A *lot*.'

I got the point. It took a few minutes longer than it would've taken most people to get it, but when I finally got it, boy, did I get it.

I Just Want Your Extra Time and Your . . . You Know What

Impressively enough, Tony Esposito was true to his word; he showed up at Beaned the following Wednesday night at nine, and parked himself in a seat about two yards from the stage. Not only that, but he brought his camcorder. It blew me away that Tony Esposito – *Tony Esposito* – ***TONY ESPOSITO!!!*** – wanted to document me on tape. I mean nobody had ever videoed me performing. Not that I wanted to watch my skinny ass on television, but it was the thought that counted.

Generally, in between sets, I liked to take a walk around the block, just to get my wind back and my head together. It would've been nice to be able to take some deep, cleansing breaths during my walks; unfortunately, this was lower Manhattan, and lower Manhattan is a No Deep Breathing Zone. Not only that, but thanks to the migration of numerous art galleries from Soho to Chelsea, that particular strip had become quite busy, and the sidewalk traffic wasn't conductive to clearing my head. But it was still better than nothing.

That night, three seconds after I stepped outside, I saw

Tony speed-walking after me. When he caught up to me, he gently took my elbow and said, 'You weren't kidding, Naomi. You guys are pretty damn good.'

Back in the day, the combination of his compliment and his hand on my arm would've turned me into a pile of goo. But this was right after a set during which I'd kicked major butt, so I felt almost cocky. 'Toldja so. And we don't even do our best tunes until later.'

'Did you write the songs you guys were playing?'

'Nope. Jenn's the composing half. I just sing. Sometimes, I suggest a lyric or two. Also, I'm pretty good at rearranging some of the stuff. Like that one we opened with, "Problem Identified".' When she first showed it to me, I loved it – I love *all* of her songs – but I thought the hook should be closer to the top, and the bridge should be repeated, so what we did was start out with a chorus instead of the verse, and made the form: chorus, verse, chorus, bridge, then repeated it. That's not a standard form, but I think it makes it catchier. Plus, I love singing the chorus, so the more times, the merrier.'

Tony scratched his shaved head. 'I have no idea what you just said. All I know is I really like that song, and the last one you played was also awesome. If you say the stuff you're gonna sing after the break is even better than that last tune, well, I *have* to stay. What was that last song called?'

' "And Then".'

'It was beautiful. And it was *hot*. I really like that part where you kept singing "And then I'm gonna . . ." What're those lyrics, exactly?'

Even back then, 'And Then' was *everybody*'s favorite Jenn tune – it was my favorite, too – so I was more than happy to give him a little taste of the mid-tempo ballad's sweet-'n'-sexy chorus, right there on the corner of 23rd Street and 8th Avenue. And I belted those six lines out, sidewalk traffic be damned. And if you know the words – and you most likely do – feel free to sing along:

And then I'm gonna wrap you in my arms,
And then I'm gonna keep you safe from harm,
And then I'm gonna cover your neck, your chest,
your legs with an endless kiss.

And then I'm gonna wrap you in my legs,
And then I'm gonna listen to you beg,
For me to never stop doing what I'm doing when
I do it just like this . . .

A couple of guys walked by, applauded, and said, 'You can wrap me with your legs any time you want!'

Tony laughed. 'Yeah, you could probably wrap any guy around your little finger with that song.'

Still feeling cocky, I said, 'Really? Any guy?'

'Probably.'

'Even a guy who used to be my high-school lab partner?'

He looked down, took a step closer to me – he was almost in the most personal part of my personal space – breathed in a lungful of tasty Manhattan air, and said, 'Naomi, you're an awesome girl, and I know we'd have a great time together, but I just got out of a really bad relationship . . .'

'So what?'

'. . . and I'm going back to school in just over a month, and I don't think a random hook-up would be good for either of us.'

Truth be told, I was ready for a hook-up of some kind, *any* kind, random or not, and Tony was my best prospect out there. (Okay, he was my *only* prospect out there, but whatever.) And for me, it wouldn't have been random; this is a guy I obsessed about for most of the latter part of my adolescence. Not too random, as far as I was concerned. 'I appreciate that, Tony,' I said. 'That's very upstanding of you.'

Tony smiled ruefully, then inched his way past that invisible line and into the uttermost personal part of my personal space. 'I'm not very good at this sort of thing,' he said, almost sadly.

'What sort of thing?' I asked.

He shrugged, kissed me on the cheek, and said, 'I should probably go. I'll come check you guys out next week, I promise.' He looked at me as if he was taking inventory of my soul, then trotted off to the subway stairs at the corner.

When I got back to Beaned, Jenn got all up in my face before I could even step inside. 'What happened? What happened? You're flushed. You must've kissed him. Didja kiss him? Didja?'

'Um, well, not exactly.'

'How do you "not exactly" kiss somebody?'

'Well, he kissed me.'

'Cool! Good kisser?'

'Hard to tell. He just gave me cheek.'

Jenn grimaced. '*Booooooo. Hisssssss*. That boy is a wuss. Did you at least give him your number? Or did you get his?'

'No and no. He said he'll come back here next Wednesday.'

'Well, don't think about that now. I'm sure you didn't notice, because you were staring at Tony the entire set, but the place is filled. I can't say it's sold out, per se, because nobody's paying, but there isn't an empty seat in the place.'

She was right. I hadn't noticed. 'Wow.'

'Yeah, wow. So I need you to focus, and sing your ass off.' And that's exactly what I did.

The following Wednesday, Tony further demonstrated his reliability, arriving midway through the first set, camcorder in hand. Beaned was again packed to the rafters, so he was forced to watch us while leaning against the back wall. After we finished, I went on my traditional half-time walk, half hoping he'd chase after me like last week, and half hoping he'd be waiting for me when I returned, and half hoping he'd be gone altogether, so I could fully concentrate on my singing. (Yeah, I know that's three halves, but I think you'd agree that based on what I've told you so far, when it came to Tony Esposito, three halves were necessary.)

As it turned out, he didn't chase after me, but he didn't leave, either. When I got back to Beaned minutes before we were supposed to go on again, there he was, propped against the wall, a rueful-but-eager expression on his face. Okay, I couldn't really discern any ruefulness or eagerness – he was too far away for that – but in light of what eventually happened with us, that's my story, and I'm sticking to it.

I apparently sang well, because the applause was ravenous, and fifteen people asked us when our CD was coming out, and Bonnie asked us if we could sing on Saturdays too, and Jenn kissed me on the lips. That was all nice, but I was dying to know the deal with Tony. I was afraid to go to him, so I helped Jenn pack up the PA. As he ambled up to us, I prepared myself for the worst.

'Hey, Naomi.'

'Hey, Tony.'

'I didn't think it was possible, but that was even better than it was last week.'

'Thanks, Tony.'

'So Naomi, I want to take you on a date. I shouldn't do it. But I'm going to.'

It blew me away that Tony Esposito – *Tony Esposito* – ***TONY ESPOSITO!!!*** – was asking me out. 'Yeah, cool, absolutely, for sure, I'm there, definitely, okay, certainly, without a doubt, fo' shizzle—'

He thankfully interrupted me, and said, 'Is Saturday night okay?' I nodded, and he said, 'Good. I'll call you tomorrow.' After I wrote down my number for him, he gave me a goodbye kiss – cheek only – then wandered slowly towards the subway.

Before he reached the top of the stairs, I called, 'Hey, Tony?'

He spun around. 'Yeah?'

'Ani DiFranco, eh?'

There was that big, goofy grin again. 'Sure. Sometimes boys like chick music.'

Hunh. I had no idea.

All I Want is Food and Creative Love

Jenn threw open the bathroom door and yelled, 'Make sure you don't tell him you're a virgin!'

I was in the shower, my halfway-shaved leg resting on the side of the tub. The entire tub was covered with Nair-saturated, stubble-filled water. 'Um, how about a "Hello"? How about a "Knock-knock, can I come in, Naomi"?'

Jenn sat down on the edge of the tub. 'No time for pleasantries. I have to leave for work in, like, two minutes. We've gotta talk.'

I was in the midst of an intense personal grooming session in preparation for date number four with Tony Esposito. Our first three outings had gone beautifully: long, chatty dinners; slow walks with some quality hand-holding; and several semi-chaste-but-promising goodnight kisses. In Naomiworld, 'semi-chaste' means a tiny bit of tongue, a teeny bit of moisture, an itty bit of teeth, a teensy bit of thigh-on-thigh, and a lot of him playing with my hair. No complaints whatsoever.

It was the best series of dates I'd ever had. (Okay, it was really the *only* series of dates I'd ever had, unless you define 'series' as 'a seemingly endless string of one-and-dones'.) After each of my nights out with Tony, the moment I set foot in the apartment, Jenn – unless she was out on a date of her own – would grill me for details.

She asked who paid. The first night, he did. The second two nights, I insisted on going Dutch.

She asked what he ate. That boy had an astounding appetite. On our second night out, for example, we went for sushi, and he ate five maki rolls, ten pieces of sashimi, a bowl of edemame, a bowl of miso soup, and two scoops of green-tea ice cream. Normally, I pig out at Japanese restaurants, but I was still kind of nervous around him, so I only had two rolls and five pieces of sushi.

She asked if we kissed. As noted, that was an affirmative. Then she asked for a painfully detailed description of the quality of Tony's kisses. I had little to compare them to, so I wasn't sure if Tony was a particularly good smoocher. But his mouth was so warm, and his lips were so full, and his breath was so tasty that, from my perspective, Tony was the best kisser in the history of kissing.

My experienced-in-the-ways-of-love best friend was pleased with the way things had progressed, so much so that she was convinced the dinner I'd prepared for him that night would, in her words, 'seal the deal'.

'What if I don't want the deal sealed just yet?'

'Inviting him to your place for a home-cooked gourmet meal is like putting up a neon sign that says, *TAKE ME, TONY! I'M YOURS*.'

I resumed shearing my legs; they were pretty badly butchered, but that wasn't a tragedy, because it was unlikely Tony would be feeling them up anyhow. 'So that's what my neon sign says, eh? *TAKE ME, TONY, I'M YOURS*?'

'Yeah.'

'I dunno, Jenn. My neon sign is more along the lines of, *I HOPE YOU ENJOY DINNER, TONY*. And that's it.'

'He's a guy. Guys don't read neon signs particularly well.'

'Well, he'd better put on his reading glasses.'

She rolled her eyes and continued on with her *Sex and the City*-like suggestions. 'See, here's the thing: when it comes to sleeping with a guy for the first time—'

'I'm not sleeping with him!'

'Whatever. When it comes to sleeping with a guy for the first time, he's gonna want some idea of what he's getting into beforehand.'

'What he's getting into? Well put.'

'Thanks. So if I were you, I'd be prepared to answer a question or three about your sexual history.'

'I have no sexual history.'

'Yeah, I know that, and you know that, but *he* doesn't have to know that.'

I knew that no matter how much I protested, Jenn would finish her pep talk, regardless of how many times I told her I wasn't going to hook up with Tony. That didn't mean I necessarily wanted to hear it. 'Don't you have to go to work?'

'When I tell Bonnie I was late because I was prepping you for your date, she probably won't complain one bit.' She was right; Bonnie knew I was a virgin, and, like Jenn, felt that everybody in the world should be having sex on a regular basis, and would be perfectly fine with Jenn taking fifteen minutes to council me. 'So when he asks how many boys you've been with, don't tell him you're a virgin.'

'But I am a virgin. And from what I gather, you can't fake virginity.'

'In theory, you're right. But guys are pretty dumb in that area. He'll be so happy he's getting some, he won't notice you're mediocre in bed.' (How did she know I'd be mediocre in bed? Humph.) 'But most guys, when you tell them it's your first time, they freak. They feel pressured. They don't want to screw up, because they know you'll always remember it. And it's not that they're concerned that they'll be crap in the sack. It's just that sometimes stuff goes wrong, especially if it's one of the partner's first time. Sometimes it's nobody's fault. Sometimes it is what it is.'

'Pretty fatalistic.'

'Pretty *realistic*. Point being, you want to alleviate as much pressure as you can.'

'What if I bleed?'

'Tell him, *Oops, I guess my period is starting*.'

'Boy, you've got this all figured out, don't you?'

'I plotted and schemed all morning.'

'And I appreciate it. Now go away. I have to finish mauling my legs, then I have to shower, then I have to put on my make-up.'

'What outfit are you wearing?'

'That black thing with the gray thing and the white thing.'

'I don't know. The black thing works, totally, but maybe you should try it with the red thing.'

'Red and black? No way. Too goth.'

'Maybe the white thing with the red thing. Oooh, no, wait, I've got it – blow off the red thing altogether, and do the gray thing and the white thing with the dark green thing.'

'The dark green thing? Didn't think of that. Good call. Okay, I have a ton of stuff to do, and you need to go away.'

'The least you could do is thank me.'

'Thank you. Now leave.'

'Oooh, I've got it – the dark green thing with the pale yellow thing.'

'*Goodbye*, Jenn.'

'Goodbye. Good luck. Love you.'

'Love you, too.'

Finally, the bathroom was mine, and mine alone. I turned on the shower, rinsed off my legs, then dumped a handful of Pantene Pro-V in my hair. But before I could even work up a full lather, the door flew open, and Jenn yelled over the wooshing water, 'Hey, Naomi, I almost forgot –'

She stuck her arm through the shower curtain and dropped six Ramses prophylactics on to the floor of the tub. The water pelted the condoms; the silvery foil wrappers glistened like a shattered disco ball. 'Be safe, honey.'

'Thanks,' I muttered, kicking the condoms away from the drain. 'You're a princess.'

Forty-five minutes later, after I was cleansed, smelling good, and more or less properly made up, I put on the black thing with the gray thing and the white thing. My fashion sense back then wasn't anywhere near as sharp as it is now, so unsurprisingly, the outfit looked horrible. After trying on a bajillion different combinations, I went with Jenn's final suggestion, the dark green thing with the pale yellow thing. I then ran around the kitchen and put the final touches to dinner. Before I knew it, it was 6.45; Tony was due at 7.00. Punctuality has always been a perverse turn-on for me, so when the doorbell rang at 6.58, my knees quivered.

The first thing I noticed was the black stubble covering his scalp and face. I kissed him, rubbed the top of his head, and asked, 'Rejoining the hair-having world, are we?'

He shrugged. 'Yeah. I've had this weird compulsion to grow it back.' Maybe that was because I'd been beaming grow-it-back vibes at him for the last two weeks. 'Right now,' he continued, 'it looks pretty crappy, and it's just gonna get worse. The in-between part is the worst.'

'That's the same thing I always say when I get a lousy short haircut, then decide to grow it out again.'

'Great minds think alike.'

I stood on my tiptoes and gave him a lingering kiss, then asked, 'Are you hungry?'

'Always. What're we eating?'

'Vegetable lasagna. Caesar salad. Some bread. Some

butter. Some wine. Y'know, nothing special. The kind of stuff I make for myself every night.'

'As long as you didn't go to any trouble.'

As it so happened, I hadn't gone to any trouble. No trouble whatsoever.

Except for when I opened up the freshly bought ricotta, I was nearly overcome with the stench of curdled milk. Turns out the stuff was way past its expiration – my fault for not checking – so I had to go back to the store and exchange it.

And when I overcooked the lasagna noodles and most of them broke in half when I dumped them into the strainer, I had to go to the store *again* and get a box of those idiot-proof no-boil noodles.

And when the tomatoes I'd bought were harder than a rock, and practically neon-green to boot – again, my fault for not paying attention – I had to go to the store *again* and pick out some new ones.

And right after I finished cutting the zucchini, and grating the carrots, and wedging the tomatoes, and chopping the garlic and onions, and slicing the mozzarella, it dawned on me that we didn't have a lasagna pan – of course we didn't; neither Jenn nor I had ever made a lasagna in our lives – so I had to go to the store *again*, and grab one of those disposable aluminum thingies.

Otherwise, no trouble whatsoever.

As it turned out, it was all well worth it – the lasagna was stellar, as was the rest of the meal. After dessert – cannoli and coffee – and after Tony did the dishes, we went into the living room, sat down on the couch (a.k.a. Jenn's bed), and talked about . . . nothing. First, small talk. Then smaller talk. Then no talk.

I hate awkward silences, so I said, 'Um, er, ah, so Tony, what do you want to do now?' This is why Jenn wrote 99.9 per cent of our lyrics.

Tony put his arm around me, drew me close, and said, 'How about we kiss for a couple of hours, and then I make love to you?'

Gulp. Jenn was right. His neon sign was blinking big-time. 'Let's just concentrate on the first part, okay?'

He played with a few strands of my hair, said, 'Okay.' Then, true to his word, he proceeded to kiss me for a couple of hours, give or take an hour and fifteen minutes. He'd just finished running his tongue up my neck, when he whispered, 'Can we go into your bedroom?'

Right away, my brain said, 'No way.' But then my mouth said, 'Mglzpajlk.' But then my brain said, 'Yes way.' But then my mouth said, 'Mglzpajlk.' Since my brain and mouth were being utterly useless, into the bedroom we went. We fell on to my bed, and our kissing became more urgent, even a bit ferocious. There were hickeys, there were scratches, there were nibbles that turned into bites, and bites that turned into harder bites. My own neon sign was blazing.

But then my brain and mouth had a quick meeting and decided things were moving a bit quickly for their comfort, so I abruptly pulled away, got up, and hoofed it into the kitchen.

Tony followed me for a few steps. 'Where're you going? You okay?'

'Everything's fine,' I chirped. 'Just need a drink.' I filled a huge stein with tap water, then guzzled the entire thing in one long gulp. Then, even though I did everything in my power to quash it, I belched.

'You okay?' Tony asked again. Apparently, my burp carried through the apartment. Lucky me.

'I'm just thirsty.' I filled the stein again. This time, I only got halfway through. 'Okay, now I have to go to the bathroom.'

'You sure you're alright?'

'Fine. Great. Magnificent. Excellent. Just have to hit the little girl's room. Be right back.'

I sat down on the toilet and pretended to pee. Thing is, I spaced out, so the pretend pee took about nine minutes. Eventually, Tony again asked, 'You okay?'

'Fine,' I sang cheerfully. I did a courtesy flush, then crept back into the bedroom.

He was calmly sitting on the edge of the bed, looking all the world like he belonged there. And looking very handsome. And not wearing his shirt. He motioned at his bare chest and asked, 'Is this okay?'

'Mmm hmm,' I sighed.

'Would it be okay if I took off your shirt?'

'Mmm hmm.' I slowly walked towards him.

He stood up and said, 'I really like this dark green thing.' Fine, he may've liked it, but he couldn't have liked it that much, because he tore it off in about three seconds.

So one thing led to another, which led to another thing, which, logically enough, led to seven or eight other things – none of which I was particularly good at.

Jenn may have been right on about the dark green thing, but she was *way* wrong about Tony asking me about my sexual past. He just kind of plowed in there. I don't mean that like it sounds – he didn't tear off the rest of my clothes and throw himself in between my legs. No, he took his time, but there wasn't any talking involved. Well, there was a little bit of talking, but he didn't ask me any questions; he just made a whole bunch of really hot declarative statements.

Honestly, I'm not particularly proud of my first lovemaking session. The overall experience wasn't horrible, but I cringe when I recall the specifics. Suffice it to say that I would've had to have been Meryl Streep to fake my non-virginity. Poor Tony Esposito handled it like a champ.

After we were finished – or at least after he was finished; I was as finished as I was going to get – I buried my head face-down under a pillow. I mentally reran the whole mess. It didn't hurt . . . much. I wasn't scared . . . much. I wasn't embarrassed about my undoubtedly lousy performance . . . much.

I wanted to try it again . . . eventually.

Tony rubbed my back and asked, 'What's going on, Naomi? Talk to me.'

'That was my first time.' I could barely get it out.

'What? Come out from under the pillow. I can't hear you.'

I removed the pillow, but kept my face pushed into the bed. 'That was my first time.'

'What?'

I sat up and screamed, 'THAT WAS MY FIRST TIME!'

After a beat, he quietly asked, 'So what you're saying is that was your first time?'

I dived under the covers. Then I threw the covers off and yelled, 'YES!' Then I dived back under the covers. Then something dawned on me, so I timidly poked my head out and said, 'Oh, wait – you're kidding. Heh.'

He pulled me on to his chest and stroked my hair. (Boy, did I love having my hair stroked.) 'It was fine. You were wonderful. And when you're ready, maybe I can be your second time, too.'

That Tony Esposito was one good calmer-downer. 'If you keep playing with my hair like that, I might just let you.'

So we tried again. And we succeeded.

A Typical Wednesday Schedule for the Magical, Musical Team of Naomi and Jenn, AKA the Intrepid Duo

9.00 a.m.: Naomi, the early bird, pads into the living room of her and Jenn's one-bedroom flat – Naomi won the bedroom in a two-out-of-three coin toss – and shakes Jenn awake. (That is, unless Naomi is hungover, a rare occurrence, but it happens, folks, it happens.)

9.02 a.m.: Jenn, the late bird, moans, then groans, then demands coffee.

9.03 a.m.: Naomi, eager to run down that evening's set list, puts together a cuppa java for Jenn. She gently guides her roommate's hands to the steaming cup sitting on the end table that doubles as her nightstand.

9.10 a.m.: Semi-properly caffeinated, Jenn – still clad in her favorite Tigger jammies – wobbles tiredly over to her keyboard.

9.11 a.m.: Naomi does a few warm-up exercises that sound strange and ugly, but loosen up her vocal cords quite nicely. Jenn does a couple of runs up and down her keys. This is all done very quietly, so as to not disturb the neighbors. (Aren't Naomi and Jenn thoughtful and considerate? Hell, yes!)

9.15 a.m.: Jenn plays the introduction to one of her many gorgeous, thoughtful original compositions. Naomi is so intimate with Jenn's songs that she doesn't need to be told the tune – she figures it out after two chords.

9.19 a.m.: They play the rest of what will be their first set.

10.15 a.m.: Each week, Jenn teaches Naomi a new tune. (Jenn is *way* prolific.) Naomi picks it up at once, loves it, and begs to perform it at Beaned that evening. Jenn hems and haws, then says, 'It's not ready yet. Could we wait until next week?' Naomi doesn't mind, because she's still in love with the brilliant new tune that was introduced the *previous* week.

11.00 a.m.: The Intrepid Duo calls it quits. Out of the kindness of her coffee-soaked heart, Bonnie over at Beaned never puts the girls on the Wednesday schedule, which gives them an entire day to kill. Jenn clicks off her Yamaha electric piano, then plops on the couch for an hour of flipping between MTV, VH-1, and *Oprah*. Naomi, wanting to look her best for that evening's performance, retires to the bathroom, where she shaves, plucks, moisturizes and exfoliates. Still not confident in her make-up-putting-on skills, she interrupts Jenn's TV time and makes her come into the bathroom for yet another tutorial.

12.00 p.m.: Jenn goes off to do Jenn stuff, which includes hauling her Yamaha keyboard and Peavey amplifier to Beaned, and setting up the shop's minuscule PA system. (Naomi, being a singer, knows nothing about sound equipment, so Jenn is the de facto mix-mistress.) Jenn isn't seen again until dinner time. Naomi has no idea what it is that Jenn does during those six hours, and while she's totally curious, she never asks. Isn't Naomi nice?

1.30 p.m.: Properly groomed, Naomi begins the long wait until seven, when it's time to meet Jenn at Dojo's on St Mark's Place for their traditional pre-gig dinner. She sometimes reads, she sometimes listens to CDs, she sometimes watches TV, she sometimes goes for a walk. She doesn't do anything that'll mess up her make-up. But no matter what she does, her mind is always thinking about the stage, the microphone, the set list, the sound of Jenn's piano, the feel of her voice bouncing off the coffee shop's walls. Her Wednesday-night performances are the highlight of her week – no, the highlight of her *life* – and it's impossible for Naomi to chill out.

7.00 p.m.: *Finally*, Dojo's. Jenn orders soup, salad, an appetizer, an entrée, and dessert. Each Wednesday, Naomi wonders how Jenn stays so thin, what with her massive appetite and lack of exercise. She doesn't dwell on it, nor does she get mad – after all, how can you get mad at metabolism? For her part, Naomi orders a salad, not because she has weight issues – remember, she's skinny (not slender, skinny) – but because she wants to stay light on her feet during the gig. Too much food makes her feel logy, and logy-ness isn't conducive to quality vocalizing.

8.15 p.m.: Unless the weather is absolutely heinous, The Intrepid Duo walks over to Beaned, a thirtysomething-minute trek during which they plot and scheme about their eventual music industry domination. Like how they'll save up their pennies and produce their own CD. Or like how they'll parlay that CD into a deal with a major record label. Or like how they'll stage their show at Madison Square Garden. Or like what they'll do after their debut album goes triple platinum. You know, that sort of thing.

8.45 p.m.: They arrive at Beaned. Jenn noodles around on the Yamaha, while Naomi takes an inordinately long trip to the bathroom. She doesn't have nervous stomach or anything; she just wants to squeeze out every last drop of pee she possibly can, because having to pee in the middle of a set isn't conducive to quality vocalizing.

9.00 p.m.: The Intrepid Duo parks at a table in the corner, right behind the stage area, where Jenn guzzles a large caffeinated drink of some sort and Naomi does some deep-breathing exercises.

9.06 p.m.: The Intrepid Duo's fan club – three enthusiastic high-school hotties named Tori, Belinda and Erica – arrive and claim the table closest to the band's performance space. One of the three – usually Belinda – guards the table while the other two visit with Jenn and Naomi and proceed to talk breathlessly about what they've been doing during the past week, which boys they're crushing on, and what songs they'd like to hear. These girls are a comfort to Jenn and Naomi; even if The Duo is having an off-night, and even if Beaned is empty, and even if Naomi feels that her voice is sounding like a garbage truck, Tori, Belinda and Erica are sincerely enthusiastic and supportive. Tori, Belinda and Erica totally rock.

9.28 p.m.: Our heroines take the stage. They like to start right on time, because they both despise bands that make audiences wait and wait and wait. (This all stems from the time when they attended a Tori Amos at the Beacon Theater, which Tori started fifty-five minutes late – which meant she had to cut that set short, in order to start the second show on time. The Intrepid Duo was way pissed off, because the second show was sold out, and they couldn't afford scalper tickets. That still irks Naomi to this day.) Granted, for the most part, there isn't much of a crowd, but The Intrepid Duo look at themselves as audience-friendly, and if one person becomes a fan because the music begins when it was supposed to begin, that's a good thing.

9.30 p.m.: The set begins.

10.22 p.m.: The set ends. Naomi is always dazed afterwards, because the fifty-odd minutes evaporate, disappear, melt away in what seems like twelve seconds. It never ceases to amaze her how incredibly lost in the music she gets.

10.23 p.m.: Tori, Belinda and Erica shower The Intrepid Duo with praise, regardless of how the Duo sounded. (By the way, here's a weird phenomenon, which all musicians who gig regularly will relate to: when you're on stage, you have very little idea of how good or how bad your performance is. If you feel you suck, you probably don't suck as badly as you think. If you feel you have kicked ass, you probably haven't done as much butt-kicking as you think you have. If you're well rehearsed – as is the case with The Intrepid Duo – your sets are more consistent than you imagine. You want proof? Record three different shows in which you use identical set lists, and don't label which show is which. Set aside the tapes for a few weeks, then listen to them. It's guaranteed they'll all sound more similar quality-wise than you would have imagined.)

10.45 p.m.: The second set begins.

11.33 p.m.: The second set ends. Tori, Belinda and Erica offer up hugs and goodbyes. Jenn packs up her gear, then breaks down the minuscule PA system. Naomi makes herself an iced chai. Our heroines treat themselves to a cab home.

12.06 p.m.: Nestled safely in the bosom of their apartment, the girls pop open a bottle of wine and dissect the evening to death. If the dissecting is going particularly well, they'll pop open a second bottle. This ritual is especially necessary for Naomi, because without the vino and the convo to help her wind down, she'd be up until four, staring at the ceiling and wishing every night could be like this.

The Intrepid Duo + 1

Our Wednesday night shows at Beaned got more and more crowded each week. While not motivated by money, Bonnie decided to institute both a $3 cover charge and a $5 drink minimum. Jenn and I tried to talk her out of it, not wanting the money issue to dissuade anybody from coming in. After Bonnie told us we could pocket half of the cover charge, we became huge proponents. Jenn even suggested bumping the entry fee up an extra two dollars. Bonnie told her not to get greedy.

We were quite money-conscious at that point, partly because we were fed up with being broke, and partly because we were so comfortable with our music that we were itching to make our own CD. We knew it would have to be a DIY affair, because the chances of getting discovered at Beaned by a big, fancy record executive were pretty minimal. The problem was it would have cost us a couple of thousand bucks to make a quality album – a couple of thousand bucks we weren't even close to having. Jenn and I had discussed one of us getting some temp work, but after much back and forth, we decided against it, not wanting to cut into our rehearsal time. Or our sleep time. Or our sex time. Yeah, that's right, I said sex time.

Ever since Tony and I glided into a pattern of regular sex, I wanted to go at it non-stop. I couldn't keep my hands off of that boy. Jenn said, 'I'm totally not surprised. We're talking two-plus decades of pent-up hormones. You'll ultimately probably be more of a nympho than I am.' I told her I doubted that, but thanked her for the support.

There wasn't as much sex time as I would've liked, though. Sometimes it was all but impossible to find a place to be alone. I couldn't bear to make love when Jenn was within earshot, so we only went to my place when I knew she wasn't going to be around. And Tony's apartment was tiny, plus his roommate, John, was a creep who stared at my ass way too much. We had to pick our spots.

The third Wednesday after the launch of the cover charge, we walked home with an extra $99 in our pockets, which, if you do the math, adds up to sixty-six people in the crowd. 'I think every cent of the Wednesday night money should go into a make-a-CD fund,' Jenn said.

'I agree.'

'Okay, maybe we could take a little bit of it, and go on a thrift store run.'

'Okay.'

'But if we're really smart about it, and if we pick up some extra shifts, we won't need to get temp work.'

'Good point.'

'But we should still buy some new clothes.'

'Yeah, you're probably right.'

'And I think we should start figuring out which songs should go on the record.'

'You're right about that, too.'

'I'm thinking fourteen tunes would be a good number.'

'Sounds good.'

'And I think if we're gonna make a CD, we need to become more than just a duo.'

I came to a halt. 'Veto.'

'Why?' She sounded surprised and a little hurt that I'd suddenly stopped agreeing with her.

As it so happened, I'd already considered, then dismissed, the concept of augmenting our group, so I was able to tick off my arguments against it just like *that*. 'First, we'd have to teach the new guys the music, which'll be a pain. Second, we'd need to integrate them into the band, which means they'd have to gig with us, and we can barely fit ourselves into the performing area at Beaned, so how're we gonna cram anybody else in there? Third, we'd have to pay them, and that would mean bye-bye to the CD fund. And fourth, where are we gonna find them?'

'I have one word that will address all those concerns.'

'And that word is?'

'Travis.'

'Your baby brother Travis?'

'My baby brother Travis.'

It turned out that Travis had taken up the bass the year before. I didn't know that. It turned out, according to Jenn, that he got pretty good, pretty quickly. Obviously I didn't know that either. It also turned out that Travis was *way* into the Intrepid Duo. Apparently he'd told his sister numerous times that he loved us. I *definitely* didn't know that.

'How could he love us?' I asked. 'I haven't seen him in, well, I can't remember the last time I saw him. And he's never once come to hear us play.'

'I burned him a CD of a gig from a couple months ago. He thought it was awesome; he learned all the tunes, and he sounds great. And he offered to play with us for free.'

'Wow. And he's really good?'

'Oh yeah.'

It was worth a shot. 'Okay, fine, let's have him come by to jam for a while.'

'He's coming over tomorrow night at eight. Cancel your plans with Tony.'

'Wait, hold on a minute. You set this up without asking me first.'

'Yeah. Deal with it.'

'But Tony's leaving for school in six weeks.'

'Yeah, I know. Sucks for you. But Naomi, we've outgrown Beaned. We're ready to move forward. I'm ready, and whether you know it or not, you're ready, too. No time to waste. Plus, I dunno, Tony's getting kind of weird.'

'Hunh?'

'Yeah, I've been getting a strange vibe from him lately. Sometimes it looks like he's giving you the stink-eye.'

Stink-eye? All I saw were goo-goo eyes. 'Whatever that means. But let's get back to this other thing. You're saying spending time with my boyfriend before he goes away for three months is a waste of time?' I loved referring to Tony as my boyfriend, even though I wasn't sure if he really *was* my boyfriend. I kind of doubted it, considering the reality of our situation was that when he got back to Harvard we'd hardly see each other, and even though I'd never been in a long-distance relationship – up until Tony, I'd never been in a *short*-distance relationship – I figured it would be virtually impossible to make something like that work. But it was still nice to say 'boyfriend', so I said it at every opportunity.

'Of course I'm not saying that Tony is a waste of time. Even though he's a little weird.'

'Back with the stink-eye again.'

'Yeah. I mean, he carries around that goddamn camcorder all the time, and up until recently, he shaved his entire body, like, every day, and he always looks like he thinks somebody's following him, but whatever. At any rate, you have to make sacrifices. Me, personally, I sacrifice sleep. Like if we get done rehearsing at one, I'll be at William's place at one thirty.' William was one of her five or six latest squeezes. He came to hear us play every Wednesday, and the best part about that was he always brought some of his cute friends. (Sure, I was coupled up with Tony, but eye candy is never a bad thing.) 'William's cool with it. I mean, I'm worth staying up late for, don't you think?'

'I guess.'

'And you're worth staying up late for, too. And if Tony doesn't realize that, well, that's his problem.'

She convinced me. And as it turned out, at first, Tony was cool about a late-night date. He was still playing the good guy role quite nicely.

Travis came over the next night, right on time, right at eight. The first thing I noticed was that Jenn's little brother wasn't so little any more. As a matter of fact, Travis had grown into a slender six-foot hottie; a tall, dark-haired, male version of his sister. He didn't glide sexily across the floor like Jenn – who does, really? – but he'd definitely become quite comfortable in his own body, and he moved a bit like a panther. His fingers were long and lean, just like the rest of him, perfect for plucking a bass – or anything else, for that matter. (And as every girl knows, pluckable fingers are not a bad thing.) And his hair flopped cutely into his face, a white-boy afro in need of some product.

As he set up his amplifier, he updated me on his life. He was in his sophomore year at NYU, majoring in film – it turned out his dream was to direct big budget, star-filled Hollywood dramas and comedies. His classes – which he loved – kept him so busy that he didn't have time for a job, thus he was always broke, thus he was living at home. 'It's not tragic, though,' he said. 'The parents are cool about it most of the time, and this girl I'm seeing, she has an apartment a couple of blocks from here, and I stay at her place at least three times a week. I'm going there after we're done here.'

'Awwwww. Little Travis Bradford had a girlfriend,' I said. 'You're all grown up now, kiddo.'

'*Little* Travis Bradford? Thanks.'

'I'm teasing. Go on.'

'Okay, she's not really my girlfriend – she's just a girl I'm seeing. I like her and all, but she's not The One, y'know? Not that I'm looking for The One right now, but me and Cheri, we're not committed. We can see other people if we want. I'm not seeing anybody else, but if another cool girl came along, I'd go out with her. I'd tell her I was seeing somebody else, though. It would only be fair.' Travis had clearly overcome his shyness. He'd become as much of a blabbermouth as his sister, albeit not as vulgar. I guess he figured if he was going to be a filmmaker, he'd better learn how to communicate.

'So, Travis, how'd you find the time to play the bass, what with you being so busy with school and girls?' I asked.

He shrugged. 'It's just something I've always wanted to do.'

'What, play bass?'

'Maybe not play bass, but play *something*.' He pushed his hair out of his face. 'Remember when I used to sit by Jenn's door when you guys would be practising?'

'How could I forget?'

'I always used to wonder what it would be like to make music with you guys. I mean, make music in general, really.'

'But bass? That's such a dull instrument.'

'I used to think so, too. But I didn't want to play a horn, drums are too annoying to carry around, and Jenn plays keyboards, so I figured I'd play bass, because *everybody* plays guitar, and every band needs a bass player – even you guys – so I knew it'd be easy to find people to play with.'

'Good thinking. Jenn says you're pretty good.'

'Like remember in *This is Spinal Tap*, when Nigel Tufnel says that his amp goes up to eleven.' Jenn and I said nothing, because we had no idea what he was talking about. '*Spinal Tap*?' Travis said. 'Rob Reiner's first flick? The greatest mockumentary of all time?' Jenn and I gave him mutual blank looks, then shrugged in unison. 'Fine,' he said, 'let's just play. Could we do "Hearts Ablaze"? I *love* that one.'

Jenn said, 'You betcha,' then counted us off.

We ran through the twenty songs that Travis had learned, then we taught him three of Jenn's recent compositions, tunes we hadn't even yet performed in public. And Jenn was right – he was good. Amazing, as a matter of fact. What was also amazing to me was having another instrument underneath me. I'd never sang accompanied by anybody other than Jenn. But having Travis there made me feel like I'd put on a pair of super-comfy shoes after having walked barefoot my entire life.

Travis had done his homework, so for the majority of our tunes, he'd already come up with bass lines that perfectly complemented both my melodies and Jenn's harmonies. But some of his stuff just didn't work, so we kicked around some ideas for what seemed like thirty minutes, but was in reality almost three more hours. But it was totally worth it, because lo and behold, the songs were *complete*. I was blown away at how fulfilling it was to make music with a fleshed-out band. I couldn't wait for Wednesday.

At 2.30, as I helped Travis pack up, the phone rang. It was Tony. 'Where the hell are you?' he roared. 'You said you'd be over here at one. I've been calling non-stop for the last hour. I was freaking out. I was about to call a hospital. You're never late—'

'Sorry, Tony,' I interrupted. 'We were rehearsing pretty

hard. It was really intense. I guess I didn't hear the phone ring.'

'Well you should've called,' he grumbled. Was the usually self-possessed Tony Esposito sounding pouty? About *me* not calling *him*? Weird.

'I lost track of time. Jenn's little brother is this really great bass player, and I'd never played with a bassist before, and it was incredible, and—'

'Sounds swell,' he said. He voice was flat, unenthusiastic. 'Are you coming over or not?'

'Tony, I just had one of the greatest musical experiences of my life. Isn't that cool?'

'Sure. Are you coming over or not?' Again, flat and unenthusiastic. Talk about a buzzkill. I'd always thought boyfriends were supposed to be, oh, I dunno, *supportive*.

'Hold on a sec.' I covered the phone's mouthpiece, and told Jenn the deal. 'Blow him off, Nay,' she said. 'If he's gonna be Mr Cranky Pants, he doesn't deserve to get into *your* pants.'

I nodded, then told Tony, 'If you're going to be Mr Cranky Pants, you're not getting into my pants.'

After a moment, Tony said, 'Excuse me?'

'You heard me. Now go to bed. I'm gonna sleep in, so *I'll* call *you*. Don't wake me up, or I'll be forced to inflict some bodily harm on you. I'll see you on Saturday.' We had a standing Saturday-night date.

'Maybe,' he said sullenly. 'And don't worry about me waking you up with a phone call. I just *won't* call. Goodbye.' Then he hung up.

I stared unblinkingly at the wall. Travis asked, 'What's wrong?'

Empowerment wasn't as much fun as I would've expected. I didn't like being in the power position. I wanted him to want me regardless of how late I showed up. He was being needy, and it dawned on me that being *needed* isn't as much fun as being *wanted*. I shook my head as if to clear the cobwebs. 'My boyfriend just hung up on me.'

'What a jerk,' Jenn said. 'You should dump his ass. You can do better.'

'Agreed,' said Travis. 'You could totally do better. Big time. You're a catch.' He again pushed his hair out of his face, which was turning out to be quite an endearing habit.

Jenn said, 'He's going back to school soon anyhow, and you don't need the excess baggage. You should be all about the music.'

'But it's *Tony Esposito*. Plus I've developed a taste for sex . . .'

'Cool,' Travis said.

'. . . and I kind of want to have it on a semi-regular basis.'

'*Super* cool,' Travis said.

'So find a nice, cute guy who wants you strictly for your body,' Jenn said. 'Over half of the people who come to hear us each week are guys, and over half of them are in love with you.'

'I bet she's right,' Travis said. 'When you're up there singing, you could probably have any guy eating out of the palm of your hand. *Any* guy.'

'But I still like Tony,' I whined. I didn't like sounding so whiny, but I couldn't help it.

'You don't need the baggage,' Jenn reiterated. 'And tunes trump boys.'

'Ya think?' Travis asked.

'I do, baby brother. At least for now.'

Travis nodded. 'Okay. At least for now. I can accept that.' He paused, clapped his hands once, then said, 'So let's talk about getting a drummer.'

Somewhat Tolerable

When he first offered up his services, Travis gave Jenn the impression he knew more musicians than he actually did, and that he'd be able to find us a good drummer. It turned out he was exaggerating. Okay, not exaggerating – *lying*. He didn't know one single drummer. As a matter of fact, he didn't know one single musician.

'You've never played with anybody else at all?' I asked him.

'Hey, you've been playing way longer than I have, and you haven't played with anybody at all either, except for Jenn.'

He had a point. 'So how do you propose we go about getting a drummer?'

Jenn raised her hand. 'I have a plan.' She whipped out a folded-up piece of notebook paper from the back pocket of her low-riding Limited jeans. 'Read this.'

Travis grabbed the paper from Jenn's hands. I peeked over his shoulder – a difficult task, as he was a tall drink of water – and scanned Jenn's plan:

Astonishingly talented singer, staggeringly brilliant keyboardist/songwriter, and somewhat tolerable bassist seek a drummer to complete their alterna-chick-pseudo-emo band. Must have drum set, the ability to groove, and a functioning wristwatch so they'll never be late to rehearsal. Auditions at Beaned, 23rd St. xxx and 8th Ave. xxx, Saturday at 10 p.m. Phone (212) xxx–xxxx to schedule.

Clearly not amused, the somewhat tolerable bassist crumpled up the page into a ball, tossed it at Jenn's nose, and said, 'Somewhat tolerable? You suck. I'm going to take a somewhat tolerable pee. Have a somewhat tolerable time while I'm gone.' Personally, I thought that Travis Bradford was more than somewhat tolerable. Even though he was still a young guy, he clearly had an old soul, an engaging sense of humor, and a developing level of maturity that would ultimately make him a solid adult. Not bad for a guy who I'd always figured would become a burnout skaterboy.

'So what's this about?' I asked.

'It's about us expanding and developing. It'll be in this week's *Village Voice*.'

'You set up a drummer audition without even asking me . . .'

'Or me,' Travis called from the bathroom.

'. . . and I'm supposed to go along with it, because you say so?'

Jenn nodded. 'Yeah, that's pretty much what I'm saying.'

Travis again called, 'Good work, Jenn.'

'Stop talking to us while you're peeing,' Jenn said. 'It's gross.'

'It's not gross,' Travis answered. 'It's somewhat tolerable.' Then he flushed.

'You could've asked me about this. How do you know I want a drummer?' I asked. 'How do you know I want to sing at this stupid audition? How do you know I—'

'Naomi, I don't know, and I don't care. I'm tired of being just a duo. I'm tired of writing songs that're being heard by only fifty or sixty people at a time. And honey, I love you, but I'm tired of your complacency. We're too good – no, *you*'re too good – to be festering away in some coffee shop. If I would've asked you about a drummer audition, you'd have spent two hours discussing it, then you would've found some random Naomi reason to say "no".'

She was probably right. And I shouldn't have been surprised. Jenn was all about pushing me: she pushed me out of her bedroom, and into Manhattan; she pushed me out of our apartment, and into Beaned. And now she was pushing me out of Beaned, and into . . . I didn't know where. But thus far, she'd never pushed me wrong. At once resigned and excited, I asked, 'Did you clear this with Bonnie?'

Jenn's face lit up. 'You betcha. She's totally psyched. And I've already scheduled five guys. The first one's right at ten, so we need to be set up no later than nine thirty. Does that work for you, Trav?'

He was standing directly behind me, almost in my personal space. I hadn't even noticed he'd come back from the bathroom. Apparently the kid moved quietly – I guess it was that panther thing. 'Absolutely. Anything for the cause.'

'You hear that?' asked Jenn. 'He's officially been in the band for, like, six hours, and he's already on board big time.'

'Wait, I'm officially in the band?' he asked.

'Yes, Travis. You're officially in the band.'

He gave a little fist pump. 'Superb. Okay, on that most excellent note, I'm out.' He gave his sister a quick hug and a little peck on the cheek, then he gave me a long hug, and a big wet peck on the cheek. 'This is gonna be so awesome, Naomi.'

I was taken aback by his embrace, but I didn't want to

make him feel bad, so I made a joking show of wiping off his sloppy kiss. 'Ewww, I already showered, Travis.'

He sort of laughed, said, 'Whatever', then took off. After I locked the door behind him, he banged a loud drum roll on the wall in the hall and said, 'Intrepid Trio in the house!' Not cool for that time of the night, but no matter how tall he got, and how floppy his pseudo-'fro was, and how long his fingers were, and how panther-smoothly he moved, and how much fun it would probably be having him around all the time, and how almost-mature he'd become, he was still Jenn's dorky little brother, and dorky little brothers do things like make too much noise after curfew, so I let it go.

Jenn smiled and shook her head. 'He turned out great, didn't he?'

I smiled back. 'He's somewhat tolerable.'

The Little Drummer Boys

Jenn scheduled ten little drummer boys to audition for our alterna-chick-pseudo-emo band, five of whom were already lined up outside of Beaned at 9.30, all bright-eyed and bushy-tailed, all armed with drumsticks and cymbals. No drums, mind you, just sticks and cymbals. One of the guys – a fortysomething black gentleman clad in a rumpled suit who looked a bit confused and out of place – poked his head in the door. 'I'm ten o'clock.'

Jenn asked, 'Cool. What's your name?'

'Ten o'clock.'

'No, your name.'

'Ten o'clock.'

'No, your *name*.'

'Oh. Paul Greene.' He stuck the fat end of a drumstick in his ear. 'My hearing's not so good.' I didn't know much about drummers, but I had a hunch that a drummer whose ears were shot probably wasn't the guy to drive our band. But he was on the schedule sheet, and who were we to deny him his opportunity for alterna-chick-pseudo-emo greatness? 'What kind of drum kit you guys got?' he asked. 'I dig Pearls.'

'Pearls?'

'What?'

'Pearls?'

'Yeah. Pearls.' He was looking at Jenn like she was the most clueless person in the world.

Jenn matched Paul Greene's clueless glare. 'You didn't bring your own drum kit? I wrote in the ad that you have to have your own drum kit.'

'What?'

'I wrote in the ad that you have to have your own drum kit.'

'Yeah, but it didn't say you had to *bring* your own drum kit. Lady, cats don't bring a drum kit to an audition. There should be one waiting there for you. We cats just supply the cymbals. And you should have Pearls. I dig Pearls.' I found out later that Pearl was the brand name of a high-end drum company. At the time, I wondered why he thought Jenn should be wearing fancy jewelry to a jam session.

'Oh, man, did I mess up,' Jenn said. She chewed on her nail and stared thoughtfully into outer space, then after a minute or three, put her hand on the small of Paul Greene's back and gently guided him towards the door. Once outside, she gave the four other drummer boys one of her killer Jenn smiles, and said, 'Gentlemen, as you can see, I'm a redhead, but I did something tonight that some might say only a blonde would do: I forgot to arrange to have a drum kit waiting here for you.' She shook her head and her gorgeous hair flew everywhere. Then she slowly slinked her left hand sexily down her chest, and rested it beside her right breast. Actually, her hand wasn't really resting beside her breast; it was all but *cupping* her breast. She ran her tongue over her upper lip, then throatily said, 'Would any of you boys be able to run home and get your drums?' As if she didn't already have them totally entranced, she flicked her nipple. She'd have been a hit at any stripping emporium.

The four little drummer boys hit her with a barrage of 'I'll do it's.' She said, 'Decide amongst yourselves. We need to be ready to go in twenty minutes.' Then she turned around, shook her ass at them, and slid back into the café. I looked outside. The boys were rioting.

'You are pure evil, Jenn.'

'Means to an end, Nay.'

Travis shook his head, clearly appalled. 'That was the single most disgusting thing I've ever seen in my life.'

'You say that only because I'm your sister. If Naomi did it, I'm pretty sure you wouldn't be disgusted.'

'One problem,' I said. 'I don't have enough boob to make that work.'

Travis said, 'Oh, I bet you could've made something happen out there.'

Fifteen minutes later, one of the drummers flew into Beaned, a luggage cart loaded down with drums in tow. When he finished setting up, I stepped outside, called out Paul Greene's name, and asked if he was ready to roll.

He shot me a confused look. 'Who, me?'

'Yeah, you.'

'Okay.' It took him about ten minutes to get his cymbals arranged just so; I'd never carefully watched a drummer set up, but it sort of struck me that it shouldn't take that long. Clearly agitated, Jenn seemed ready to send him on his way, when he said, 'Okay, let's go.'

Jenn was pissed. 'Okay, Mr Greene,' she snarled, 'this one's called "Problem Identified". Play it with a funky backbeat, almost a hip-hop thing. Okay?'

'What?'

'*Play a fucking funky backbeat!*'

Paul Greene stared at the ceiling and said, 'Okay.'

'Great. I'll count it off. One, two, uh-one two three four . . .'

Paul Greene didn't play on the intro. Paul Greene didn't play on the verse. Paul Greene didn't play on the chorus. Finally we realized Paul Greene wasn't going to play at all. We stopped, then Jenn said, 'What gives?'

Paul Greene swallowed and said, 'Ladies, I haven't touched a drum set in fifteen years. Plus I'm very, very drunk.'

The next guy was a new-agey frizzy-haired, Kenny G.-looking guy who, after sucking out loud on 'Problem Identified', continued to play for almost three minutes after the song was over. And it wasn't like he was playing the song – no, he was taking a full-out solo, a loud, arrogant, obnoxious, un-new-age-like solo. He stopped only after Jenn threw a balled-up napkin at his head.

The next guy was a teenaged punk with a green Mohawk, who, mere seconds after slapping his cymbals on to the respective stands, took a long, loud solo. His solo was better than New Age Boy's, but at least New Age Boy had the courtesy to play the song before launching into his barrage. After Mr Mohawk was done, he threw his sticks across the room, yelled, 'EMO SUCKS! CHICK SINGERS SUCK! I SUCK!' then calmly removed his cymbals from the stands, and quietly went on his merry way, leaving his sticks for us as a souvenir. Jenn, Travis and I stared at each other silently for a few seconds, then we all burst out laughing. It took us about five minutes to get control of ourselves; it was at that moment – a non-musical moment, ironically enough – that I felt we became a true band.

I decided I was going to like being in a band.

The next guy was a hulking, apple-cheeked man-child who claimed to have played with [Gravelly Voiced Bob Dylan-ish Female Singer-Songwriter] '. . . when she was still an alkie', and with [Allegedly Virginal Ho-Bag-Looking Blonde Diva] '. . . before she came up with that whole schoolgirl thing', and with [Tortured Folkie One-Hit Wonder] '. . . before he topped himself'. Looking mildly impressed, Jenn counted off the tune.

Unlike Paul Greene, he started playing at the beginning of the song. Unlike New Age Boy, he stopped playing at the end of the song. Unlike Mohawk Boy, he didn't take a solo or tell us we sucked. But there's no way he told the truth about his résumé, because there was no way any of those singers would have hired a guy who played that awfully.

The next guy was the little drummer boy who was kind enough to lend us his drum set. I was rooting for him, but unfortunately, he played really softly, and boringly, and stared up at the ceiling the whole time – a true bummer, because he was really cute. The next guy told Jenn, 'When you did that thing with your hands, I wanted to stick my face in between your tits.' Travis threw down his bass and physically launched the guy out the door. I told Jenn, 'That's what you get for playing with yourself on the sidewalk in Chelsea.'

Finally, just after 1.00 a.m., we got to the last guy, who was . . . good.

He wasn't particularly cute. As a matter of fact, he was quite average in every respect: average height, average weight, average hair, average dress. He wasn't particularly chatty. He wasn't particularly warm and fuzzy. But once he started warming up with a fast bebop beat that would've fit nicely on a Miles Davis record, I knew there was a chance he was a winner.

We ran down six tunes, finishing up with 'And Then'. I looked at Jenn. Jenn looked at me. Jenn looked at Travis. Travis looked at Jenn. We all looked at the drummer. Jenn said, 'I'm sorry, what was your name again?'

'Frank. Frank Craft.'

'Well, Frank Craft, how'd you like to join our band?'

He gave a little shrug. 'I'm mostly a jazz guy, but your stuff is nice. It's not Cassandra Wilson, but it's not *not* Cassandra Wilson. You know what I mean?'

We did. Thus, the Intrepid Quartet was born.

But not until after a certain little drummer boy strode into Beaned and said to Jenn, 'Hey, you, redhead, yeah, you with the boobs, gimme my drums back.'

The Famous Naomi Porno Tape

I shouldn't even mention this, but there's a website called NakedNaomi.com. Right before I started writing this book, I surfed over there out of morbid curiosity. It consisted mostly of pictures featuring my head pasted on to the bodies of fake-boobed pin-up girls, which, as anybody who's ever looked at my skinny self for even the briefest of moments knows, is ridiculous. But I guess some guys get off on that kind of thing, so whatever.

At the bottom of the NakedNaomi.com front page, there's a link to what the webmaster of this pathetic site calls THE FAMOUS NAOMI PORNO TAPE. When you click on it, it takes you to a page that says in big red letters, 'There's a reward of $50,000 for any information leading to the capture of THE FAMOUS NAOMI PORNO TAPE. Please email Tape@NakedNaomi.com if you can help.'

When I read that, I broke out in a cold sweat. Fortunately, I'm the only person in the world who has any information that would lead to the capture of said tape.

The day after the drum auditions, I met Tony for lunch at the Ray's Pizza on Sixth Avenue and Eleventh Street. New Yorkers know that there are a bajillion different Ray's pizzerias, none of which have anything to do with the others in terms of ownership. This particular Ray's was by far the best one, if only because their mushrooms and eggplant were always fresh.

I suspect as payback for me postponing and/or canceling our three most recent dates, Tony showed up twenty-five minutes late. For a guy who was always on time, that was a pretty passive/aggressive move. Actually, it wasn't a passive/aggressive move – it was flat-out aggressive. 'Hey, Naomi,' he said breezily, as if he hadn't left me sitting there with my slice for almost half an hour. He offered no apology or explanation.

'Hey, Tony.'

He gazed around the restaurant. 'This isn't what I'd call an ideal date spot.'

'This is my favorite pizza place in the whole world. Besides, I thought we were at the point where *every* spot was an ideal date spot.'

'I thought we were at the point where we didn't blow each other off all the time,' he said in a tone and volume I found inappropriate for the time and place. A cancellation here and a postponement there, and the guy goes nuclear. Alarm bells sounded.

Yeah, things had been tense with Tony, and yeah, the Intrepid Quartet had come to dominate my time, my thoughts and my life, but I wasn't ready to give up on him just yet. After all, this was Tony Esposito, my high-school dream guy, the boy who used to have the blackest hair ever. And right at that particular moment, in his tight, faded DKNY jeans, his navy blue Fresh Jive T-shirt, and his black, clunky boots, he was looking *good*. 'This isn't about me blowing you off,' I patiently explained. 'It's not even about you. It's about the band. Our band is a *band* now. I thought you liked my music thing.'

He softened a bit. 'I do like your music thing. And I'm

happy that your band is doing well. But I don't get to see you all that often, and I'm going back to school soon, and I miss you.'

I dramatically batted my eyelashes, and said in a mock Mississippi accent, 'Wah Tony Esposito, ah do declare. Tell me more, suh. Tell me exactly what y'all miss about me.'

He stared down at his hands, suddenly all shy. 'I dunno; I miss your face, and your laugh, and the way you chew on your lower lip when you're listening to me really carefully, and the way you get all excited when you talk about whatever song was just on your iPod, and the way you look when we're having sex. That sort of thing.'

My desire for Ray's was replaced with my desire for Tony. 'Is your roommate home?'

'John? I think he's at his parents' place in Westchester. Why do you ask?'

I reached under the table and gave him a little squeeze in the area where all boys liked getting squeezed. 'Why do you think?'

He leapt up from his seat and said, 'I think we should go back to my place.' I followed him, not even the tiniest bit upset that I'd only eaten half of my excellent Ray's slice.

We jumped into a cab, and groped each other for the entire ride to Chez Tony. We took the stairs up to his place two at a time; I'd turned him on so much that he had trouble getting his hands to stop trembling long enough so that he could open his front door. Once we made it to his bedroom, he ripped my clothes off, I ripped his clothes off, and we had the roughest, hottest, smokiest, wettest sex I'd ever had in my life.

After we finished, I padded off to the bathroom. As I attempted to regain some semblance of composure, I stared into the mirror. For a change, I liked what I saw: I was flushed; my neck and shoulders were covered with love bites; my hair had that I-just-got-laid look that women all over New York pay their beauticians, like, $500 to achieve. This was one of the first times as an adult I ever felt proud of my body. Yeah, I was skinny, but I had decent muscle tone, clear skin, and a cute little butt. My boobs were minuscule, but you can't have everything.

When I came back to earth, I heard a voice coming from the other side of the apartment. I assumed John had made it back from Westchester. I wrapped myself in the toweling robe that was hanging on the back of the door, and headed into the living room, hoping I'd be able to sneak across the floor quietly enough so John wouldn't hear me.

As it so happened, John didn't hear me because John was distracted. *Very* distracted. Tony's creepy roommate was parked in a chair in front of the television, leaning forward, his face inches away from the set, his hand wrist-deep down the front of his khakis. And what was he watching? That's right, ladies and gentlemen, THE FAMOUS NAOMI PORNO TAPE – a tape, I soon found out, that was produced, written, directed by and co-starred one Tony Esposito. Yours truly was the female lead, and suffice it to say, I wouldn't have gotten any Oscar nominations for my performance.

I gasped loudly, totally destroying John's concentration. He shot up out of the chair and turned to face me. 'Oh. Hi, Naomi,' he said sheepishly, removing his hand from his pants. 'Um, you look very nice today.'

My mind went into crisis mode. I didn't freak out. I just calmly walked to the VCR, ejected the tape, and told John, 'It would be wise of you to leave this apartment. Immediately.'

My deadly quiet tone must've scared him, because he flew out the door even before he'd buttoned his pants. I cinched the robe around my waist, cleared my throat, and called – again very calmly – 'Tony, can I see you for a minute?'

His bedroom door slammed shut. 'Just cleaning up,' he said. 'Be right there.'

I tiptoed across the living room and threw open his door. Tony Esposito – my high-school dream guy, the boy who used to have the blackest hair ever – was standing on his bed, pulling a tape out of the camcorder that he'd surreptitiously mounted on his ceiling.

I'll spare you the exact details of how I tore out a handful of Tony's pubic hair, then hurled his camera against the wall, then threw the chunks of broken camera at his face, then bashed his head with one of my black Pumas, then told him if I ever saw his black-hair-having, X-rated-film-making face again, I'd gouge out his perverted little eyeballs.

As I flew out of Tony Esposito's apartment, after pulling on my clothes, my white-hot anger morphed into sadness, then back into anger, then into naked rage, then into utter depression, then into an intense eight-second crying jag, then back into anger. I stomped down the sidewalk, rhythmically mumbling, 'Douchebag, douchebag, douchebag, douchebag' with each step. On the subway, still douchebagging, I accidentally made eye contact with this older guy, who clearly thought I was douchebagging him, and clearly didn't care for it, and clearly would have thrown me on to the tracks given the opportunity, which was fine, because I was just about ready to throw myself on to the tracks.

Anyhow, long story short, the only existing version of THE FAMOUS NAOMI PORNO TAPE is somewhere at the bottom of the Gowanus Canal. Take that, Mr Tape@NakedNaomi.com.

Jenn Gives me Her Calm Assessment of the Tony Situation

'I told you his camcorder thing was weird.'

I Give Jenn My Not-So-Calm Assessment of the Tony Situation

'I hate boys!'

Jenn Gives Me Her Assessment of the Manner in Which I Dealt With The Tony Situation Later That Week

'It's been three days, four boxes of tissues and six bottles of wine, and all you can tell me is, "*But I love-hove-ed him-m-m!*" I say stick with the "*I hate boys*" approach. Much more dignified.'

12

Bye-Bye Beaned

Travis's bottom-end elasticity and Frank's jazz-soaked percussive sturdiness helped the Intrepid Quartet grow into an honest-to-goodness rock band, slick and sincere, professional and potent, intelligent and engaging. It was what Jenn and I had sought to do back in her bedroom all those years ago, and we did it, damn it, we totally did it. But with the growth came a serious growing pain. And boy, did it hurt.

The fateful Wednesday – after we roared through a couple of smoking sets, after we closed with 'And Then' to tons of gracious applause – Jenn leapt up from behind her keyboard, ripped the microphone from my hands and said, 'Thanks for coming. We love playing for you. We love that you support us. We just flat-out love you. Do you agree, Nay?'

I nodded emphatically. 'Absolutely.'

'That's why this announcement is so hard for us. Next Wednesday is gonna be our final night here at Beaned.' There was a mild uproar from the crowd; Jenn put her hand up and shushed everybody. 'It's a bittersweet thing for us, to leave after all this time, but it's time for the Intrepid Quartet to move on to bigger and better things. Keep your eyes and ears peeled for us. Trust me, you'll be seeing and hearing a lot of us. Please give us your email addresses and we'll keep you in the loop.'

Virtually everybody in the place rushed to sign up for our e-newsletters. The crush of people claustrophobed me, so I tiptoed through the crowd, towards the back of the room. I would've gone outside, but the door was being unwittingly blocked by our awesome fans. I went behind the back counter and made myself an iced chai. Just as I was about to take my first sip, somebody whispered in my ear, 'I'm gonna miss you guys sooo much!'

It was Bonnie, and her face was a picture of unabashed sorrow. 'You look like you just found out there's a Starbucks opening next door,' I joked.

She stroked my cheek, and, still whispering, said, 'Hush, Naomi. Don't try to be funny about this. Please. This is really hard for me. I've known about this for a month now, but it didn't really hit me until Jenn made the announcement.'

'Yeah, we're still trying to wrap our brains around it ourselves. But you'll be fine. You'll find some other awesome servers, and you'll find an awesome band, and three weeks from now, you won't even remember our names.'

'That's not the point, and you know it,' she said, pawing a tear from her cheek.

'Jeez, don't cry, Bonnie. You're gonna make *me* cry,' I sniffled.

Jenn snuck up behind me, draped her arm over my and Bonnie's shoulders, and said, 'What're you two blubbering about.'

Bonnie took a deep, hitching breath. 'You're my little sisters. You're my Pied Pipers. You're the soul of this place. And I'm losing you.'

Jenn nodded. 'Yeah. You are losing us. And it sucks on a

bunch of different levels. But on a bunch of *other* levels, it's incredible. I mean, aren't you psyched for us?'

'Of course I am.'

'You'd damn well better be. Because if you're not, I'll have to do things to you with your espresso machine that're too awful to put into words.'

Bonnie laughed – Jenn was great at making people laugh when they thought they didn't want to – then reiterated, 'Of course I'm psyched for you. But if you two disappear from my life forever, well, I'll have to do stuff to you with a ten-pound bag of French roast that's too awful to put into words.'

Jenn cracked up. 'Touché. Now get over here, you.' She pulled us into a group hug that lasted for a long, long time.

Flaunting Our I.Q.

A couple days after that group hug, our little group underwent a name-ectomy. Frank had commented at our first post-Beaned band meeting that he had thought, ever since day one, that 'Intrepid Quartet' was a silly moniker, but he hadn't said anything because he didn't want to hurt our feelings.

Jenn gave him a steely glare and said, 'But it's okay to hurt our feelings *now*. Thanks a lot, Craft.' Frank clammed up and looked incredibly uncomfortable.

'Jenn,' Travis said, 'stop it. Frank, she's messing with you. I've dealt with it my entire life, and, trust me, you get used to it whether you like it or not.'

Jenn put her arm around Frank, kissed him on the cheek, and said, 'Seriously, I have no problem changing our name. Hell, you're the voice of experience in this unit. You're the only guy who has performed someplace other than a coffee shop.' Frank forgave her. No surprise there. Jenn could run over some guy's foot with a car, but if she kissed him on the cheek and gave him a little ego-boosting compliment, he'd forgive her.

It took Travis about two seconds to come up with our new name: 'I.Q'. That beat my suggestion of 'Little Babies'

– the title of one of my favorite Sleater-Kinney songs – by a landslide vote of three-to-one. So, just like that, we were I.Q. Ta-da.

'Good work, Travis,' I said. 'This reaching puberty thing has done wonders for your creativity.'

He said, 'Ha.' And it seemed to be more of an annoyed 'ha' than a laughing 'ha'. I wanted to tell him I was kidding. I wanted to tell him that I figured if he could handle Jenn's teasing, he could handle my teasing.

But I didn't.

Our second post-Beaned move was to put together a demo CD. We still didn't have the means to make an entire album, but we needed to have *something* to give to the clubs who would hopefully be booking us. One of Frank's friends gave us four hours of free studio time, so we banged out versions of 'And Then', 'Hearts Ablaze', 'Generic' and 'Problem Identified'. We had to rush through the tunes – recording four songs in four hours is tough for any band, let alone one that had never set foot in a studio before – but the whole thing came out pretty well.

Jenn was our de facto musical director, so she appointed me business director, and, in I.Q. Land, the business director was in charge of getting us gigs, which involved putting together a bajillion press kits, and dialing up club after club after club until the nail of my right index finger was a nub, and pounding the pavement so hard that my black Pumas became sole-less. Shockingly, eight clubs almost immediately called me back and asked to book us. I knew our demo was pretty good, but it wasn't as good as the photo we had included in the press kit. Check that: the demo wasn't as good as the photo of Jenn we included in the press kit.

Don't get me wrong – it wasn't a solo shot of her. But she was front and center, completely sexed up in a short skirt, thigh-high fishnets, clunky boots, and a tight little tube top. I can't deny the rest of us looked pretty good, too: Travis was staring at the ground, his hair flopping in his face, looking very mysterious. (The funny part was that Travis wasn't mysterious in the least. But image is everything, and it never hurts to have one guy in the group who's at least somewhat enigmatic, because being an enigma generally equals being a sex bomb, and struggling bands need all the sex bombs they can get. And, dare I say it, Travis did look kind of sexy. It was weird to equate Jenn's baby brother with sexiness, but I figured that since I always equated Jenn herself with sexiness, it was okay – but still weird.) As for Frank, he was sitting on the ground, leaning up against Jenn's leg, looking straight up her skirt. That was Jenn's idea, her reason being that we could position him as the goofball of the group, I.Q.'s version of Ringo Starr. But he was goofy the way Travis was mysterious, that is to say not at all. It would've made more sense for their roles to be reversed in the picture, but Travis didn't want to be photographically documented staring up at his sister's privates.

As for me, well, not to sound arrogant, but I looked excellent. As you can tell by now, back then, I wasn't too enamored with my physicality. But this picture was a huge step in helping me get over that.

Jenn put me in a black Miu Miu button-down shirt she'd found at a Salvation Army thrift store in Brooklyn – it cost $3, and it had never been worn; ya gotta love the Salvo – and made me unbutton enough buttons to make me feel very unbuttoned. 'Listen, the camera'll be so far away that nobody's going to see your boobs . . .'

'I have no boobs to see.'

'. . . but the cleavage will blow them away . . .'

'My cleavage will *never* blow *anybody* away.'

'. . . because it's all about imagination. Trust me.'

She slapped a ton of make-up on to my face – she was still a big proponent of cosmetics – and she made me go out and get a Louis Brooks haircut. I kicked and screamed during the entire makeover process, but it worked. And no matter what happened for the rest of my life – if I gained 100 lb, or if I broke out in permanent king-sized zits, or if my nose fell off – I'd always have this one picture of me and my best friend looking beautiful, and, dare I say it, sexy. *En fuego*, even.

I suspected a lot of club owners would hire us based on how we looked rather than on how we sounded, but a gig was a gig no matter how we got the gig, and I was more-than-ready to gig. If that required a new hair do and some 'cleavage', so be it.

It was a tough decision, but the joint I chose for us was called Upper East. It was an ironic name, because the place was located on the Lower West side of Greenwich Village. On the surface, Upper East looked like a questionable decision for us; it was a new place, and even though it had developed a solid buzz among Greenwich Village club goers, it didn't have the same cachet as, say, the Mercury Lounge or C.B.G.B.'s. But Upper East's owner, Billy Rogers, offered us a guarantee of $500 a week, a number that could increase if he made a certain amount of money at the door. Most importantly, he asked if we'd be interested in doing a two-month residency, i.e., could we play there the same night for eight consecutive weeks.

'How about Wednesdays?' I asked during our first face-to-face meeting. Wednesdays had worked quite well for us at Beaned, so why mess with success?

'Done,' Billy said, without even consulting a schedule.

On opening night, a bunch of the Beaned regulars came by, and Jenn's newest boyfriend brought his entire gang, and Bonnie brought a handful of her Phish-loving pals, and the Intrepid Trio got some fake IDs and finagled their way in. And since Upper East was getting more hip 'n' happening by the day, there were also a goodly number of random people I didn't recognize at all.

That evening was kind of a turning point in my musical career. Up until then, I'd performed at exactly three venues: Beaned, my apartment, and Jenn's childhood bedroom. The crowds at Beaned were decent, but the place only squeezed in seventy-five people, tops. The crowd in my apartment consisted of Travis and Frank. The crowd in Jenn's bedroom consisted of about two dozen stuffed animals, and, periodically, Travis.

But that night, the crowd at Upper East was BIG. Not big. BIG.

If you'd have asked me right after we quit Beaned, 'Naomi, how do you think you'd perform in front of a BIG audience at an almost-trendy club in the Village?' I'd probably have said, 'Okay, I s'pose, assuming I didn't have a nervous breakdown after the third tune.' I'd have been wrong. At our Upper East debut, nary a nervous breakdown was seen. Yours truly, Ms Naomi Braver, kicked ass like she'd never kicked ass before.

I paced the stage like a tiger. I looked my audience in the eyes. I sang with passion, with assuredness, with *balls*. Each tune was better than the last. And I had so much fun. I don't know whether I was having fun because I was singing well, or if I was singing well because I was having fun, but it didn't matter, because I owned the Upper East.

I could spend hours trying to explain to you how it felt, but the only way you'll really know what it's like to have an audience eating out of the palm of your hand is . . . to have an audience eat out of the palm of your hand. And I hope that each and every one of you gets to have that experience.

It's better than Double Stuf Oreos and a cold glass of milk. (Double Stuf Oreos, by the way, are the greatest cookie created by mankind.) It's better than mediocre sex, but not quite as good as great sex. It's fantabulous, and I'd recommend learning how to sing, or to play an instrument, or to act, or to juggle, or to do *something*, whatever it takes to get on a stage and command a room.

In any event, that's pretty much the way it went for the next six months.

A One-Act Play Starring Naomi, Jenn, Travis, Two Awesome Fans & a Mysterious Stranger

The scene: our heroine Naomi and her band I.Q. have just finished two sweaty sets at a hip-'n'-happening night club in Manhattan called Upper East. Naomi sits at a table to the right of the stage, basking in the adulation of several listeners, doing an excellent job of not letting their praise go to her head.

AWESOME FAN NUMBER ONE: Can I have your autograph, Naomi? I know this probably sounds weird, but I have a hunch it'll be worth something someday.
NAOMI [*excited, because A.F. #1 is an astonishingly Kissable Boy*]: No problem. But if I see this on eBay, I'm going to track you down, Mister.
A.F. #1 [*laughing and – is it possible? – blushing*]: Don't worry. I'm holding on to this – although it probably'll be eBay-worthy in a year or two. Make it out to Karl. That's Karl with a 'K'.
AWESOME FAN NUMBER TWO [*elbowing Karl away the second Naomi hands over her John Hancock*]: I promise not to sell mine on eBay, too. All I have is a cocktail napkin. Can you sign this?

NAOMI [*rubbing her eyes, because A.F. #2 is also an astonishingly Kissable Boy, possibly even more kissable then Karl, and never in her life have two random Kissable Boys initiated conversation with Naomi in a single night, let alone a single minute*]: You betcha. But if you want, you can come next week with something less napkin-y for me to sign, okay?
A.F. #2 [*laughing and – is it possible? – blushing*]: I'll be here!
Two more Kissable Boys and a girl – whom Naomi would also, if she was so inclined, consider to be kissable – ask Naomi for autographs. With no more autograph hounds in the house, Jenn and Travis sneak up behind Naomi.
TRAVIS [*in a high-pitched, pseudo-mocking voice*]: Oooh, Naomi, you're the best singer in the history of singers. Can you sign my butt?
JENN [*in a low-pitched, pseudo-mocking voice*]: Oooh, Naomi, sign my boobs first.
TRAVIS: No, my butt!
JENN: No, my boobs!
NAOMI: Ah, the comedy stylings of Bradford and Bradford, a.k.a., Butthead and Butthead. Maybe you two should do some stand-up before the show next Wednesday.
TRAVIS [*to Jenn*]: Actually, that's not a bad idea. I've seriously been working on some stuff. I'm not kidding. I'd be up for it. I have this bit about—
NAOMI & JENN: Travis, shut up!
TRAVIS: You two suck. Naomi, you can sign my butt. Jenn, you can kiss my butt. [*He skulks away.*]
JENN [who, it should be noted, is a tad buzzed]: Nay, I love you. I love playing with you. I wanna play with you for ever. I wanna marry you. I wanna have, like, a million of your babies. And I want us to be rock stars.
MYSTERIOUS STRANGER [*sneaking up behind the girls, and scaring the pants off them – figuratively, of course*]: I want you babes to be rock stars, too.

JENN [*putting her hand on the back of Naomi's neck*]: I bet you want her autograph. Shit, I want her autograph, too, and I live with her.
M.S.: You bet I'd like Naomi's autograph . . . at the bottom of a contract. Here. [*M.S. reaches into his pocket and pulls out a business card.*] Let's cut to the chase – I wanna be in business with I.Q.
NAOMI [*rolling her eyes as she takes the proffered card*]: I bet you say that to all the girls. [*Naomi is about to say something way sarcastic, but then she reads the card.*]

Mitchell J. Busey
Director of Artist & Repertoire
Éclat Records
A Division of Universal Music Group

This quickly shuts Naomi up. She shows the card to Jenn, who, possibly for the first time in her life, is also speechless. After the girls regain their capacity to talk, they pepper Mitch with questions, but since they were screaming at the same time, Mitch most likely had no idea what they were saying.

MITCH [*cutting off the girls in mid-pepper*]: Babes, babes, babes, call me tomorrow. All will be answered then.

Mitch saunters off, leaving the girls shell-shocked and slack-jawed. The joint empties, but the girls remain at the bar, drinking, plotting, scheming, freaking, until two hours later, when the club owner good-naturedly tells them to take a hike.

THE END

Part Two

Mitch's First Monologue

I rang up Mitch Busey the next day. His assistant put me right through.

'BAAAAAABE!' he roared. 'Glad you called. I'm crazy busy right now, but how'd you and your posse like to come up to my lair for a summit meeting?'

If nothing else, the guy was energetic. 'Yeah, sure. But I won't have the, um, posse with me, just Jenn. You met her last night, and—'

'Actually, babe, that's what I meant by posse. Just the chicks. This'll be a chicks-only *mano a mano*. I don't need to see your sweaty-dude rhythm section. How's tomorrow at noon? Works for me, too. Talk to Rachel. Wait, you just did talk to Rachel. Talk to her again. She'll firm up everything. Gotta run. See ya *mañana*.' Then he slammed the phone down. Part of me wanted to call back and tell him that Travis and Frank were important members of our group, that they should most definitely be there.

But I didn't. I felt okay about it being just the chicks. Couldn't tell you why. I just did.

Mitch was only thirty minutes late – and I say *only* thirty minutes, because, as I eventually learned, Mitch never shows up anywhere close to on time. Lateness grates on me, so by the time he breezed in, I was a bit irked. But I kept it under wraps. After all, this guy wanted to make us rock stars.

He looked exactly like you'd expect a record biz guy would look – or at least a record biz guy who's just slightly out of step with all the other record biz guys. He's tall and stooped over, with a paunch that probably grew in relation to his expense account. He has a tanning-salon tan, a single gold hoop earring in his left ear, and a ponytail that our resident movie nut Travis Bradford described as 'Steven Seagal-esque'. Travis also said he resembles 'a porky Quentin Tarantino'. Can't say I disagree with him on that one.

Mitch has seemingly dozens of affectations: berets, red-tinted glasses, leather vests, leather pants, and the ostentatious medallions. Sadly, I could go on. His voice is deep and resonant, and he affects the sound of a late-night deejay. It's a fine, soothing voice – that is, until he starts calling you 'babe'. Unless you're a star of Madonna-like proportions, Mitch will never, ever, ever call you by your given name: you're 'babe'. And it's not a sexual harassment thing; in Mitch Busey's world, *everybody* is 'babe', men and women, boys and girls, cats and dogs.

He's an okay guy, but it's tough to be around him for too long, because he doesn't converse: he monologues.

'BabesBabesBabesBabes,' Mitch said as he burst into the conference room, breathing heavily as if he had sprinted up from two floors down. 'Thanks for coming. Did Rachel bring you drinks? You want a Diet Coke? Water? O.J.? Wine? Yeah, that's right, I said wine, because at Éclat, it doesn't matter what time of day it is. If you're on my team and you want booze, you've got booze. I don't care whether it's noon or midnight.'

'We're fine, Mitch,' Jenn said. 'Thanks for asking us up.'

'Thank me? Thank *you*, babes. Now let's talk. Can we talk? Cool, let's talk.' And then *he* talked.

'Okay, first off, you guys are the bomb, the straight up *bomb*!' He pointed at me, and raved, 'Especially you, babe. The way you move, the way you connect with the crowd, the way you sing, it's insane, babe, *insane*!' He pointed at Jenn. 'And you, babe, I couldn't take my eyes off you. You're *hot*! Your keyboard playing – *hot*! Your outfit – *hot*! Your rack – *hot*! That's part of the reason I want to be in business with I.Q. You two effing *ooze* hotness!'

Jenn flicked my knee under the table. I somehow managed not to laugh.

'But your music is also *hot*! And that's what it's about – the music. Yeah, looks are pretty important – okay, looks are *very* important but if there's nothing to back them up with, then you're looking at an empty vessel who'll deliver *maybe* one hit single, *maybe* one good tour. But if you can't bring the noise night after night, album after album, looks mean dick.'

This time I flicked her. She *did* laugh. Mitch didn't notice.

'And clearly you guys can bring it – you have the tunes, you have the presence, you have the skills – but when we sign you, we'll need to make some changes. And notice I said *when* we sign you, not *if* we sign you, because I want it to happen, and when I want something to happen, it happens, damn it, it happens. But I need to warn you up front, when you become an Éclat recording artist, you're gonna put yourself in Éclat's hands. I don't want you coming to me in three months and saying, "Mitch, you didn't tell me this" or "Mitch, you didn't tell me that." I'm telling you now.

'And I don't think I'm being arrogant when I tell you that our hands have molded some pretty amazing successes. So to repeat, *there will be changes to your group*. Some musical. Some stylistic. Some internal. Some external. And I'm not gonna lie, here – this ain't about altruism. I wanna get *paid*. I want you to get *paid*. And if we're gonna get *paid*, we need to come correct with the whole package – and by *we*, I mean I.Q. and Éclat. And I.Q. will listen to Éclat. I.Q. will accept these changes, and I.Q. will embrace these changes.'

Jenn whispered to me, 'Watch this.' Then she unbuttoned her top button and leaned forward. Her boobs were *out there*. Mitch didn't notice. She rolled her eyes, buttoned up, and flicked me again. This time, I laughed.

'Okay, now let's talk about these changes. I know I told you I wanted to be in business with I.Q., but the fact of the matter is I want to be in business with you two. I want you two to be the faces of the band. Actually, babe' – he pointed at me – 'I want *you* to be the face of the band. Musically, with you, no changes are necessary. You're a pre-packaged goddess, a songbird sent to me from heaven – which is why you'll be your group's public face, the "it girl".' He pointed at Jenn. 'No offense to you, babe – you're a stone fox, and looking at you makes my knees tremble like they haven't trembled since I made out with Madonna back in '88. Now *there*'s an effing hot chick. But the thing is, you're an instrumentalist, and the problem with that is your average fifteen-year-old male music buyer doesn't jerk off while staring at a picture of a piano player – unless she can sing, like Alicia Keys. No, they yank it to Mariah, or Christina, or Britney. Some people even whack to Whitney. But not me. That'd be nasty. I mean, maybe I whacked it to Whitney back in the day, but that's not important here. Anyhoo, that's part of the reason we need to drop the name I.Q.' He pointed at me again. 'The public perception should be that this is your band, and that's why we're gonna rename you. We're gonna rename the group, and your name is gonna be . . .' He snapped his fingers four times then pointed at me again and said, '. . . *your* name. It's not even like it'll be a group name – it'll *just* be your name. That's what your group will be called. Got it? And we're gonna come up with a one-name name for you. Like Cher. Like Madonna. Like Mariah. Okay, Mariah isn't a one-name name, but when's the last time you heard anybody say "Carey"? Yeah, I don't remember either. But for you, I'm thinking it shouldn't be a name, or at least not the kind of name you'd give to a child. Although I have a hunch that after you blow up, there'll be tons of babies named, well, named whatever name we decide on. Maybe it'll be a nickname, maybe even something wacky. Maybe "Sweets". Maybe "Toots". Maybe "Babe". That's it! *Babe!* You're Babe! I love it!'

Suddenly I didn't feel like laughing. Jenn's face was a blank.

'Now, let's talk fashion.' Mitch pointed to Jenn. 'Your look is great, babe. Your figure is the bomb, and you dress awesomely – I mean that publicity photo of yours? Effing yummy!' He pointed at me. 'But your look needs some work. You're hot, but you're *raw*. You need some of that special Éclat molding. We're gonna fix you up. You'll be our Eliza Doohickey. We're gonna get you red-carpet ready. We're gonna get you MTV Video Awards ready. We'll give you an assistant, who'll also be your stylist and masseuse. Her name is Marnie Lake, and she is the bomb. She'll make you look effing gorgeous. And Marnie won't cost you one cent. That one's all on Éclat, babe.

'Another issue: your band. Two hot babes and two goofy-looking dudes doesn't cut it. Your boys play good, but there're hundreds of thousands of hot chick drummers and hotter chick bassists who'd cream themselves for a chance to get on a stage with you two. Hell, if you get a couple more hot chicks on stage with you, I'll cream myself. We'll get auditions going, like, the day after you sign the contract.

'Okay, so that's it for right now. We'll hammer out a deal, you'll sign on the dotted line, you'll change your name, you'll change your look, you'll change your band, you'll record a badass record, you'll tour the world, you'll play on *Saturday Night Live*, you'll get paid, I'll get paid, and if we play our cards right, next year you'll be taking home the Grammy Award for Best New Artist, Best Vocal Performance by a Female, and – drum roll, please – Best Album!'

He took a huge, noisy slurp of his coffee. 'So. You two have any thoughts?'

I looked at Jenn. 'Yeah, I have a few thoughts. And you?'

Jenn looked at me. 'Oh, yeah –'

A One-Act Play Starring Naomi, Jenn & Mitch, Although Mitch, Shockingly Enough, Just Sits There and Doesn't Say Much of Anything

The scene: our heroine Naomi and her partner Jenn are dazed by the barrage of verbiage thrown their way by Mitch Busey, the high-powered record-industry maven who wants to make them internationally revered music goddesses. He insists they make some major changes to their band, but even though the girls are itching to achieve goddess status, they still have some semblance of integrity.

NAOMI [*to Jenn*]: Would you like to share your thoughts with Mitch?
JENN [*to Naomi*]: No, no, you take the floor.
NAOMI: Well, if you insist. [*to Mitch*] First off, nobody in our band is leaving. *Nobody.* If you fire our band, you may as well fire us. Neither of us would care if Frank was five feet one inch tall and weighed three hundred pounds. Neither of us would care if Travis had green skin and blue hair, and smelled like roadkill . . .
JENN: Ironically, sometimes my brother *does* smell like roadkill.

NAOMI: . . . because they're our friends. They're our family. They know our music. They're loyal. They're punctual. And I don't care if you call our band I.Q., or I.D., or A.B.C.D.E.F.G., but at the end of the day, it's *our* band, and all decisions as to who's on stage are ours. We're happy to listen to your suggestions – we respect your track record – but the final verdict is ours. Period.
JENN: Preach on, sistuh-girl!
NAOMI: Second off, like I said, the name of our band doesn't matter. We've gone from the Intrepid Duo to the Intrepid Quartet to I.Q., and we've managed to survive. But this isn't going to be 'The Naomi Show' or 'The Jenn Show'. If you don't like I.Q., we'll come up with a list of names, and you'll come up with a list of names, and we'll put them all in a suggestion box at Upper East, and we'll pick a name at random. I don't really care.
JENN: Well, Naomi, if you don't really care, I have no problem with making it so you look like a solo artist.
NAOMI: Really?
JENN: Yeah. I think Mitch is right. There're hardly any bands that have boys and girls in them that aren't under a girl's name. It wouldn't bother me if I were Babe's back-up – at least I don't *think* it would bother me – and if it makes Mitch happy, and it makes everybody here at Éclat happy, then that's good, because they'll work that much harder on the record. Besides, that'll probably mean way less work for me. I can sit around and be a lazy-ass. You can do the out-front work, and I can do the in-back work.
NAOMI [*at once surprised and resigned*]: Okay, fine, but I refuse to be Babe. Or Sweets. Or Toots. Especially *Toots*.
JENN: Couldn't agree more. We'll compromise. If Mitch wants you to do the one-name thing, do what Cher and Madonna did.
NAOMI: Which is?

JENN: Use your first name as your whole name. You'll be Naomi. Even Mitch wouldn't deny it's a gorgeous name.
NAOMI: Are you sure?
JENN: I'm sure.
NAOMI: Okay, Naomi it is. Now let's talk makeover.
JENN: Yeah, let's.
NAOMI: I don't know how you intend to Eliza *Doohickey* me, but I want final say over *everything*. If you try to put me in clothes I'm not comfortable with, I'm not gonna wear them. If you try to put me in make-up that makes me look like a whore, it's coming off. If this Marnie person turns out to be a pain in the ass, she's gone. I've only just started getting comfortable with how I look, and I'll leave it at that, because frankly, my self-image is really none of your business, Mitch. I'll try it your way, but if I don't like it, it ain't happening.
JENN: Ahem.
NAOMI: Yes?
JENN: Maybe you could be more open-minded about this.
NAOMI: Excuse me?
JENN: Don't get me wrong, honey – you look great, better than ever. You glow. You're not pregnant, are you?
NAOMI: Not as far as I know. Misconstrued: doctrine of 'Immaculate Conception' is about Mary being conceived without 'original sin' – *not* about Mary conceiving Jesus without an earthly father . . .
JENN: Funny. But Naomi, you have unrealized physical potential. Whatshisface over here is right on this one. You're beautiful. A killer make-up artist could make you . . . breathtaking.
NAOMI: But I don't want a killer make-up artist. If anybody's going to make me over, it'll be you.
JENN: No way. I'm good, but you need a pro.
NAOMI: I thought you said I was beautiful. Why would I need a pro?

JENN: I want as many people to hear our music as possible, and if turning you into a goddess will sell, like, five thousand more records, well, isn't that worth it?
NAOMI: I dunno—
JENN [*to Mitch*]: Great. Done. So let's get Naomi and this Marnie chick together ASAP.

Mitch then explains to the girls how their contract will work, the details of which are far too boring to recount here. Suffice it to say that once the group formerly known as I.Q. starts selling records and performing to packed houses, the girls will be compensated to the point that they won't have to worry about having a day job for at least the lifetime of the debut recording by Naomi.

THE END

Simon Says

Mitch told us we wouldn't be performing at Upper East – or anywhere else, for that matter – until our record release party, which struck me as record company illogicality at its finest. Part of his reasoning, he explained, was that he wanted us in a rehearsal room, focusing on getting our material, as he put it, 'studio solid', so once it got time to record, we'd be 100 per cent ready to roll. The thing is, our material *was* 'studio solid' – as a matter of fact, we had too much great material to choose from. We're talking forty-two songs, enough for three albums. And all the tunes were really good.

Jenn's songwriting skills, already stellar, had somehow improved. I don't know whether it was because she had more life experience to draw from, or because practice makes perfect, or because she was in the midst of a string of purely sexual, mostly emotionally void pseudo-relationships and songwriting was the only way she could tap into her as-of-late-untapped well of passion. I don't even think *she* knew where the tunes came from.

'And Then' was still her magnum opus. Mitch recognized this, and decided it would be our first single, and that he wanted it in stores a full two months before the album was released. Mitch then told us we were to choose twenty of our favorite Jenn tunes, all of which we'd record, after which we'd eliminate the lesser performances. He also insisted we record a cover tune. I wanted it to be Suzanne Vega's 'Tom's Diner' except done with a samba beat. Jenn wanted to do 'Kung-Fu Fighting' as a ballad. Frank wanted to do a hip-hop version of Billie Holiday's 'Strange Fruit'. We ended up going with Travis's suggestion: a no-frills rendition of Stevie Wonder's 'Knocks Me Off My Feet'. You can't go wrong with Stevie.

Mitch's choice for the producer of the album was a guy named Simon. That's it – just Simon. Mitch wouldn't tell us his last name, even with Jenn's threat of a knee to his boy parts. Simon was Éclat's ace producer, and had worked with Mitch for over a decade. Our first meeting with Simon was at his house-slash-studio in Brooklyn, which, as it so happened, was located practically around the corner from where I grew up.

Once our material was studio ready, the group formerly known as I.Q. trekked to Brooklyn and trooped to Simon's door. We were a bit nervous, because none of us had ever worked with a producer; for that matter, we'd only been in a recording studio that one time when we recorded our demo, and we were only there for a grand total of four hours. But we weren't going to Simon's place for a recording session that day; we were there to pow-wow. And when Simon opened up the door, 'wow' was the operative word.

I pegged Simon No-Last-Name to be in his early thirties. (I was a few years off there; he was thirty-eight.) He was a shade over six-feet tall, he was lean, he had shaggy, light brown hair, blue eyes, some wonderful facial stubble, and a smile that could melt an entire grocery freezer of Ben & Jerry's. Put all that together, and you've got one of the most gorgeous creatures I'd ever laid eyes upon. Simon No-Last-

Name knocked me off my feet. Simon No-Last-Name knocked Jenn off her feet. If Stevie Wonder was a woman and wasn't blind, Simon No-Last-Name would've knocked him off his feet, too.

He gave Jenn and I separate, brief once-overs, so brief that I wouldn't have noticed had I not been paying close attention. It kind of gave me the quivers, but in a good way. It didn't seem to faze Jenn, but she'd had an entire lifetime of getting once-over'd. Simon stuck out his hand and introduced himself. Jenn and I reached for his hand at the same time, and both of us started babbling. I couldn't hear what Jenn said over what I was saying, and I don't remember what I said, because my brain was totally fogged with lust. But Simon No-Last-Name had that effect on women.

Simon held up his hand, laughed, and said, 'Whoa, whoa, whoa. Which one of you is Naomi?'

I raised my hand, and said, 'Naomi service at your Braver, um, I mean Naomi Braver at your service, um, I mean Naomi at your service, that's right, I'm just Naomi, because Mitch took away my last name the other day, but I guess he did the same with you, because you're only Simon, but how long have you been only Simon, and was it your decision, because I'm on the fence as to whether I like being just Naomi, I mean on one hand, I suppose I can see the appeal in it, but it's weird having all the attention focused on me, see, I like being part of a band, but I guess it makes sense from a marketing standpoint, but I don't know how much I agree with the decision, but at any rate, it's great to meet you, and I can't wait to start working with you, and for that matter, neither can the rest of I.Q., oops, we're not I.Q. any more.' I hadn't had an attack of the run-ons in a long while. Frank hadn't experienced it before, and gave me a look that was at once confused and mortified.

Jenn put a gentle hand on my right forearm and said, 'Naomi doesn't usually babble that much. I think my girl is psyched. Are you psyched, girl?'

'Of course I'm psyched,' I said, 'I mean, aren't you, c'mon, Jenn, we're making a record that's going to be in record stores everywhere in the world, so how could I not be psyched?'

Simon put a gentle hand on my left forearm. His touch sent a spark up past my elbow, past my shoulder, past my head, and all the way around to my other forearm – and then parts south. 'So starting next week,' he said, 'I guess you guys are virtually gonna be living here, so I may as well give you *el grande* tour. Follow me.'

I whispered to Jenn, 'I'd follow him anywhere.'

Jenn whispered back, 'Calm down, Nay.'

'I'll try. But it'll be hard.'

She stared at his butt and nodded. 'I hear you.'

Simon's lair was a combination of comfy and high-tech. The high-tech part was the studio and the recording room. I hadn't known there was a difference; I thought the entire thing was called a studio. I was wrong. The studio was where all the recording equipment was located: the mixing board, three sets of speakers, four laptop computers, a huge multi-CD burner, and a bunch of other stuff that I didn't understand and, frankly, didn't really care to learn about. (I didn't want to get too involved in the technical side of our little project; I wanted to focus solely on my singing, and wasn't about to overflow my already overflowed brain with equipment specs.) There was a big picture window above the mixing board that enabled the studio folks to see the musician folks in the recording room. The walls were covered with a bajillion photos of Simon semi-canoodling with his female clients, most of whom, coincidentally enough, were vocalists: there was Simon with his arm around [Sassy Underage Soul Crooner], Simon hugging [Super-Sexy Junk-in-the-Trunk Boob-Hanging-Out Rapper], and Simon being kissed/licked by [Mega Mega Super Super Hot Hot Hoochie Shaker]. I could go on.

The recording room was filled to overflowing with *stuff*. Stuff like a dozen amplifiers, and a bunch of exotic percussion instruments strewn on the carpeted floor, and a grand piano, and two electric pianos, and a bajillion microphones, wires, cords and headsets. Simon pointed to an enclosed glass booth in the corner. 'That's gonna be your home for the next few weeks, Naomi. Feel free to decorate it as you see fit.'

I stared at it nervously. 'I hope I don't get claustrophobed.'

Simon patted me on the shoulder. 'Nobody's ever had a panic attack in there. You'll be fine.' I hoped he wouldn't touch me all that much during recording. It'd mess up my concentration big time.

Frank asked a few questions about the drum set, and got very excited when Simon told him most of the drums once belonged to a jazz drummer named Art Blakey. Jenn was very excited, too, because she'd have access to a grand piano, plus she wouldn't have to haul her Yamaha electric keys back and forth from the East Village to Park Slope.

Simon then took us to his enormous 'chill-out room', and what a chill-out room it was: two overstuffed couches, two overstuffed reclining chairs, a plasma television, an X-Box, a full-sized refrigerator, and a coffee table covered with munchies – including a package of Double Stuf Oreos. I never asked him how he found out about my Double Stuf Oreo fetish – I'm sure Mitch or Mitch's assistant must've mentioned it. But I preferred to think of it as serendipity.

Simon motioned for us to sit down. 'Okay, we start

recording ten days from today,' he said. 'Mitch tells me you haven't been in a studio before.'

Travis said, 'No, we've been in one studio.'

Jenn said, 'Yeah, Trav, for like six seconds.'

Simon nodded. 'Okay, so since for all practical purposes, you've only performed live, it might be difficult for you to layer your tracks.'

'What do you mean, layer?' I asked.

Frank said, 'He means we'll record each instrument separately. We'll probably do the drums first using scratch bass, scratch keys, and scratch vocals, then we'll do final drums, then final bass and keys over the drums, then final vocals, then harmonies, then any extra instrumental overdubs. Right, Simon?'

'Exactly.'

I snatched up a pair Double Stufs and said to Frank, 'Speak English, please.' Then I asked Simon, 'What're "scratch vocals"?'

Simon explained, 'A "scratch track" is kind of a template. For you, Naomi, your scratch track will consist of you singing everything at half power – we don't want to blow out your voice this early in the process. You'll just bang out one take of each tune, so Travis and Jenn can listen to you while they're playing their parts. When the rhythm section tracks are all done, like Frank said, you'll get back in that booth and give me Grammy-winning performances.'

'I dunno, Simon,' I said. 'It'll be weird for me to sing all by myself. Wouldn't it make more sense for me to do it the same way I've been doing it for the last however-many years? Like with Jenn by my side.'

'I'll still be by your side, honey,' Jenn said. 'I'll even sit in the booth with you if you want. Would that be okay, Simon?'

'Absolutely,' Simon said. 'So long as you don't make one iota of noise.'

'I can do that.'

Travis mumbled, 'I'll believe that when I see it.'

I then asked Simon, 'Does it have to be that way for the whole record?'

'What way?' he asked.

'Like do we have to do every song all separately like that? Can't we do a couple of songs with us playing at the same time?'

Frank said, 'Yeah, that's a good idea. It'll change up the sound a little bit. I hate records where every tune is recorded exactly the same.'

After thirty seconds of running his fingers through his hair, he nodded. 'Yeah. Yeah. That's a good idea. Good call, Frank.'

Jenn stood up, slowly walked over to Simon, and said, 'I want to do "And Then" like that. I want to do it live.'

'No way,' Simon said. 'That one needs to be perfect. It's the centerpiece of the album.'

'As well it should be. It's my best song. But I've been dreaming of the day I'd record it, and that dream didn't involve Naomi being tucked into a corner all by herself.' Her eyes were laser beams, boring holes in Simon's head.

Simon said, 'I appreciate that, but this is the producer's call. You have to trust me on this one.'

Jenn kneeled down, put her hand high on his knee, and softly said, 'Simon, *you* have to trust *me* on this one.' She moved her hand farther up his thigh. 'I know this song.' Further up the thigh. 'I know how this song makes people feel.' Further up. 'It has to be . . . intimate.' Even further up, then she pulled away.

He said okay. Damn, Jenn was good.

Simon clapped his hands together. 'Okay, gang, any questions? Comments? Concerns?' I raised my hand. 'Yes, Naomi?'

'I'm freaking out. I was fine when it was just this abstract thing, but now that it's here, I'm kinda scared.'

After an awkward pause, everybody started talking at once, offering up their version of, 'You'll be great.' Simon sauntered over, did the forearm touch again, and said, 'I'll get you through it. Promise.' I wonder if he knew what kind of effect his hand had on me.

Travis sauntered over, then gave me his own forearm touch. 'I'll help get you through it too, Naomi.' Then he kissed me on the cheek.

Simon jumped up, again clapped his hands together, and said, 'Okay, Travis, that'll be enough. Naomi'll be fine. Kids, how about I buy you lunch. Thai food okay with everybody?' We'd yet to receive one cent from Éclat, so if somebody was picking up the check, *any* cuisine was okay with us. 'Great. Let's go out the front door.' He led us out of the chill-out room, and into the foyer of his living space. We walked past his living room, and I noticed an Ani DiFranco CD on the coffee table. Yikes. Tony Esposito was an Ani DiFranco guy. I briefly wondered if all Ani DiFranco guys were gross sex-taping freaks.

'Hey, Simon,' I called.

He spun around. 'Yo.'

'Ani DiFranco, eh?'

There was that big, sexy grin again. 'Sure. Sometimes boys like chick music, too.'

So I'd heard.

More of Jenn's Awesome Advice and Encouragement, Much of Which I Ultimately Ignored

It's midnight, and Jenn and I are curled up on her futon. Jenn speaks.

'Do *not* sleep with our producer. Yeah, I know he's gorgeous. I mean, don't you just love his hair? Wait, don't answer that. Don't think about his hair, or his ass, or his hands, or his eyes, or his stubble. *None* of that. He's our producer. What he does with us over the next few months is gonna have a huge impact on what our lives are gonna be like over the next couple of years. If he helps us make an amazing record, there's a chance we won't ever have to play places like Upper East again. I don't know if we'll be doing Madison Square Garden, but I *could* see us on stage at Irving Plaza.

'I mean, there's a chance that if you do Simon, he'll be even *more* inspired, and want to do right by you – and even want to do you right, heh heh heh. And I know you're horny, I know you haven't gotten any since you dumped Tony. Hey, didn't I tell you that since you started late, you'd be a total nympho?

'Oooh, here's an idea: I know I said you shouldn't think

about Simon in *that way*, but maybe if you lusted after him from afar – or a-near, since we'll be in the studio with him – that might be great. Nothing fuels passion more than unrequited love. And I bet you think I don't know about unrequited love. Well, I do. What do you think I think about when I'm writing? Sometimes I make up a fantasy about my perfect guy – a guy who probably doesn't even exist. Sometimes I think about you, about how much I love you. Sometimes I'm more practical, and I'll go out of my way to write a song solely because I think it'd sound awesome coming out of your mouth.

'But when I need to come up with something intensely emotional, with something that resonates more than usual, I think about that guy Eric. Remember him? That tall black guy with the cornrows? We had one excellent date, and he never called me back. I wanted him sooo badly. So once in a while when I get writer's block, I think about our one kiss. It was electric, and there wasn't even any tongue involved.

'You probably think I'm being a total bitch, but I can't emphasize enough how truly awful it would be for you to hook up with Simon – for *either* of us to hook up with him, really. Seriously, take all your lust for him and channel it into your singing. God, even if you *don't* do something like that, you're gonna sound so great anyhow. Imagine how much fun it's gonna be to sing in a place with a real sound system, a place with great acoustics, not to mention that grand piano. It's gonna be fucking amazing. But imagine also what'll happen if you hook up with Simon only one time, and it's really bad. Imagine if he's *done* in, like, three seconds, then imagine if he leaves, like, three seconds after that. Then imagine having to share space with him six days a week for weeks after that. That'd suck on so many levels.

'Just sing, honey. Just sing your heart out. There're plenty of guys out there with Simon's stubble, and eyes, and great voice, and nice butt, and long fingers. I know you think I probably shouldn't be saying stuff like this, but I want you to feel longing when you're in that booth singing "Problem Identified", and "Strong One", and "Viable", and "You're Not Done Until I'm Done", and "Bring It, Bring It", and "Sweeeeet", and the other thousand songs we're gonna record. I birthed those songs, and I want you to raise them right. And I know you'll make a wonderful mother to my tunes.

'So when we get to work, you go out there and kick ass. And don't forget to not sleep with our producer.'

The Effing Gorgeous, Effing Wonderful Marnie Lake

'Babe, meet Marnie. Marnie, meet Babe. She's straight up the bomb. Actually, both of you are straight up the bomb. I'll leave you two bombs alone to bond. Later.'

As it so happened, we'd already bonded, because Mitch, as usual, was insanely late. Marnie Lake, on the other hand, was insanely early, and I knew that because I, too, was insanely early.

The 'F' train moved astonishingly well that morning, so I made it to the Éclat conference room at 12.45, thirty minutes before my meeting with Marnie and Mitch was to begin. Marnie was already there – and had been for fifteen minutes – chilled out, head buried in the latest issue of *Billboard* magazine, her platform-shoe'd feet resting on the conference-room table. She was the picture of cool.

As Mitch might say, she was effing gorgeous, even hotter than Jenn in some ways. She was petite, just about five feet, two inches tall, with piercing, ice-colored eyes, light chocolate skin, a blonde mop of dreadlocks piled on her head, impressively muscled arms and legs, boobs out to *here*, a tiny waist, and a butt out to *there*. Between her and my roommate, I felt like somebody smacked me upside my head with an ugly stick.

Marnie leapt up and gave me a hug. 'Ohmigod, Naomi, it's amazing to meet you. You're even cuter than your picture. And I *love* your demo. I can't wait to hear your finished CD. You're working with Simon, right? He's the *best*. And what a cutie he is, right?' She was a bubbly one, alright; her personality matched her looks to a 'T'.

'It's nice to meet you too. But I have to admit, I'm kind of weirded out by the concept of having a, a, um, a—'

'A personal bitch? What, you've never wanted you own personal bitch?'

'Wait, I didn't mean—'

'Nah, I'm messin' with you, it's all good. I'm happy to be your personal bitch. It's my job.' She pulled her card from her pocket; sure enough, it read *Marnie Lake, Personal Bitch*. She chuckled and said, 'Keep the card; but I'm sure you'll have my celly memorized soon enough. And use me. That's what I'm here for.'

Who'd have thought that singing would lead to me having a personal bitch? It was awkward for me at first, but I could tell right off the bat that Marnie was cool. She was so upbeat, and she had such an innately positive vibe, that I couldn't help but smile and relax – at least a little bit. 'The thing is, Marnie, it'll be really hard for me to use you, because I don't know what I'm supposed to use you for.'

'Girl, from this second on, my job is to make your life easier, to make sure all you worry about is your singing. 'Cept from what I can tell, you don't have much to worry about in that department.'

'Thanks, Marnie. That's sweet. But right now, I'm not worried about anything *except* my singing. I have nothing else going on: no job, no boyfriend, just free time. All I do is watch TV, or read, or sing, and even when I'm not singing, I'm thinking about singing.'

She nodded. 'Enjoy your free time now, because this is the last quality free time you'll be seeing for a *long* while. Your life is about to get *busy*, and in about six months, if I wasn't here to help you, your life would be nothing but worry.' She ticked off the next year of my life on her fingers. 'You'll have an album to record, you have a ton of photo sessions to get ready for, you'll have a video to shoot, you'll have tours to prepare for, you'll have a bunch of interviews to do, and you'll have late-night talk shows to appear on. Enjoy the calm while you can, Naomi, 'cos before you know it, it'll be all storm. Éclat is gonna pump a bunch of money into you, and they'll want to see a return on their investment, so girl, you'd better prepare to *work*.'

'Yeesh. You're making me tired already.'

Marnie gave me a broad grin – she had a great grin – and jokingly yelled, 'Well, you'd best not fall asleep, girlfriend!'

I laughed. 'Okay, okay, I'm awake, I'm awake.' I regarded her for a silent moment. 'How'd you get into this anyhow?'

'You mean how did I become a professional bitch?'

'Uh, yeah, something like that.'

She sat down again and put her feet back up on the table, leaned back, and said, 'I have over four thousand CDs. I have two 80 GB iPods. One of 'em is filled, and the other is halfway there. I have a stereo system that cost me almost $10,000. And that's just the listening stuff; I also have some playing stuff. I have four guitars, a bass, a Fender Rhodes, and a saxophone – none of which I can play for shit. And I can't sing for shit, either. You ever heard the saying, "Those who can't do, teach"? Well I can't *do*, and I can't *teach* . . . but I can *help*. I want to do my part for music, 'cos I'm all about music.

'I worked for a management company for a while, which

was pretty cool. I was at a show, like, every night, meeting excellent people, hanging with the bands – and, to be honest, being sort of a groupie. At one point, I hooked up with the bass player from [Out-of-Step Grunge Band Who Insist On Still Playing Grunge]. But we dug each other in more than just a hook-up way, so we started dating *for real*. This was right when [Out-of-Step Grunge Band Who Insist On Still Playing Grunge] got really huge, and he was on the road all the time, and he was always *mad* busy. He was the most disorganized dude I ever met, so I figured if I kept his shit together, we'd get to hang out more. Well, he loved me doing that, and I loved doing it, too. Doing my part for the music, you know? He was the guy who started calling me his personal bitch. It's funny, right? But as time went on, I started being less his girlfriend, and more his personal bitch, so I quit.'

I asked, 'Quit what?'

'I quit being his girlfriend. No acrimony. No anger. It was all good. But I stayed on as the [Out-of-Step Grunge Band Who Insist On Still Playing Grunge'] personal bitch.'

'And that's how you met Mitch Busey.'

'And that's how I met Mitch Busey.'

And that's when Mitch Busey burst in and said, 'Babe, meet Marnie. Marnie, meet Babe. She is straight up the bomb. Actually, both of you are straight up the bomb. I'll leave you two bombs alone to bond. Later.'

I wasn't sure if I was the bomb, but Marnie Lake sure was.

My Fair Naomi

'My first assignment', Marnie said, 'is to give you a makeover, to give you a *look*.'

I knew this was coming, but I didn't think it would come this quickly. 'We haven't even recorded the album yet. Don't you think this can wait?'

'Girl, you think you can come up with a *look* overnight? Unh-unh. We're gonna take our time and get it right. I don't want to just haul you over to Barney's or wherever, slap some expensive clothes on to that cute little body of yours, and call it a day. I want to get to know you, and I want you to get to know me, so we can come up with this look together. I don't want your look to be contrived. It has to be legit. People can tell if you're a poseur. I want your shit to be *real*.'

It all sounded a bit pretentious to me, but I knew Marnie would do her best to, as she put it, keep it real. Ironically, when Mitch first mentioned the Eliza Doohickey thing, I thought it would indeed involve a trip to Barney's, which, frankly, would've been embarrassing. Parading around a huge, high-tone store like that in outfit after outfit? Being peered at by a stylist, as well as everybody else in the place? Staring into a mirror and looking at clothes of all shapes and colors hanging off my skinny frame? No, no, and no. But hanging out with a cool chick like Marnie – somebody who sincerely seemed to want to do right by me – well, that might make it okay.

Marnie further proved her mettle when she recounted an exchange with Busey: 'I have to tell you, Mitch asked me to ask you to consider plastic surgery,' Marnie said.

'Excuse me?'

'Yeah, he hinted to me that he wanted you to think about a boob job.'

I looked down at my chest. 'Depressingly enough, I guess I can see his point. But no way. I saw this thing on MTV a couple years ago where they filmed this girl getting an augmentation, and it was so disgusting . . .'

'Hey, I saw that too! Nasty shit, girl. Nasty.'

'. . . and I won't go under the knife unless I absolutely, absolutely have to. No elective surgery for Naomi.'

Marnie gave me a nod. 'I told him I'd never allow that to happen. But –'

She didn't say anything for a good thirty seconds.

'But what?'

'But, well, we *have* to get you some cleavage. I know, you are who you are, and you should be proud of who you are, because you are a cutie. But you don't have much . . .' She pointed at my chest. '. . . down there. We have to create the illusion. Quality boobage in your video, or on your album cover, or at a club, will move tens of thousands of more units. Like it or not, that is the sordid truth.'

I pointed at my double As. 'Hate to break it to you, but there is absolutely zero quality boobage here.'

'I know some people who'll hook you up. Trust me on that one. You'll dig it. But let's forget about that for now. Our first step is a trip to the spa. A mud bath. An aroma body wrap. A body masque. A hot-stone massage.'

Hmmm. Maybe this whole makeover thing wouldn't be so bad.

'We need to relax you,' Marnie continued. 'Your skin has to shine, and be blemish free; I don't wanna have to pancake you with make-up whenever you have a one-on-one with some journalist dude from the *Iowa Cowshit Weekly*. I want you to look as natural as possible. Because if you look natural, you'll feel natural, and if you feel natural, you'll sing better. We're gonna make weekly spa trips while you're still here in New York. When we're on the road, we won't have enough time to look around for a local spa, so I'll hook you up, at least massage-wise. I'm certified and everything.'

'Wow,' I marveled. 'What with all this being catered to, I hope I don't turn into a diva or something.'

'Not gonna happen on my watch,' Marnie said. 'No divas allowed. Got it?'

'Got it.' And I did get it. I hoped.

The Scarlet 'A'

Marnie had this thing about white pants. It didn't matter if it was after Labor Day, or before Memorial Day, or on Presidents Day, or during Arbor Day – she thought my tush looked great in white. I'm a pale chick, so I have no idea why she felt that white worked, but she was the professional, so I rolled with it. She went out and bought me a whole bunch of solid white pants, including some skin-tight white Calvin Klein slacks, some baggy white Kimora Lee Simmons denim jeans, and some white Isaac Mizrahi linen pants. She also presented me with a rainbow of Kangol hats, and purple Converse high tops, and black Puma low tops, and bajillion-inch Manolo Blanik strappy sandals, and some slinky La Perla bras and thongs, et cetera, et cetera, et cetera. I wasn't with her for any of these shopping sprees, so it would stand to reason that I didn't try on any of the clothes. Impressively, she got my sizes *exactly* right. Marnie had quite the eye.

'I want your ass in white every day for the next two weeks,' Marnie said as she handed me bags and bags of white bottoms, and boxes and boxes of multicolored everything else. 'I don't care if you're just going to the bodega down the street for some fruit, or to that Mexican bakery around the corner from the studio for a muffin. You put this stuff on. I want your body *and* your mind to get used to 24/7 hotness.'

'Um, Marnie, I live in New York City,' I pointed out. 'You never see people dressed in white pants here. You know why? Because it's a filthy place, and white pants get gross, like, two seconds after you step out the door.'

'Yeah, I know, but we're not going to always be in New York City. We're going to be all over the world, and no place'll be as filthy as here. And you're not wearing this to look good now – like I said, this is about body and mind. Body and mind. Body and mind –'

'Okay, I get it, I get it.'

The next day was my first official day of official vocal-tracking. That night I tossed and turned, and I had a nightmare about showing up at the studio and forgetting all the words to 'And Then', then blowing out my voice, then being naked in front of everybody. And yes, Simon was in the dream, and yes, he was looking at my nude body, but the dream was so frightening that he could've been naked himself, and it wouldn't have made things any better.

I finally got out of bed – it would be technically incorrect to say I 'woke up', because I hadn't slept – made some coffee, then hopped into the shower. After I dried myself, I put on a Marnie-selected red-black-checked Gama Go babydoll T-shirt that showed off my too-skinny tummy, a white Arianne thong that made its presence known if I bent over even the slightest, a pair of tight-ish white Barry Bricken linen slacks, a pair of red, shiny Sergio Rossi sandals with insanely high stilettos, and a red Kangol hat. We're talking a couple of thousand dollars' worth of junk for me to wear while encamped in a tiny vocal booth. Great way to spend the record label's money, right?

I gave myself a once-over in the mirror and was pretty

pleased with what I saw. Maybe Marnie was right about white pants. The only thing I had issue with was the thong – to me, having it on display was more awkward than having nothing at all – so I stripped off my pants and went commando.

After I stepped out of the bathroom, Jenn checked me out top to bottom, bottom to top. 'Damn, girl, you're a vanilla ice cream cone. With sprinkles.' She poured herself a cup of coffee and asked, 'So are you ready for today?'

'Absolutely not.'

She took my hand and guided me to the couch. 'Listen, Nay. This album is going to be by Naomi. Not by Jenn – by *Naomi*. You're going to have your own bin card at every record store in the world. It's on your shoulders. You have to go in confident. I'm confident in you, and Simon's confident in you. *You* should be confident in you. But if you can't get confident in you, then pretend, because if you screw up, we're screwed.'

'Gosh, Jenn, thanks for freaking me out even more. 'Preciate it.'

'No prob. And don't forget, I'll be in the booth with you, giving you moral support.'

When we got to the studio, Simon gave Jenn a lingering hug. I thought he was going to do the same for me, so I opened my arms, and closed my eyes, and . . . nothing. When I opened my eyes, he was standing directly in front of me, checking me out top to bottom, bottom to top, just like Jenn had done, back at the apartment.

He audibly gasped, then tentatively stepped into my arms and whispered super-softly in my ear, 'You're lovely, Naomi.' Then he released me, and, as if that sexy little moment had never even happened, said, 'Ladies, I've been waiting for this day since the moment I heard your demo.'

He squeezed my shoulder and said, 'I'm dying to get this magic voice of yours on wax. You ready?' he asked me.

I shrugged, and without a word, Jenn and I retired to the recording room and ducked into the booth. I did some warm-ups, slapped on my headphones, and spoke into the microphone. 'Okay, Simon, what do you want me to do?'

Even though I was in a glass booth, and Simon was behind a plate-glass window, I could see him perfectly. The sightlines in the studio were ideal – just like everything else in Simon's lair. Simon, who was pretty damn ideal himself, leaned into the talkback mic above the mixing board and said, 'What's the first song you want to tackle?'

I asked Jenn, 'What do you think?'

'Your call, honey.'

Travis's voice replaced Simon's in my headsets. 'How about "Hearts Ablaze"?'

'Hi, Travis,' I said. 'You didn't need to be here this morning.' In fact, I'd specifically told him *not* to be there that morning. In fact, I didn't want *anybody* there that morning other than Jenn, Simon, and one of Simon's assistant engineers. Everybody knew that. Or at least I thought they did.

'I wanted to be here,' Travis said. 'Wouldn't miss it for the world. Moral support and all that.' More moral support from a Bradford. Yahoo. 'Frank's here, too.'

'Hey, Naomi,' Frank said into the talkback. Both the bassist and the drummer were waving at me; both had huge smiles plastered on their faces. It was rare to see Frank smile, so my level of annoyance diminished. Somewhat.

Simon piped up, 'Naomi, I'm sending Scott, Brian, and Ella in. I'm getting some buzz from your channel. They're gonna suss it out. Won't take but a minute or three.'

'Guys,' I said, 'I thought it was gonna be a skeleton crew today. I didn't want the entire world watching me.'

Another voice from the talkback. 'It's not the entire world, babe. Just your band, the sound posse, and your A&R guy.'

I took a deep breath. 'Hi, Mitch.'

'Hey, babe. Thought I'd come and give you some moral support.' At this rate, I'd never need moral support ever again.

I then had what Jenn would later refer to as 'a diva fit'. 'I *specifically* told our producer that I wanted nobody here except for him and Jenn and one assistant, and correct me if I'm wrong, Simon, but a producer's job is to make sure the singer is happy, and I'm the singer, and I'm not happy, and you could've made me happy by sticking to your word, and keeping everybody out of here, and that means Brian and Ella too, and frankly, I really don't feel like singing right now, and I don't care if that puts us behind schedule. Okay, I guess I care a little bit if we fall behind, but I won't be able to sing until everybody clears the hell out.'

There was a stunned silence from the studio that lasted a good minute. Then I heard Mitch's voice in my headphones: 'Babe, are you on the rag or something?'

I was about to tell him he was, among other things, a sexist pig, a Neanderthal, and a hammerhead, when Jenn covered the microphone with her hand and said, 'Actually honey, you *are* on the rag.' She pointed at my pants, my nice new white Barry Bricken pants, which were now dotted with menstrual blood. And not just a few dots. A bunch of dots. Going commando sometimes sucks.

'Oh, fuck me, you've *got* to be kidding,' I said. 'What am I gonna do?'

Jenn put her hand on my shoulder. 'You're not gonna do anything. I'll run out and grab you a pair of pants, then I'll go to CVS and get you some tampons. Just stay here and chill out. I'll be back in ten minutes. I'll tell everybody to give you some space, and that you need some time to get your head together. They'll believe that.'

'It's the truth.'

She gave me a hug. 'You'll be fine, honey. I'll be right back.'

'Hurry. Please. Pretty please.'

She took her hand off the microphone and said, 'Guys, Naomi needs some chill time. Leave her alone for a while, okay?'

All the guys in the studio okayed us. Jenn had one foot out of the vocal booth, when I grabbed her sleeve. 'Hey, don't tell anybody about this,' I stage whispered. 'Especially Simon.'

'Puh-leez, Nay, you think I'd mention this? Chill out.'

After she left, I removed the headphones so the guys couldn't access me. I plopped down on the floor and leaned against the wall. The top half of the booth was glass and the bottom half wasn't, thus, I couldn't see anybody or anything. I had quiet and solitude. Beautiful.

Not one minute later, the door burst open. It was Scott. 'Naomi, I just need to check out this connection, so—' He noticed my bloody pants. 'Oh, shit.' Then he turned on his heel and sprinted off. That's right – sprinted. It's amazing how many guys are frightened by menstrual blood.

Like Frank. How do I know that? Because two minutes after Scott scooted away, our drummer poked his head into the booth and said, 'I'm gonna split, so good luck today, Naomi. I hope we didn't, um, oops. See you around.' He spun around and galloped off.

A few minutes later, there was a knock on the door. 'Is that you, Jenn?' I asked.

'No, it's the other Bradford. Just wanted to see if you're okay.'

'I'm fine, Travis. Don't come in.'

He ignored me and threw open the door. 'I –' He couldn't even get one full word out. He checked me out top to bottom, bottom to top. I wanted to literally die. Not figuratively. Literally.

He audibly gasped. 'Naomi. You're lovely. My God.'

'Thank you. Go away. Immediately.'

He didn't go away immediately. He was giving me this weird little smile. His forehead got damp. He took a deep, hitching breath, repeated, 'You're lovely', then left. Very sweet of him, but very mistimed.

A little bit later, the door burst open, and who was there? None other than Mitchie-boy Busey and Simon No-Last-Name. 'Babe, I gotta split,' Mitch said. 'Just wanted to say you're the bomb, and I know you'll kick tail today.' He got a gander of the spreading stain between my legs, and yelled, 'HOLY SHIT, I WAS RIGHT! SHE IS ON THE RAG! TOLD YA, SIMON! I KNEW IT!' I should note here that the microphone was still open, which meant everybody in the entire studio knew. Actually, considering how well Mitch's voice carried, probably everybody in Brooklyn knew.

I jumped up, ran all the way outside, and all the way into a taxi, which I took all the way home.

Fine German Engineering

After the period-while-wearing-expensive-white-pants debacle, suddenly everything seemed more manageable. I guess suffering through the single most embarrassing event of your adult life puts things in perspective. The next day, at Scott's behest, Jenn and I arrived at the studio early so we could iron out any logistical issues before everybody else showed up – everybody else, in this case, meaning Simon. You see, the second I got home that afternoon, I called Travis, Frank, and Mitch, and told them in no uncertain terms that if I saw their faces in the studio at any point in the next three days, I'd, well, I'd do something bad. Three days was how long I figured it would take before I was relaxed enough to sing in, shall we say, mixed company.

Frank of course, said, 'No problem.' That's it. Just, 'No problem.' You could always rely on Frank to be succinct, to get to the heart of the matter. For his part, Mitch monologued me for a while – at one point, just as an experiment, I put down the phone to go pee and change my tampon; when I got back four minutes later, he was still going.

Travis was bummed out when I gave him the edict, and

I was a little bummed out for him. He'd been nothing but encouraging and sweet, and he wanted to be there not just to be there. He was legitimately sincere about giving me 'moral support'. But he was nothing if not a team player. 'I'll drop by the studio next week,' he said. 'Just sing great, okay? I'll be thinking about you.' He spoke with such heart that I told him he could come by two days from then, rather than three. That cheered him up immeasurably – which actually cheered me up immeasurably.

It cheered me up so much that I called Marnie and told her I'd be up for both hanging out and shopping, something she'd been pestering me about for the last week. 'Good timing, girl,' she said. 'I was three seconds away from calling you. I can't do anything today, but keep tomorrow night free.'

'Tomorrow's my first day of tracking. I'll probably just want to come home after and crash.'

'I thought today was your first day.'

'Yeah, well, today was kind of a bust. I don't want to talk about it. But I have to tell you, Marnie, I'm not sure about the all-white-pants plan. Wait, let me rephrase that: I *am* sure about the all-white-pants plan. I'm sure I don't want to wear white pants ever again.'

'Why not? Somebody say something? Somebody say they didn't dig the way it looked? That couldn't be. You look money in white. Was it Mitch? I bet it was Mitch.'

'No, that wasn't it. I just had a traumatic experience. I'd rather not go into it. So can we put tomorrow off?'

'Nope. Sorry. Nine o'clock.'

'We probably won't be done at the studio until at least eight. Too bad. Guess we'll have to postpone.'

'Sorry, girl. You *have* to get there by nine. My designers are in town for only a hot minute. They came in from Europe just for you.' She gave me an address in Soho, and told me to be right on time, because her designers were always on time. At least there was that.

As it turned out, my first official, honest-to-goodness recording session the next day was awesome. With Jenn by my side, I ripped through 'Hearts Ablaze' and 'Problem Identified' before noon. We took a break and ordered up some Middle Eastern food. While we waited for the delivery person, we listened to my work. All I could say was, 'Wow.'

When I first sang at Beaned, even though the crowds were thin – so thin, they couldn't really be called crowds – people would tell me how much my singing touched them. At first, the compliments weirded me out, but then I realized they were only trying to express their gratitude, the same way I'd express my gratitude to, say, Joni Mitchell if I was to run into her on the street. This isn't to say I'm putting myself anywhere near Joni's class – that'd be heresy. It's just a matter of thanking an artist for making you feel good.

Well, during that first playback – the first time I could *really* hear what my singing voice sounded like – I wanted to thank *me*, because I made *myself* feel good. And in some ways, that's the most important thing you can do as an artist – make yourself feel good, feel fulfilled, feel *happy*. There's much to be said about the purity of art for art's sake, but right that second, in that studio, listening to my voice pour out of a pair of bajillion-dollar speakers, sitting next to my oldest, dearest friend – not to mention behind a guy whose bones I wanted to jump – I was pretty damn happy.

That happiness lasted until about 8.30, which was when I remembered I had to meet Marnie in Soho in half an hour. Jenn asked if I wanted her to come with me. I told her she didn't need to be subjected to an evening of me parading around in budget-busting clothing, and sent her on her merry way.

At 8.58, I flew out of a cab, and rang the bell of a ratty-looking building that stood kitty corner from the Angelika Film Center. Somebody buzzed me in, I jumped into the elevator. At the top floor, I stepped out of the lift and into an enormous loft, we're talking over two thousand square feet. The place was virtually empty: there were two sofas, a square metal platform that stood about three feet high, and a scary-looking contraption that looked vaguely like an MRI machine.

Marnie greeted me with an effusive hug. 'I just spoke to Simon, and he was bubbling!' she said. 'He said not only are you a kick-ass singer, but you're one of the most professional, focused people he's ever worked with. I think he's a little bit in love with you.'

My tummy did three topsy-turvies. 'Ex-ex-excuse me?'

Marnie laughed. 'But he falls a little bit in love with every female vocalist he works with. He's got a thing for you guys. He doesn't dig us stylist types. Too bad for me, eh?'

On a certain level, it was too bad for me. I hadn't fully gotten out of my 'I hate boys' mode, and it wouldn't be fair for Simon to suffer the brunt of my Tony Douchebag Esposito hangover. But on the other hand, maybe he could wash that all away. My tummy did one more topsy-turvy, then settled down. 'I'll keep all that in mind.' How could I keep all that *out* of mind? I glanced around the loft. 'Quite a place you've got here.'

'Oh, this isn't my place. Don't I wish. No, it belongs to Buestenhalter Gesellschaft.'

'Busten-whozit Gizelle-whatzit?'

'Buestenhalter Gesellschaft. Loosely translated from German, "Bra Company".' She motioned over my shoulder and said, 'Naomi, meet Otto and Ernst.'

I spun around and almost crashed into two tall, pale,

skinny guys who'd managed to sneak up right behind me. I let out a scared squeal, then said, 'Um, hi guys.'

They said in unison, '*Guten abend*, Naomi.'

'Um, *guten abend*.' The one on the right had long hair and round John Lennon glasses, and the one on the left had short hair and square Buddy Holly glasses, but despite that, they were almost identical. I asked, 'So are you guys brothers?'

Lennon monotoned, 'Yes.'

Holly monotoned, 'We are twins.'

'Have been since birth.'

'And we always will be.'

'That is the way it is.'

Marnie slapped Lennon on the bicep. 'Otto, chill.' She said to me, 'Feel free to ignore them. They do great work, but they're weird. Ernst, explain to Naomi what's going on here.'

Ernst, a.k.a. Lennon, gave me a once-over. Then a twice-over. Then a thrice-over. I'd never been examined so unashamedly; *I* didn't even look at myself as closely as he did, and I looked at myself pretty hard. 'Naomi,' he said, 'please remove your top. Immediately. Thank you.'

'I'm sorry? Could you repeat that? Because it sounded like you just told me to take my shirt off.'

'That is correct. Do it now. No dilly-dallying, *mein lieber*.'

I said to Marnie, 'These guys are creeping me out.'

'Yeah, they creep me out, too. Ernst, quit being creepy.'

Ernst was nonplussed. 'I am a businessman and a scientist, and your feelings are of no consequence to me, and it is late in the evening, and we have a deadline, and I wish to attend to my business and my science. So may we proceed?'

Marnie sighed. 'Proceed.'

'Thank you. Now Naomi, please remove your shirt,' Ernst said.

'Yes. We cannot proceed until you remove your shirt,' Otto said.

'We must examine your breasts.'

'Very closely. We must examine your breasts very closely.'

'For that is what we do – examine breasts.'

'We are experts in our field. You're in good hands.'

'Yes, your breasts will be in good hands.'

'Marnie,' I asked, 'what's going on?'

She asked the twins, 'Would you guys like to explain, or should I?'

Otto said, 'You begin the explanation, Marnie.'

Ernst said, 'And Otto and I shall finish.'

Marnie rolled her eyes, then looked at me and took a deep breath. 'Naomi, I have a hunch you're not going to like this, but it's not really that big a deal. I mean, everybody complains about it at first, but ultimately, they come to love it.'

Otto said, 'Please hurry up, Marnie.'

Ernst said, 'You are boring us.'

'We do not appreciate being bored.'

'We can be bored back in Stuttgart.'

'Okay,' Marnie said. 'Shut up already. Naomi, in a nutshell, Ernst and Otto are going to fit you with a bra.'

I asked, 'Um, couldn't we just go to Victoria's Secret?'

'Well, this isn't *just* a bra,' Marnie explained. 'Otto, you want to take over from here?'

'Naomi, I will be blunt,' Otto said. 'Your breasts are tiny. We understand you have the talent to be an international star. But you will be a slightly bigger star if you have slightly bigger breasts. And in the American entertainment industry, being a slightly bigger star means much more money. Ernst and I have developed a brassiere that will make your breasts bigger. Thus your bank account will be bigger.'

Ernst said, 'Thus our bank account will be bigger.'

'Because we get commission.'

'And referrals.'

'And more referrals mean more commission.'

'And more commission means more money.'

'And we enjoy money.'

'Thus we enjoy commission.'

I said, 'That's wonderful, guys.' I turned to Marnie and said, 'I'd be perfectly happy buying a Wonderbra. I'll even pay for it myself, and—'

'The Wonderbra is not good enough,' Otto interrupted. 'Our bra is a miracle of modern science. Observe.'

He reached into his lab coat and pulled out what looked to me like a transparent strapless undergarment. 'Not to state the obvious,' I said, 'but isn't that just a clear bra?'

'On one level, you are correct,' Ernst said. 'But it is so very much more.'

I don't want to bore you recounting Otto's long-winded scientific babble, so I'll give you the short version: the Buestenhalter Gesellschaft wonder twins were going to customize me a padded bra that would be the next best thing to plastic surgery. As I mentioned, the bra was clear, but somehow when it touched a human body, it adopted both the wearer's skin tone and musculature – kind of like a chameleon. The material also soaked up the wearer's body temperature, so it felt 98.6 degrees, thus it felt real. And the nipples, well, they *worked*. If it got cold, they got hard. If they got rubbed, they got hard. If Simon stared at them, they'd probably get hard.

'Please don't freak, Naomi,' Marnie said after Otto's speech. 'I know it's bizarre, and superficial, and kind of lame, but trust me, plenty of other celeb types have used it.'

She reeled off the names of five film stars, three sitcom actresses, and eight – count 'em, eight – singers who've hired Buestenhalter Gesellschaft. Decorum prevents me from revealing their identities. 'They all love it,' Marnie continued, 'believe me. I bet you wouldn't have even guessed in a million years that [Curvy Revered Eighties Female Pop Star] used it. Or [Super Curvy Flash-in-the-Pan Nineties Female Rock Star]. Or especially [Height-Challenged Pseudo Punk Female Pseudo Singer].

'[Height-Challenged Pseudo Punk Female Pseudo Singer]? Really?'

'Really,' Marnie said. She gestured at Ernst and Otto. 'These weirdos do some great work. Now I know you're probably totally against this, but let me—'

'You know what? It sounds fine,' I said. 'If it's good enough for [Height-Challenged Pseudo Punk Female Pseudo Singer], it's good enough for me. Let's do it.'

Marnie blinked her eyes in surprise. 'Really?'

'Sure,' I said. 'Bring on my new boobs!'

Otto said, 'Very good.'

Ernst said, 'We look forward to making you more beautiful than you already are. If that is possible.'

'Now remove your shirt.'

'Yes, remove your shirt.'

'Yes, remove your shirt.'

Imitating the twins' robotic monotone, I said, 'I am now removing my shirt.' Then, as you might've guessed, I removed my shirt.

Otto said, 'Now step over to the machine.'

Sure enough, the MRI-looking contraption worked just like an MRI contraption. I lay down on a movable platform that eased me into the enclosed tube. I was in there for about thirty minutes. It was confining but tolerable, tolerable because sweet Marnie lent me one of her MP3 players. It was her 'all jazz machine', and the tunes, none of which I recognized, were soothing and smart. I'm sure our jazz-loving drummer would've approved.

After the Buestenhalter Gesellschaft boys were done doing the voodoo that they do, they ejected me from the tube, and Otto said, 'You will return here in eight hours.'

Ernst said, 'That is approximately seven in the morning.'

'We will work overnight to complete your bra.'

'Tomorrow morning, you will have new breasts.'

'Perfect full C cups.'

'Perfect.'

'Perfect.'

I came back at seven on the dot. It took Ernst and Otto ninety minutes to demonstrate how to put on the bra – but it was worth it. They *were* perfect C cups. If you looked at our album cover, or our videos, you'd have never guessed.

This, dear readers, is information that you'd never find in *Naomi: A Woman, A Singer, An Artist*, or *Diving Inside Naomi's Head*, or *Songbird: The True Naomi Story*. Aren't you glad you bought this book now?

And Speaking of Videos

Things were going so swimmingly in the studio that the following week, Simon took the entire band out for a celebratory dinner at a fancy-schmancy, amazingly yummy French place in Soho called Balthazar. He told us to order whatever we wanted, and we did – an enormous platter of oysters, an insanely expensive cheese plate, chi-chi salads, the priciest entrées on the menu, multiple servings of steak frites, a bottle of Château Lafite Rothschild Pauillac, a bottle of Château Margaux, and a bottle of Château Haut Brion Pessac-Léognan. I'm embarrassed to tell you exactly what the bill came to; suffice it to say it would've covered three-plus months of Jenn's and my rent. But we hadn't seen much money from the fine folks at Éclat Records, thus we were still semi-starving artists, thus – as had been the case since day one of recording – when free food came along, we grabbed at it.

Over dessert and coffee, we mused about our soon-to-be-produced video for 'And Then'. Neither Jenn nor I had any good ideas as to what the video should look like. Travis, film geek that he was, had a bunch of concepts, all of which were impressive and creative – and expensive. During a brief lull in the conversation, Simon, who'd been relatively quiet all evening, said, 'I have an interesting story about a video shoot.'

Up until that point, Simon hadn't offered up *any* interesting stories – it wasn't that he was reticent, it's just that he talked about what was happening in that moment, most of which had to do with recording. But he'd been in the game for so long that we knew he had a ton of great tales buried somewhere. I leaned forward and said, 'Let's hear it, Mr Producer.' (I should note that Mr Producer was looking exceptionally cute that night, which is why I made sure to grab a seat next to his. I felt his leg touch mine under the table a few times, but I didn't think much of it – that is, until I got a few glasses of Château This And That into my system. Then I thought about it *a lot*. I thought about skin on skin, and mouth on mouth, and tongue on tongue, and sweat on sweat, and heartbeat against heartbeat. I felt as sexy as I'd ever felt in my life. I felt like I was Jenn.)

'Hear it you shall, Ms Vocalist. This one's about a certain singer/songwriter who will remain nameless. He was like you guys in that his label had huge hopes for him, and they wanted to rush his single out, which meant rushing his video out, too. He was also like you guys in that he'd never been in front of a camera before. But he wasn't like you guys in that he was kind of odd looking.'

Jenn said, 'Is "odd looking" a euphemism for "ass ugly"?'

Simon smirked, 'You said it, I didn't. He was skinny, but he had a bit of a gut. He had a deadly combination of a bad complexion and chubby cheeks. And to make matters worse, even though he was in his early twenties, he had a badly receding hairline.'

Travis piped up, 'Ooh, I bet I know who it is. It's [Goofy-Looking Underrated Male Singer], right?'

Simon nodded. 'Yeah, I guess it wasn't really that hard to

figure out. So as you know, his music is beautiful, just gorgeous. Man, what a voice. I hope this doesn't sound harsh, but it was hard to believe that that voice came out of that face.'

'That's the exact thing I thought when I saw him at Mercury Lounge right after his album came out,' Travis said.

I said, 'And that's the exact same thing I thought when I saw him on *MTV Spring Break*.'

Travis gently punched me lightly on the arm. 'Hey, great minds think alike.'

Simon continued, 'The director was told to do everything possible to make this guy look okay. Thing is, even though the label wanted to break him big, the video budget was tiny – they only had eighteen hours to shoot the entire thing. Unfortunately, no matter what they did, they couldn't make the poor guy look good. They put him in baggy clothes, then in tight clothes, then in vintage clothes, then in a suit, and nothing worked. Ultimately, he wore blue jeans and a white T-shirt – boring, but functional.

'They sent in Marnie to work on his face.' He turned to me and said, 'She tried everything. I don't know anything about make-up, so I have no idea exactly what "everything" means in cosmetics lingo. But I'm sure if Marnie couldn't make him look right, *nobody* could've made him look right.'

'Hear, hear,' I said. 'She's the best.'

'They even tried putting him in a wig,' Simon marvelled. 'Marnie showed me a Polaroid of that, and it wasn't pretty. She ended up spending nine useless hours on his "look", which gave them only nine hours to shoot the clip. Marnie finally told the director, "I can't do it. I can't make him look good. This guy is a sweetheart, and he sings his ass off, but I just can't do it!"

'The director says, "Well, do *something*. I'm over it. At

this point, I just want a presentable and professional video in the can."

'Sara Rogers was the director, by the way, and if you know anything about videos, you know that Sara's one of the best—'

'*Ohmigawd!*' Travis screamed. 'She's *incredible*! Did you guys see that documentary she did for PBS? It was about drummers. Frank, you know which one I'm talking about, right?'

'Hell yeah I do. Incredible. Amazing. I have it on DVD.' That was the most animated I'd ever seen Frank.

Simon said, 'So anyhow, Sara goes off into the corner, scribbles on to a legal pad for a while, then jumps up and says, "I've got it! I've *totally* got it. Marnie, get me a female heroin chic model who can dance. And get her *fast*."

'Marnie knows everybody in town, so three phone calls later, she had [Anorexic Overexposed Model/Socialite] on the soundstage. Let me repeat that: Marnie got [Anorexic Overexposed Model/Socialite] to the soundstage in *under an hour*. When [Anorexic Overexposed Model/Socialite] got there, Sara calls everybody into the middle of the room, and says – and I'm paraphrasing here, but this is the general gist – "[Goofy-Looking Underrated Male Singer], you sit on this here bar stool. We're gonna kill all the lights except for the ones behind you. We're going to backlight your ass to death. Marnie, get [Anorexic Overexposed Model/Socialite] a diaphanous gown. We're gonna have her dance all around him. If she can't dance, make her prance. She'll touch [Goofy-Looking Underrated Male Singer] in an intimate way, and look adoringly at him, and that's it. I'll shoot it with a hand-held, and we'll do as many takes as we can before we have to get out of here. We'll do it in black and white, and I'll edit it to death, and we'll have something like that Chris Isaak video."

'You guys know which Isaak video I'm talking about, right?' Simon asked. 'The one with Helena Christensen? The two of them rolling around on the beach?'

Jenn nodded. 'I sure do. Massive hotness.'

Simon said, 'Indeed. As I'm sure you remember, all you saw of [Goofy-Looking Underrated Male Singer] on the final cut were his hands, and his silhouette, and a brief shot of his face. The thing ended up looking like softcore porn, but everybody loved it – except [Goofy-Looking Underrated Male Singer], of course, poor guy. The irony is that he and Sara won an MTV Video Music Award for the thing.'

The table was quiet for a minute, then Travis broke the silence by saying, 'That's kind of a depressing story. But inspiring. All at once.'

'Well put, Trav,' Jenn said. 'But why did you tell us that?'

'Why?' Simon said. 'Oh, I guess Mitch didn't tell you. Sara Rogers is gonna direct the video for "And Then".'

Travis yelled, '*Cool!*'

A Weird Marnie Thing That Really Doesn't Have Much to Do With Our Story, But it's Just So Weird That I Can't Not Mention it

The day after our Balthazer outing, Marnie dropped by the studio at around 9.00 p.m. and invited Jenn and me out for dinner. She said she'd been wanting to check out Cucina, Brooklyn's legendary Italian restaurant, which was just down the street from Simon's place. I'd been there dozens of times, and was happy to go again – especially since Éclat was footing the bill.

After I polished off a huge plate of rigatoni with a red pepper and basil sauce, Marnie asked if we'd like to come back to her place in the city and play with her make-up. I was pooped, but Jenn said it sounded like fun – remember, she's a bit of a make-up queen – and that I'd better come or she'd kick my butt, so off to Midtown we went.

Marnie had a huge condo in one of the high rises on Central Park West. After a quick tour – during which Jenn and I couldn't even speak, we were so blown away by the enormity of her home – Marnie took us into her 'art studio'. Jenn and Marnie pored through the dozens of types of eyeliner, mascara, blush, moisturizer, lipstick and *everything*. I had a good old time watching Jenn have a good old time, which got me to thinking that Jenn and I hadn't had a girl's night out since we signed our record contract.

After an hour, I got kind of bored with the cosmetics seminar, so while Marnie explained to Jenn the merits of various lipsticks – like what's prettier, Shiseido Pied Nus or Nina Ricci Soupir De Rose? – I went exploring. Marnie had told me that I had free rein to check out anything, so I looked into any box I stumbled across, I peeked under sheets, and I opened all the drawers and closets. Nosy Naomi.

The last place I poked my nose was the skinny closet right beside the bedroom door. Not only was it skinny width-wise – probably about one foot across – but it was shallow, only four or so inches deep. There were a couple of dozen shelves, all covered with a baffling array of perfume bottles.

'Holy crap, Marnie,' I said, 'do you think you have enough perfume?'

She turned around and shrugged. 'I have a bit of a perfume fetish.'

'Will you be perfuming us while we're out on the road?'

'Absolutely.'

'How do you decide what to use?'

Marnie started playing with her fingernails. 'I have a method.'

Jenn asked, 'And that method is?'

'It's a trade secret,' Marnie mumbled.

'Oh, come on, Marnie,' I said. 'I'm the one that's going to be wearing the stuff. You have to tell.'

After almost a minute of silence, Marnie mumbled, 'Mlafubetis.'

'Speak up, woman,' Jenn said.

'Elfumbsvem.'

'*What?*' I asked.

'I ALPHABETIZE THEM!'

After a bit of silence, Jenn said, 'You're kidding.'

'Well, how else do you think I could keep track?'

I closely examined the closet, and sure enough, each and every one of those bottles was set in alphabetical order.

Like here are some of the As – A La Française. Acqua Di Gio. Adolfo. Adrianne Vittadini. Aimez-Moi. Anne Klein. Arpège.

And like here are some of the Gs – Gai Mattiolo. Gieffeffe. Gold Mania. Gucci Rush 2.

And like here are some of the Zs – ZOA. Actually, that was the only Z.

I stopped counting the bottles when I hit a hundred – and that put me only about a quarter of the way through the closet.

'Marnie,' I said, 'this is enough perfume to get me through six US tours, four European tours, and a trip to Japan. Tell me you won't bring all of this with you.'

'Of course I won't bring it all with me.' Then she looked thoughtfully at the closet and mumbled, 'Maybe only half.'

The Intrepid Duo . . . But Not That Intrepid Duo; We're Talking a Different Intrepid Duo. Thing is, it's an Intrepid Duo That Wasn't Supposed to Exist

Finally, after three weeks of blood and sweat and tears – okay, there wasn't any blood after the white pants incident, but there was sweat and tears all over the place – all my vocal tracks were in the can. All the tracks, that is, except for 'And Then'.

Mitch wanted us to record that first so he could get it out ASAP. Simon, on the other hand, felt it was too important to rush into, thus he decided to save it for last. I agreed with Simon. But of course I did. I was Simonized from the get-go, so if he'd told me that zebras had dots rather than stripes, I'd have agreed with him there, too.

Sweat and tears notwithstanding, I ultimately got into a groove recording-wise, such a great groove that my three weeks behind the mic turned out to be pretty fun; way more fun than I ever imagined. Jenn and I would show up at the studio between nine and ten, then we'd munch on whatever Simon got us for breakfast. Sometimes it was bagels, sometimes he'd make us oatmeal from scratch, sometimes it was a fruit salad. At Jenn's and my behest, there was *always* some strong, strong coffee. After we ate and digested, Jenn and I would retire to the vocal booth, where I'd sing, and she'd cheer me on. Simon was a doll throughout the whole process, consoling me when I felt insecure, cheering me on when I kicked ass. Also, his production skills were astonishing; he made my voice sound so good, so crystal clear, that I wept with gratitude during three of the playbacks. And he was so cool that when the tears came, he never asked me what was wrong, he'd just rub me in between my shoulder blades. It was like he knew exactly what I was thinking, knew exactly what I needed.

Travis was there practically each day. He'd roll in around noon, plunk down on the couch in the studio, grab whatever was left over from breakfast, then for the rest of the day offer up his own special brand of moral support. Frank popped in only a few times, because he was generally busy rehearsing and gigging with his other bands. We wanted him for ourselves, of course, but we couldn't begrudge him for doing the other work – after all, we hadn't seen much money yet.

We procrastinated for a few days before we dived into 'And Then', tweaking whatever could be tweaked. Eventually, it got to the point where we couldn't wait any longer to cut the single. Remember, we were going to do two versions of it, one with me singing to the pre-recorded track, and one live with the band. Considering how well everything had gone up to that point sound- and comfort-wise, we opted to stay our course and do the pre-recorded take first.

I was primed to sing that song, that beautiful song, that romantic song, that sexy song, that song I'd sung a bajillion times but had never grown tired of. So the big day, the hopefully fateful day, the hopefully magical day, the day that

I was to lean into a state-of-the-art microphone and sing the words that would make the whole world sing, I ate my bagel, I did my warm-ups, I strutted confidently into the vocal booth accompanied by my brilliant best friend, and I proceeded to blow the whole thing spectacularly.

I still don't know what happened, whether it was fatigue, or over-preparation, or some bad cream cheese, but I stank. And once I start stinking, I start thinking. I got lost in my head, trying to work out what was wrong, and how to fix it, and what Simon thought about the whole thing. When it happens, it's like bad sex, i.e., if you're making love, and things start going awry – and you know exactly what I mean by 'going awry' – you get trapped in your head, working out a way to make it better. Which, of course, makes it worse.

Jenn, in a very un-Jenn-like display, freaked out. I guess I could understand why. 'And Then' was her favorite child. But, after realizing I was freaking just as much as she was, if not more, she did her best to keep her freak flag under wraps. Unfortunately, her freak flag wouldn't *stay* under wraps, and she had a minor meltdown. Okay, it wasn't minor.

'Naomi, we've done this song dozens and dozens of times, and you've never messed it up, not even close, and you haven't messed up anything else in three weeks, nothing at all, so why do you have to pick today to lose it, I mean, this is the most important day of our artistic lives, and you go and get a case of brainfreeze, and I've seen you get brainfreeze, but never this badly, and never on something you know this well, and I can't believe it, I really can't believe it—'

Hey, I'm supposed to be the queen of the run-on sentence!

Jenn finally ran out of steam and headed towards the door. 'Where're you going?' I asked.

'I'm sorry, honey, that was uncalled for on my part. I'm just a little burnt. I need to get away. Maybe we should take a break from each other for a while. You stay here, okay?'

'A break?' I asked. 'Are we getting a divorce? Should I stay at a hotel tonight?'

'That's not what I meant, and you know it. I mean a few hours, not a few months. Stay here and work alone with Simon for a while; see if you can make anything happen. I'm gonna go and get trashed.'

'It's only three o'clock. Isn't it a bit early?'

'Oh, sorry, *mother*. I'll wait until five. Would that make you feel better?' She rubbed her forehead as if she had a migraine. 'I'm sorry. I'm really sorry. I guess I want this to be perfect. Stay here. Work. Make it happen.'

'I'll get it together, I swear. Tomorrow, I promise you'll walk into the studio and be blown away.'

Hurricane Jenn downgraded to a light drizzle. 'I know, Nay. And I can't wait to hear it. But right now, I'm in desperate need of three pitchers of Guinness. Maybe four. Don't wait up for me.'

After she left, Simon said, 'So. What now?'

It dawned on me then that was the first time I'd been alone with Simon for more than just a few minutes. It was both kind of cool and kind of disconcerting. I looked at him, *really* looked at him, and wanted to kiss him, and I marveled once again at how damn handsome he was. Beautiful, really. And he seemed like a good man, kind, talented, and supportive. Would it be so awful to kiss him? But I wondered if he was too good to be true, if he was even *real*? Were any guys *real*? Would he make me feel safe? *Could* he make me feel safe? Was he the anti-Tony, or merely a Tony in producer's clothing?

But then I figured who cares, what the hell, one little kiss wouldn't ruin my career.

But I wimped out. 'Let me walk around the block and clear my head,' I said. 'When I get back, we'll give it a couple more shots. Sound good?'

'Take your time. No rush at all.'

I hiked up to Prospect Park – Brooklyn's version of Central Park – and found a nice spot under a nice tree. I emptied my head as best I could, closed my eyes, and took ten nice, deep breaths. Two seconds later, I was asleep.

I woke up an hour or so later, refreshed, revitalized, and hungry. On the way back to Simon's, I stopped by the local Italian deli, and bought myself and my producer overstuffed turkey subs with buffalo mozzarella.

Simon rushed to meet me at the door. He looked pissed. 'Where the hell were you? I was getting worried.'

'No worries. Just took a little nap in the park,' I said, then handed him his sandwich.

The pissed-ness dissipated. 'I've never had an artist buy me food. I've always been the food procurer.'

'Well, I'm not your average artist,' I said.

'You sure aren't,' he said, staring right into my eyes.

I stared right back, and was so entranced that I slipped into run-on mode. 'And you aren't an average producer, although I can't really say that with certainty, because I've never worked with any other producer before, and to be honest, I don't even know what a producer's supposed to do, I mean you're our den mother, and our engineer, and our chef, okay, you're not *really* a chef – you don't cook for us, but then again, you make us oatmeal, and it's not like I'm an oatmeal connoisseur or anything, but I appreciate the effort, I mean doing oatmeal from scratch is way more time-consuming than dumping a packet of powder into a bowl and adding hot water, but you can use milk, too—'

'Naomi.'

'Yes.'

'Shut up—'

'Hey, you're not supposed to tell me to shut up,' I joked. 'I'm the diva, remember?'

'You didn't let me finish. I was gonna say, "Shut up and kiss me." '

Our first kiss wasn't one of those slo-mo movie kisses. We didn't take each other's hands, and then stare deeply into one another's eyes, and then gently move our faces closer and closer and closer until our lips grazed, then grazed some more, then grazed even more until we fell into a gentle embrace. No, our first kiss was *fast*. We went straight from 'Shut up and kiss me' to frenetic tongue wrestling.

And it was very, very good.

We collapsed on to the floor and made out like high-school kids. (Actually, I'm not really sure if we were making out like high-school kids, having never made out in high school.) He tasted amazing, like bubblegum and bagels. His stubble scraped my neck, which both tickled and hurt, the combination of which drove me nuts. His hands ran up and down my side, all the way from my shoulder to my knee, and that man had great hands, electric hands, hands that I'd be happy to let stroke me for days at a time. We flailed around for I don't know how long, the sandwiches and my hunger forgotten. It was way better than anything that happened with Tony Douchebag Esposito, more intense, steamier, hotter, and, frankly, better tasting. I was so in the moment that Douchebag was *gone* – at least for the moment. I figured the more I kissed an upstanding citizen like Simon, the quicker my memories of Douchebag would fade into oblivion.

Right then, right at the point where the stakes were seconds away from being raised – with us tangled up on the ground, with my shirt half off, with Simon's shirt unbuttoned, with Simon fully aroused, and with me *almost* fully aroused – in walked Travis. He stared at us. We stared at him. Silence.

Finally, after what seemed like an hour, Simon said curtly, 'Travis, we're done recording for the day. Now get.'

'Fine,' Travis said, then he stomped out.

I disentangled myself from the NaomiandSimon human pretzel, and attempted to stand up. My legs, weakened by lust, weren't having it, and I plopped back into his lap. 'Simon, be nice. I'm like his surrogate older sister, and imagine walking in on your older sister. I know if I had a brother and I walked in on him, I'd freak. I'm gonna go chase him down and talk to him. Don't go away. And leave your shirt just like that, okay?'

'Fine.'

Yikes. Harsh tone. Had his pissed-ness returned?

If it had, I ignored it.

A Fairly Short One-Act Play Starring Naomi & Travis

The scene: our heroine Naomi – having just made out with somebody she probably shouldn't have made out with and feeling a bit, shall we say, rubbery – runs after Travis, who, having just witnessed said make-out session, is totally weirded out. She catches up with him just as he's about to walk down into the subway.

NAOMI: Trav! Hold up!
TRAVIS: Why?
NAOMI: Listen, what you just saw, that's the first time that ever happened.
TRAVIS: Yeah, whatever.
NAOMI: Really, it's not that big a deal. You work closely with somebody, and things happen.
TRAVIS: I've worked closely with Simon. I don't think anything's going to happen with me and him.
NAOMI: Very funny. Seriously, this isn't a big deal. And please don't tell your sister or Frank about this.
TRAVIS: I won't tell Frank. He wouldn't care, anyhow. But I have to tell Jenn. Really, *you* should tell Jenn. And, I

mean, by tomorrow. If you don't, I will.
NAOMI [*surprised that Travis had put his foot down so hard*]: Um, okay.
TRAVIS: Okay. Goodbye.
NAOMI: Bye.

Travis stomps off to catch his train. Naomi goes to make out some more with that person she probably shouldn't have made out with. For the moment, everybody is happy – or so our heroine thinks.

THE END

I Do Exactly What Jenn Told Me Not To Do

That's right, folks, I ignored my best friend's advice and slept with the producer.

And it was very, very good.

The Day After

'Jenn, I was a bad girl.'

I knew she'd gotten in *very* late. I knew she'd gotten *very* drunk. I knew she hadn't had her coffee yet. What better time to break the news that I didn't want broken?

'What'd you do?' she grunted.

'I did exactly what you told me not to do.'

'Hunh?'

'I slept with the producer. And it was very, very good.'

I think it was the tone of my voice – dreamy, smitten, and, dare I say it, sexy – that pierced through her booze-fogged brain. 'You did *WHAT*?!' She sat up and pushed her sleep-tousled hair out of her face. 'Did you say what I thought you said, or am I still drunk?'

'I said it. I slept with the producer. And it was very, very good.' I took her shoulders and pulled her close so her face was just inches from mine. 'Jenn, this was the best it's ever been. By far. Nothing I ever did with Tony Douchebag came close.' I ran to the futon, jumped up and down on it, and chanted, 'The best! The best! The best!'

She sighed, chuckled despite herself, then said, 'Honey, I'm happy for you, I suppose. I just want you to be happy. But there're a million guys out there who're just as cute as

Simon. And let's say you ended up dating one of those millions of guys, and then the relationship ended badly. That wouldn't have any effect on your professional life – or mine, for that matter. Whereas if your relationship ends badly with Simon, that will have a huge effect on everybody, and that's not—'

I interrupted, 'Don't you think I thought about all that? Don't you think I want to *stop* thinking about all that? Just be happy for me. Please.'

She gave me a rueful smile. 'I already told you I'm happy for you. I am, truly, I guess. But can you do me a favor though? Try to keep it kind of quiet. I don't think Travis, or Frank, or Mitchie-boy, need to know about it. And frankly, I don't want to hear about it.'

'Yeah, well, it's kinda too late for that.'

'What do you mean?'

'Well, your brother kinda walked in on us.'

'TRAVIS WALKED IN ON YOU?!'

'Stop yelling. And yes, he walked in. But we still had our clothes on. Or I still had my clothes on, for the most part. Simon's shirt was unbuttoned.' I zoned out for a second, remembering how nice his bare chest felt against mine.

'Was he okay?'

'Was who okay? Was Simon okay? Absolutely.'

'No, was Travis okay?'

'Of course he was. Why wouldn't he be?'

'Forget it. Just do your best to keep the Simon/Naomi romance separate from the Simon/Naomi recording sessions, okay? And like I said, I really don't want to hear about it either.'

'Why not?' I asked.

'Just because. Okay?'

'Okay. No problem.'

*

But naturally, it *was* a problem. That day, all I wanted to do was touch him, and all I wanted for him to do was touch me. But whenever my hands drifted over to the small of his back, I'd feel Jenn's bloodshot eyes on the back of my neck, even when she wasn't in the room. I did a pretty good job of keeping my hands to myself, but Simon, well, not so much. Every time we got near each other, he'd run his index finger across my butt, or he'd put his thigh against mine, or he'd purposefully breathe into my ear. Finally, dizzy with wanting, I had to say something. I dragged him into the chill-out room, and, of course, started up with a whispered run-on.

'Simon, yesterday was the best it's ever been for me, granted, there hasn't been much, but it was special, really special, and I hope it was special for you, and I want to kiss you right now like you wouldn't believe, but we should try to keep this between ourselves for a while, I mean Jenn knows, and she's concerned that it'll have some sort of effect on our record, but I know that won't be a problem, because you're a professional, and I'm a professional, and we're both smart people, and we know what's important, and what's important is making a good record, but what happened yesterday was important, too, but in a different way, and—'

He held up his hands as if to ward off a ghost. 'Mellow out, Naomi. Relax. Keep it cool.'

'Okay. I'll relax. I'll keep it cool.' Was his telling me to 'relax' and 'keep it cool' his way of saying, 'I've changed my mind, and I don't want to sleep with you any more'?

That question was answered soon enough. 'Let's lie back,' he said, 'and get to know each other, and have fun together. No pressure. No worries. If you wanna keep it on the down low, that's fine.'

I believed him. I depressurized. I left my worries on the doorstep – at least for the time being. I didn't want to fall too far into the Simon Abyss. So far, he wasn't being at all Tony-like: no poutiness, no clinginess, no attitude. So far he liked me (I thought). So far he liked my singing (I knew). So far, he was warm for my form (I figured). So far, he was all chocolatey goodness.

So far. But who knew what would happen tomorrow. Or next week. Or next millennium.

Anyhow, I was relaxed enough that I grabbed him by the collar, stood on my tiptoes, and gave him a huge, exploratory kiss that must've lasted three minutes. We were both out of breath when we were done. Simon was obviously aroused – *very* obviously – so I gave his little man a squeeze and said, 'You stay in here for a while and cool off. I'll go warm up.'

He blushed. How about that? I made Simon No-Last-Name blush. I must've been doing something right.

'And Then'

You've probably heard the version of 'And Then' we recorded the following day about a bajillion times.

Which means you know about Jenn's piano intro, somehow at once funky and danceable, mellow and sexy.

And Travis's confident, booming, looooong note that crashes in sixteen bars later, a note that makes both your stereo and your stomach rumble with bliss.

And Frank's cymbal hit that crashes in four bars after that, announcing the imminent arrival of something sort of wonderful, sort of mysterious, sort of new, sort of special.

And the deep, audible breath I take during the two-beat pause before the first verse – a happy accident that we decided to leave in the final recording. As a matter of fact, not only did we leave it in, but we cranked it up in the mix.

And the way I caress that first verse as if it was delicate and breakable, even though the lyrics and the melody are solid as stone.

And Frank's one-bar drum fill announcing the arrival of the chorus, a fill full of anticipatory oomph.

And Jenn's neck-bobbing, two-fisted counter-melody to my gritty, ballsy rendition of the chorus.

And the rhythm section's collective mellow-out while I

all but whisper the final three words leading back into the verse: *Just like thisssss*.

And the rapid, almost jarring rise in volume two seconds later.

And the ever so slight jump in tempo during the second chorus – which, contrary to what some snobby music critics might have thought, was purposeful, and not because Travis and Frank weren't able to keep a solid groove.

And Jenn's perfect, just *perfect* vocal harmony to my melody that kicks in at the same time that we dial the tempo up.

And the notorious unison bass-and-drum lick that propels us into the bridge. (Said notoriety shall be explained momentarily.)

And the stick-in-your-head improvisation Jenn bangs out behind me during the bridge.

And the Beatles-y, anthemic 'la la la's' that me, Simon, Jenn, Travis, Frank, Scott, Brian, and Ella overdubbed over the climactic four trips through the chorus.

And the liberties I take with the chorus's melody as Jenn's soon-to-be-smash pop/rock opus fades to a close.

That's the stuff you already know. Here's what you might *not* know.

You might not know that it took us a mere four takes to get the song perfect, a feat that astonished our seen-it-all producer no end.

Or that halfway through the first verse during the ultimate take, Travis started pogo-ing up and down – at which point, Jenn and I caught each other's eye and almost broke out laughing.

Or that Frank was so uncharacteristically animated during the second verse that he almost knocked over a microphone stand.

Or that after we finished the last take, Jenn, Travis, Frank and I had a love-scrum that culminated with us rolling around on the floor, and me knocking my head on the piano bench.

Or that Simon jumped into that pile and 'accidentally' cupped my right butt cheek.

Or that Scott, Brian and Ella also jumped into that pile – and one of them 'accidentally' cupped my left butt cheek. I suspect it was Scott, because Jenn told me that at some point during the fray, he 'accidentally' grabbed her right breast.

Or that after that pseudo orgy, Simon demonstrated his mettle as a producer when he suggested off-the-cuff that we put together an ad hoc choir and crank out the aforementioned 'la la la's'.

Or that the vast majority of the aforementioned ad hoc choir – specifically Frank, Travis, Scott, Brian and Ella – had never before sung in public, let alone in a recording studio.

Or that Simon threw a digital camera at Scott and said, 'Get a picture of Naomi kissing me for the Wall of Fame.'

Or that after he declared us finished for the night, Simon sprung for some Cristal. Lots and lots of Cristal.

Or that Jenn and I staggered home that evening and talked and laughed and cried and ate and drank and didn't sleep; and generally acted like a couple of dorks. Ecstatic dorks, mind you, but dorks nevertheless.

Jenn Licks the Piano

Travis fell in love. No, Travis fell in *lurve*. The second he laid eyes on video-directing goddess Sara Rogers, he was *gone*. I guess I could understand why he went cuckoo over her: she was gorgeous in a preppy sort of way, she was hyper-intelligent, she was cool, and her videos rule – especially the one she did for [Multi-Grammy-Award-Winning Jazz/Pop Female Crooner]. Sara was just the kind of girl that a young, cute, on-the-prowl guy like Travis would be attracted to.

'Isn't she a bit old for you?' I asked, pegging her to be in her early thirties. 'She's even older than I am.' I reached over my shoulder to scratch my back. The German bra was making its public debut, and I was itching like mad.

'First of all, you're not even close to old,' he said. 'Second of all, I dig older women. It's that whole Mrs Robinson thing. Anne Bancroft is awesome. Back when she did *The Graduate*, she was *smokin*'.'

Jenn asked, 'So how're you gonna go about wooing our director, baby brother?'

He shrugged. 'I dunno. I've never really had to woo anybody. You have any ideas, Naomi? Like what would I have to do to woo you?'

'Woo *me*? I might not be the best person to ask,' I said.

'Yeah, that's true.' Jenn said. 'She's pretty easily woo-able. If she's attracted to a guy, he doesn't even have to try that hard.'

I didn't think I'd have to suffer through any veiled jibes from her about the Simon issue. I was wrong. 'That's not true, Jenn,' I said. 'Why would you say something like that?'

'Oh, I don't know, Naomi. Why *would* I say something like that?'

Travis asked, 'What're you guys talking about? Simon?'

'Yeah,' Jenn said. 'It's about Simon.'

I said, 'You know, we don't need to advertise it. Really, it's not that big a deal.'

'Oh, c'mon, Naomi, it's a huge deal,' Jenn said. 'This is only your second boyfriend.'

'You've only had two boyfriends?' Travis asked. 'I don't believe that.'

'He's *not* my boyfriend. He's our producer.'

'Who you're messing around with,' Jenn said.

'Yeah, who I'm messing around with.' Why did she feel the need to go there? And in front of Travis, too. It's not like we were back in her bedroom and he was sitting in the Bradford hallway with his ear glued to the door. Travis was a big boy now – a *very* big boy, actually – and he didn't need to get wrapped up in our drama. I guess that's why I went there right back. 'But you yourself have messed around with about three thousand guys. How many of them reached boyfriend status?'

She nodded. 'You do have a point there.'

Travis said, 'Naomi, if it's okay with you, I'd rather not talk about this right now. And Jenn, frankly, I never want to hear about your messing-around habits. Yuck.'

'Hey, I always have to listen to you whine about your love issues,' Jenn said, 'so don't start in.'

He nodded, then mimicked his sister: 'You have a point there.' He then gave me a confused once-over. 'Naomi, you look different. Did you get a haircut or something?'

I stole a quick peek at my chest to make sure the fine German engineering was doing its thing. So far, so good. 'Nope. Nothing's changed. Nothing at all.'

Jenn snickered, and said, '*Achtung*, baby.'

Somebody snuck up from behind and put their hands on my shoulders. I nearly jumped out of my bra. 'Oh, sorry I scared you, Naomi.' It was Sara.

'No problem. So what should we be doing right now?'

'Would you guys like a tour around the soundstage?'

'Hell, yeah.' Travis smiled.

We pulled Frank and Marnie away from the breakfast buffet – if you could call an overflowing tray of H&H bagels, a gallon of Tropicana orange juice and a coffee pot a buffet – after which Sara walked us around the enormous structure. 'To your left,' she said in a pitch-perfect tour guide voice, 'you'll see the apartment mock-up where we'll set the first part of the clip. To your right, you'll see the crane we intend to use for the sweeping overhead shot of Jenn and Naomi in said apartment. Straight ahead is the fake jazz-club-slash-bar we'll be using for the second part of the clip. Next to that is the stage that, through the magic of editing, will appear as if it's inside the fake jazz-club-slash-bar.' She gave us all once-overs and asked, 'Are you guys prepared to work late tonight?'

Frank asked, 'How late is late?'

'Definitely after midnight, because as you know, our buddy Mitch Busey came up with a budget that only allows for one day of shooting. Isn't that right, Mitch?'

'You betcha, babe,' Mitch said. At some point, he had snuck in without us noticing. He seemed to enjoy making those unannounced pop-ins. 'But I have faith in you, babe.'

'Which babe are you referring to, Mitchie-boy?' Jenn asked.

'Each and every babe in the joint. Now that I think about it,' he said, motioning to the plethora of women who were manning the equipment necessary to make a big-time video, 'this is quite the hoohah house here.'

Sara snarled, 'Mitch, isn't it time to come up with some new material? I swear, if I hear you say "hoohah house" on one of my sets again, you're outta here.'

'C'mon, babe. Hoohah house? That's classic stuff.'

'What's a hoohah?' I asked.

'Forget it,' Sara said. 'Naomi, let's go shoot ourselves a video.'

Frank then sidled up beside me and said, 'Naomi, you look different. Did you get a haircut or something?'

I stole a quick peek at my chest to make sure the fine German engineering was *still* doing its thing. 'Nope. Nothing's changed. Nothing at all.'

Jenn snickered, and said, '*Achtung*, baby, part two.'

Sara turned to Marnie and said, 'Get Naomi and Jenn dressed and beautified for the apartment stuff. While we're shooting the apartment stuff, figure out the guys' wardrobes.' She said to Travis and Frank, 'After you're done trying on clothes, you'll have a couple of hours to kill, so go chill out somewhere. Marnie'll call you on your cells when we need you back for make-up.'

Travis said, 'Oh, I'm staying, Sara, because before I started in with the band, I was taking film classes at NYU, and it's gonna be amazing to watch you work. I was hoping I could sorta follow you around a little bit. I won't get in your way or anything, I promise; it's just that it'd be like a huge lesson for me. Would that be cool?'

Sara laughed, visibly tickled by Travis's naked display of enthusiasm. 'Of course you can look over my shoulder. And feel free to pipe up with any suggestions. This is your band, after all.'

'It's really Naomi's band, well, not really Naomi's band, because Jenn writes the music, so it's mostly her band, but Jenn doesn't sing all that well, I mean, she harmonizes pretty okay, but she couldn't do lead – okay, maybe she *could* do lead, but probably not as well as Naomi, but then again not too many people could do lead as well as Naomi, because Naomi is—'

Everybody was catching the run-ons. 'Travis,' Jenn said sharply, 'she gets the idea. Marnie, Nay, let's retire to the dressing area.'

Marnie dressed me in crisp new Blue Cult blue jeans and a tiny white Jack Wills T-shirt with red trim that showed off about two inches of my tummy. Jenn's costume was sexier than mine, which made sense, because she's way sexier than I am: low-riding faded blue jeans – also Blue Cult – that barely covered a red L.A. Rose Delight thong, and a pale blue baby-doll Diesel T-shirt that showed off about four inches of her tummy. She looked super hot. I suppose I looked pretty okay, too.

Sara didn't give us any specific direction; she just pumped 'And Then' over the sound system, and told us to act like a couple of goofy girly-girls preparing for a big night on the town. No problem there. After two hours, Sara said, 'Okay, cut. You're naturals. Grab some lunch, and we'll start the bar stuff when you're done.'

The 'bar stuff' was a bit more difficult, because Frank wasn't able to relax. He looked jumpy, and nervous, and kind of creepy. After an hour of shooting what was most likely unusable footage, Sara called a halt to the proceedings, stepped into the faux club, and said, 'Frank, can I speak to you alone for a few minutes?'

Frank blanched. 'I guess.' She put her arm around his

waist and guided him into a corner. When he got back about five minutes later, he had a silly grin plastered on his face.

Jenn asked, 'What're you smiling about?'

Frank ran his hand through his hair. 'She knows how to flatter a guy.'

'What'd she say to you?' Travis asked, looking quite jealous.

'Nothing really. Just some encouraging words.'

'What kind of encouraging words?'

Frank grinned evilly. 'Nothing dirty, Travis. Don't worry, I won't steal her away from you.'

'I didn't ask if it was anything dirty. I'm just curious because I'm trying to learn about directing from her, and part of directing is dealing with actors. Not that you're an actor or anything. And what do you mean, "steal her away from me"?'

Jenn said, 'Honey, it's obvious to the entire room that you're crushing on her big time.'

'So what if I am,' Travis said. 'She's incredible. Any guy with half a brain would crush on her. As a matter of fact, I think I'm gonna ask her out when we're done. What do you say to that?'

And who should walk up to us right at that moment, but Sara. 'Oh, Travis, I think that's very sweet.'

He wheeled around, his eyes wide with horror. 'Wh-wh-wh-what?' he stammered.

'I said, that's sweet. And I'd go out with you in a heartbeat, if I wasn't seeing someone.'

Travis looked crestfallen. 'You're not just saying that as a nice way to blow me off, are you?'

'My partner's right over there.' Sara cocked her thumb over her shoulder. 'See? She's working camera one.'

'She?'

'Yeah. She.'

'Ah, crap,' Travis mumbled.

Sara said, 'It's all good, Travis. You can still follow me around when we're not shooting you. And if you want, you can come by the editing room next week.'

Travis brightened a bit. 'Yeah? That'd be cool.'

'Not a bad consolation prize, I'd say,' Jenn pointed out.

Sara said, 'Okay, now that we've got that cleared up, could we get back to work, please? Time's a'wasting.'

With Frank settled down and Travis no longer distracted by *lurve*, we banged out the bar scene in a couple of hours. We then went to wardrobe and got all gussied up for our moment on the tall stage. Marnie put Travis and Frank in matching Corneliani black tuxes with red cummerbunds – cummerbunds that matched my gorgeous silk Gianfranco Ferre gown. Jenn looked amazing in a low-cut, gravity-defying black Stefano Pilati dress and Nicole Miller Vamp stiletto heels.

Once we were in our places – Travis behind his bass, Frank behind his drums, Jenn perched on the piano stool, and me behind an old-timey microphone – Sara jumped on to the stage and said, 'Okay, guys, I want to get this out of the way right up front. For this, it's all about Naomi. No offence to the rest of you – you're all looking terrific on camera – but that's the directive we were given by the label, and that's the way it has to go. Travis, Jenn and Frank, you three seem professional enough so this won't bother you. Am I right?'

After a minute of silence, Jenn said, 'If doing that gets this song of mine on MTV and VH-1, I don't really care if I'm in it for one minute or one second.'

'You rock, Jenn. Now let's get this done, and get it done *right*.'

At first it was rough going – Sara kept asking me to be sexier. I'm not a particularly sexy person in real life, so playing sexy on television was virtually impossible. After three times through the song, Sara yelled, 'Cut! Naomi, get you ass down here.'

She guided me to the same corner where she'd given Frank his pep talk several hours earlier, draped her arm over my shoulders, and asked, 'Okay, what's the problem? I know you can be sexy.'

'No, Sara, I really can't. I'm possibly the least outwardly sexual person in the world.'

'Doesn't matter. Here's what you do: give the microphone head.'

'Excuse me?'

'Don't really put it in your mouth, but go ahead and pretend that the mic is a dick that's attached to the hottest guy you've ever seen. Do that, and we'll have a phenomenal video. Okay?'

'I suppose.'

When I got back behind the mic, I pictured Simon. I pictured his face, his chest, his eyes, his mouth, and, of course, his, y'know, *thing*. And apparently Sara was right. According to everybody, I came off as a smoky sex goddess.

Oh, it also bears mentioning that the last take was when Jenn licked the piano. Not the entire thing, mind you. Just the keys. Mostly the black ones, oddly enough. Sara and Mitch liked that a lot.

If you bought this book, chances are you've seen the thing a bajillion times, but in case you forgot, here's a recap: it starts out with me and Jenn in our apartment, getting ready for a night out. After some power-primping, we find ourselves at a jazz club where who do we see on stage? None other than . . . *us*! Jenn and I then sit down at the bar, where a bunch of guys hit on us. Frank played the bartender, and Travis, one of the hitter-onners. At that point, it starts cutting back and forth between me and Jenn sending the guys on their merry way, and the entire band tearing it up on the stage. At the end, I give a super hot model guy my phone number, Travis gets a phone number from a super hot girl, and Frank gives Jenn his phone number, and all six people go their separate ways. The final shot is the four band members on stage, gazing down on the whole scene with knowing, I've-seen-it-all looks. It didn't really reflect what the song was about, but we all loved the concept anyhow – especially the thing where we're sitting at the bar watching ourselves on the stage.

We were correct in believing it would be something we'd always be proud of.

Can I Have Your Autograph? Please? Can I? Huh? Huh? Pleeeeese?

The video debuted on VH-1 only one month after the shoot; I now know that that's an astonishing turnaround time. We were thrilled, because it was the first tangible display of Éclat's commitment to Naomi. And I'm not talking about myself in the third person; remember, 'Naomi' was the name of our group. I was finally getting used to that.

We invited everybody in the band and their parents over to our apartment to watch the premiere. I threw together a veggie lasagna. (This one went much smoother than the one I made for Tony Douchebag; then again, *anything* would've been smoother than that almost-fiasco.) We had no idea exactly what time the video would air – all we knew was that it would be shown at some point between eight and midnight. By the time ten rolled around, all three sets of parents were tired and, since VH-1 kind of blows, bored and antsy. For that matter, I was bored and antsy. And nervous. And excited. But mostly bored and antsy.

Finally, at 10.38, guest veejay [Precocious Child Television Star Turned Sexpot Film Slut] introduced our video to the world: 'And now, here's a new one from a new band from right here in New York. The group is called Naomi. The song is called "And Then". Check it out.' Then, after a seemingly interminable pause, Jenn's and my faces filled the screen.

Four minutes and eighteen seconds later, the song faded out, and everybody in the room burst into applause – except for Jenn and I, who were too busy hugging each other and bawling to do much of anything. Travis clicked off the television, after which our respective families barraged us with questions.

'How long did it take to shoot?'

'Did you bring your own clothes?'

'Who's that girl Travis was talking to? She looked familiar.'

'Is it gonna run on MTV, or just VH-1?'

'Did you get to keep those dresses?'

'Was it fun?'

'Jennifer Marie Bradford, why in God's name did you lick the piano? What's your grandmother going to think when she sees that?'

We four band members answered each question patiently and thoroughly – that is, until Jenn crashed. She let out a huge yawn, and said, 'Okay, people. Time to take a hike. We have a photo session tomorrow, and the girl half of this band needs its beauty sleep. Actually, Naomi needs her beauty sleep – I look fine.'

I grabbed a pillow and whipped it at her head. 'Screw you, Miss Thing. Go find a piano to lick.'

The power that television could effect was evident the next morning. After a quick phone debriefing at the Éclat offices in midtown, we all took a train to Soho for yet another photo shoot. We still hadn't gotten a significant amount of money from Éclat – just enough to cover rent, utilities and food, really – so we were still stuck using the subway. As usual, the 'F' train was running slowly. There was supposed to be a train every seven-to-ten minutes, but we waited for over twenty minutes, which meant unless our conductor drove like a maniac, we would be late. And you all know how I feel about punctuality.

There weren't any empty seats on the train, of course, so we stood squashed up against our fellow riders. A couple of minutes into the trip, I felt a hand on my shoulder. Taken more than a little aback, I spun around, and saw the hand was attached to an arm that was attached to a semi-cute guy. Still, I despise getting touched on the subway, the cuteness of the toucher notwithstanding. I flicked his hand away, and said, 'Lay off, creep.'

Travis got into the guy's face and said, 'If you put another finger on her, I'll knock you into tomorrow. Got it, buddy?'

He held up his hands as if he was fending us away. 'Sorry. I just wanted to ask, did I see you two on VH-1 yesterday?'

Jenn and I looked at each other and raised our eyebrows so high that they practically grazed the subway car's ceiling. 'Um, as a matter of fact, you probably did,' Jenn said.

He peered at her. 'You licked the piano, didn't you?'

She nodded, then mumbled into my ear, 'Maybe that licking thing wasn't the best idea.'

'And you,' the guy said nervously, 'you were terrific! Your voice was, um, terrific! And that dress was, er, terrific!' He reached into his pants pocket and pulled out a pen and a tiny piece of paper. 'Can you sign my business card? I don't have anything else to write on. I don't even know your name, but I have a feeling this'll be worth something someday.'

I can't describe to you how weird that felt, having some random stranger ask for my signature. It was one thing to have somebody compliment you after a live performance, but having some guy on a train randomly tell you how swell you were, then request an autograph? That's like making a veggie lasagna, then having your across-the-hall neighbor knock on your door and tell you how amazing the lasagna tasted, after having only smelled it.

He exited the train at the next stop. When he was good and gone, Jenn grabbed my bicep and whispered excitedly, 'Ohmigod, ohmigod, ohmigod. You're a star. You're a rock star. You're a shooting star. You're a shooting rock star. I can't believe it. That is so amazing!' She then let go of my arm, ran her fingers through her red mane, and said, 'I hope I don't get to be known only as the slutbag who licked the piano.'

On the way to the photo session, three people stopped us on the street and asked for autographs. It was surreal. But I got used to it. Pretty quickly, actually.

I was wearing the magic bra for the photo session; it was uncomfortable, but I grudgingly admit that it made me look pretty hot. Jurgen, the photographer, was German (just like my bra), and the gayest person I've ever met, and he couldn't stop talking about how 'fabulous' we all looked. He especially took a shine to Travis. Travis wasn't the least bit offended – he even seemed sort of flattered – but took me aside he asked me, 'How come gay guys love me, but gay women don't?'

'You're still thinking about Sara Rogers?'

'Yeah,' he said. 'When you don't have a girlfriend, and you find somebody you dig who doesn't dig you back, well, it's hard.'

I nodded. 'I can relate. I don't know if you knew this, but I had a total thing for Tony Esposito when we were in high school together. And look what happened – a few years later, we hooked up. It took a while, but there it was.' I sort of wanted to give him the scoop about how Douchebag jerked me over, but something told me not to. For some reason, I didn't think Travis would take it particularly well.

'So you're saying that possibly at some point down the line, Sara might come around?'

'Well, Travis, I've gotta say in this case, probably not. She seemed pretty happy with her girlfriend. But you never know. Stuff like that happens.'

'So you're saying that if I wait around long enough, if I bide my time, maybe somebody else who I dig might come around?'

'Could happen, Trav.'

'Good to know.'

The photo session was relatively painless, and even, at times, somewhat fun. Jurgen focused his cameras on me more than he did the rest of the band. It was still odd to be the total center of attention, but Jenn, Travis and Frank still seemed okay with it.

We finished up just after sunset. Marnie offered to take us out to dinner. As usual, we couldn't refuse a free meal. On the way to the restaurant, two girls and two guys stopped us for autographs. At the restaurant, our waitress told us she'd seen the video that morning, then she went on and on about how much she liked the song, and how pretty she thought I was, and how cute Travis's floppy hair looked, and how much it turned her on when Jenn licked the piano.

Jenn playfully banged her head against the table and mumbled, 'That . . . was . . . such . . . a bad . . . fucking . . . idea.'

A One-Act Play Starring Naomi & Simon

The scene: our heroine Naomi – who's just made passionate, hot, sticky, sweaty love to Simon – is happily cuddled in Simon's king-sized bed, basking in post-coital bliss. Her head is resting on Simon's chest, and Simon is playing with her hair, something she enjoys immensely.

NAOMI [*purring*]: You can keep doing that hair thing. That is, if you want to.
SIMON: I want to.
NAOMI [*still purring*]: Yeah, I want you to, too.
SIMON [*after a long pause during which Naomi continues her purring*]: So what do you think?
NAOMI [*still purring*]: About what?
SIMON: About us.
NAOMI [*her purring screeches to a halt, because she's very curious – and also a tad wary – about where this conversation is headed, and curiosity generally kills the purr*]: I dunno. What do you think?
SIMON: Well, I'd like to try to be your boyfriend.
NAOMI [*excited, but confused, and again wary*]: Simon, we've only really gone out on two dates, and I think that might be kinda quick for boyfriending. Actually, we haven't gone out on

any dates. Both times we've been together by ourselves, we've spent the entire time in your bed. Oh, we were on the floor next to your bed for a while, too. Plus, if I remember correctly, we hung out in your bathtub for some time. And then there was that bit on the floor of the recording room—

SIMON: You know what I'm saying.

NAOMI: Yeah, I do. But we don't need to declare anything, to put a label on this. Besides, I thought we were gonna keep it on the down low.

SIMON: Yeah, I know that's what I said, but I kind of changed my mind. I like you, and I feel comfortable letting everybody know that I like you. It'd be cool to introduce you like, 'This is my girlfriend, Naomi.'

NAOMI: Um, I don't think so. Makes me feel like things are moving fast. Can't we just say we're dating?

SIMON: Isn't that the same thing?

NAOMI: No way. I'm surprised that a guy your age doesn't know the difference between boyfriend/girlfriend, and just dating.

SIMON: What do you mean, a guy of my age? I'm not *old.*

NAOMI [*rolling her eyes*]: I don't mean you're old. I'm just saying I assumed you had enough experience to know something like that.

SIMON: I guess I don't. So please, O grand exalted voice of experience, explain the difference between boyfriend/girlfriend and dating.

NAOMI: You can't define it. You just know it when you see it.

SIMON: I guess I'll have to figure it out by myself. [*Gently removing Naomi's head from his chest and sitting up.*] So I have some good news.

NAOMI: Ooh, I like good news.

SIMON: Mitch Busey told me yesterday that you'll be touring with a full sound crew.

NAOMI: As opposed to what? A partial sound crew?

SIMON: Sort of, yeah. Usually for budgetary reasons, when a band goes out on its first tour, they'll just take one guy to do everything – the front-of-the-house mix, the monitor mix, and sometimes also some live recordings.
NAOMI: Front of the house?
SIMON: That's the mix the audience hears.
NAOMI: Ah. So why can't the guy who does the front-of-the-house thingie do the monitors?
SIMON: He can, but if there's another guy there to handle that, everything will run smoother and sound better.
NAOMI: Gotcha. So what's this about a live recording?
SIMON: Mitch loves the way you guys play in concert, so he's going to record a bunch of your shows. He can use those songs to put together a live album, or to use as B-sides, or as iTunes exclusive songs.
NAOMI: Cool. That's not common?
SIMON: Nope. They're going to throw around piles of money on you guys. Be prepared. And there's even better news.
NAOMI: And that is?
SIMON: I'm gonna be your monitor mixer. I'll be with you for the entire tour.
NAOMI: Really?
SIMON: Really.
NAOMI [*at once hyper-pleased that she'll be able to have regular sex on the road, but hyper-concerned about the possibility of over-Simonization*]: That'll be so much fun . . . I think.
SIMON: That's kind of why I was hoping I could tell people you were my girlfriend. Things with us could be solid, y'know? Plus, when all the models and actors start hitting on you, you can say to them, 'I have a boyfriend. And he's right over there. And if you don't step off, he'll be very upset.'
NAOMI: Simon, believe me, that won't happen. Nobody's gonna hit on me.

SIMON: Naomi, believe me, it will.
NAOMI: Well if it does, I'll just say, 'The guy I'm dating is right over there, mixing the monitors', and point to you.
SIMON [*sighing*]: I guess we could try that for a while. But if things progress as I hope they do, I'm gonna bring this up again.
NAOMI: Okay, then. Now lie back down, and let's do more stuff, okay?
SIMON [*grabbing the back of Naomi's head and kissing her neck in a way it's never been kissed before*]: No problem.

They do some more stuff, none of which is appropriate to discuss in this play. After they finish their stuff, Naomi promptly falls asleep. Simon later tells her that she snored.

THE END

The Stars Are Out

The days leading up to our record release concert/party at Manhattan's own Irving Plaza were dizzying; they were when both the band Naomi and the person Naomi became famous. Not nearly as famous as we'd become a few months later, though, but famous enough that our lives were permanently altered.

Personally, I think it was Jenn's piano lick that compelled MTV to put our video into heavy rotation. (At least, that is, when they rotate, because as we all know, MTV plays about four videos a day.) I mentioned this to Marnie at one of the many photo shoots we'd been forced to endure over the previous two weeks. 'No, girl,' she said. 'It's all you. I know that for a fact.'

'And how do you know that?' I asked.

'Mitch told me. The programming dude at MTV has a total hard-on for you. A literal hard-on, apparently.'

'*Ewwww*,' I squealed.

'Yeah, I've met the guy. He's pretty skanky. But if he digs your ass, then roll with it.' She tweaked my German-manufactured nipples. 'I bet he digs these, too.'

My cell vibrated in mid-tweak. Mitch. 'My phone's been ringing insanely for the past seventy-two hours, babe,' he roared. 'Peeps are begging to get put on the guest list, just begging! There're gonna be some heavy celebs there, let me tell you. The joint only holds just over a thousand, so there're gonna be a lot of disappointed people. Man, that place'll be a zoo.'

'Will any movie people be there? Travis was asking.'

Mitch said, 'Are you kidding? We're talking [Perky Blonde Actress Who Sleeps With All Her Directors], and [Neophyte Oscar-Nominated Director and Her Criminally Unsung Director Husband], and [Porno Star Turned Mainstream Film Goddess], and [Young Audrey Hepburn Clone Actress], and [Television Comic Slash Filmic Second Banana Actor]. That's all I can remember off the top of my head. But I'll tell ya, babe, the hottie factor'll be off the hook! We're talking models galore! If your bass player wears something nice and smiles a lot, even he has a good shot of getting his johnson sucked.'

I was uncomfortable with the concept of Travis getting his thingie sucked.

Since we'd been stuck in the recording studio, and photography studios, and, in my case, a bra studio, we hadn't performed in front of a living, breathing audience in five-plus months. And now I find out that the entire island of Manhattan was trying to crash our record release party. So that night at the apartment, I had a bit of a meltdown.

'What if I suck, Jenn? What if I suck so bad that the tour gets cancelled? What if I suck so bad that [Television Comic Slash Filmic Second Banana Actor] curses me out in front of everybody? What if the stupid bra explodes? What if my face breaks out? What if I'm allergic to whatever perfume Marnie spritzes all over me?'

'Speaking of which, what letter is she up to in perfume land?' Jenn asked in an obvious attempt to derail me.

'Um, let me think. The last one I remember was Fleur de Diva. So I guess we're at G.'

Finally, after a seemingly interminable afternoon, the evening was upon us. Mitch sent a limo out down to the Lower East Side to pick us up and deliver us to Irving Plaza, which was a grand total of one mile away. None of us formerly-starving-but-soon-to-be-not-so-starving artists had ever ridden in a limo before, and we all agreed that it wasn't particularly exciting.

'My parents have an SUV that's bigger than this,' Frank pointed out.

Travis joked, 'I've been in cabs almost this big.'

'And there's not even a mini-bar,' Jenn noted.

'Don't you guys think the label could've found better ways to use the money than this?' I asked. 'We could've walked.'

Jenn said, 'Not in these dresses, we couldn't have.' My dress was a white Vera Wang off-the-shoulder number, and was painted on. Jenn's was a black Dior that was cut down to *there* both at the front and the back. Marnie had done her hair and make-up, and Jennifer Bradford looked astonishing. I was happy just to look a tenth as good as she did.

It took fifteen minutes to drive that one mile. We could've hoofed it in less time, even in our Jimmy Cho four-inch stilettos. The limo pulled around the back, where we were met by a tall, ripped, Mr Clean-looking guy. He threw open the car door and said, 'Get moving, plebs. I got your backs.' He hustled us into the stage door and slammed it shut. 'Okay,' he said in a very scary, very booming voice, 'which one of you is Braver?' Travis and Frank whimpered and pointed to me.

Mr Clean stuck out his hand. 'Aaron Gibson. Call me Gib. Just Gib. Pleasure to meet you.'

His hand completely engulfed mine. 'Um, pleased to meet you, too. And who are you?'

Still holding on to my hand, he said, 'You weren't briefed?'

'Clearly not.'

'Nobody at Éclat said anything to you about me?'

'Not so much.'

He said in a clipped, military fashion, 'The communication level at that place is simply unacceptable.' Finally, he dropped my hand. 'I'm your road manager. While we're on tour, I make sure you get checked into your hotels safely. I make sure you get to and from the shows safely. I make certain you are not hassled before, during, or after performances. I'm also your security detail. If you want someone disappeared from any situation, I'll disappear them. If someone you don't want touching you touches you, I'll touch them back, and it won't be a nice touch. I've been handling bands for a long time, and I'm very good at what I do, so follow my instructions, and we'll have zero problems.' He motioned to Jenn. 'You're Bradford, correct?'

Jenn stuck out her hand and did a purposely lousy impression of Gib's baritone voice. 'Yeah. But you can call me Jenn. Just Jenn. Pleasure to meet you.'

His left cheek twitched, which, I eventually found out, is the closest that Gib ever got to a smile. 'Are you being insubordinate, Bradford?'

'Hells yeah.'

Gib nodded. 'That shows spirit. I appreciate spirit. But I don't like being mouthed off to, even by the talent. Got it?'

Jenn gave him a killer smile and leaned forward. I guessed she wanted to see if her cleavage had any effect on him. 'Mr Clean, I'll mouth off whenever and whatever I want to. Got it?'

You had to have been paying close attention to notice Gib's eyes sneak the briefest of peeks down Jenn's dress, but sneak he did. He must've liked what he saw, because his cheek twitched again, then he said, 'If I'm not mistaken, there's another Bradford here.'

Travis, who stood nearly as tall as Gib, but was a bajillion pounds lighter, raised his hand and croaked, 'Me.'

Gib nodded. 'Good to meet you, Bradford. Your bass playing on the album is spot on. I dabble on the bass myself, and look forward to watching you perform on a nightly basis.' He rubbed his hand over his shiny scalp. 'I'll have to call you Male Bradford.' He pointed at Jenn. 'And you're Female Bradford.' He pointed to Frank. 'And by process of elimination, you're Craft.'

'Yeah.'

He gave Frank a quick up-and-down glance. 'You look like a troublemaker. I don't like troublemakers. Will you cause trouble?'

'Probably not.'

'You'd *better* not,' Gib snarled. 'Now let's get you to the dressing room.' As he led us through the backstage maze, he said, 'You hit at 9.45 on the nose. I expect the rhythm section in the stage left wings no later than 9.40. I'll be there to get you at 9.32. Braver, you can wait in the dressing room until 9.44. I know you divas like some extra time alone.'

'Hey! I'm not a diva!'

'Not yet, you're not,' Frank kiddingly mumbled. At least I thought he was kidding.

Gib wheeled around. 'I knew you were a troublemaker, Craft!'

Jenn grabbed Gib's arm and said, 'He was joking. He makes jokes once in a while. Humanoids do that.' She gave his elbow an extra squeeze, which seemed to calm him down.

Gib took my hand then walked us over to the dressing room. 'Get on in there and relax, plebs. Enjoy a cold beverage. See you at 9.32. Good luck.'

After she was sure he was out of earshot, Jenn said, 'I think I'm in love with Mr Clean.' We all laughed, then she said, 'No, I'm *serious*. He's got this hot G.I. Joe thing going on. Nay Nay, I wish he'd held my hand for as long as he held yours.'

'Don't call me Nay Nay. And you *are* kidding about that guy,' I said. 'Aren't you?'

'I'm not. Not at all. And I get to see him every night. We can double-date when we're on the road: me and Gib, and you and Simon.'

Travis perked up. 'What do you mean, her and Simon?'

'Naomi didn't tell you? Mr Simon No-Last-Name is gonna be traveling with us as our monitor man.'

'I thought he was just doing it for tonight.'

'Nope. The whole tour.'

'Swell,' Travis said sullenly. 'That's just fucking swell.'

Frank asked, 'What's wrong with that, Trav? He knows his stuff. He's a cool enough guy. It'll be helpful, no doubt.'

Travis shrugged and composed himself. 'I guess.' He took a deep breath, clapped his hands, and said, 'Okay, is everybody ready to rock the hee-zay!'

Jenn, Frank, and I screamed 'YES!' in unison.

'Frank, are you ready to bash the hell out of your traps?'

'Sir, yes sir!'

'And Naomi, are you ready to sing so loud they can hear you back in Brooklyn?'

'I s'pose.'

'And sister dear, are you ready to . . . lick the piano?'

'Oh, screw you, Trav,' Jenn laughed.

We settled down after a few minutes of yelling and screaming and generally acting goofy – or at least Jenn,

Travis and Frank settled down. Me, I couldn't turn my brain off. *What if I suck?* I thought. *What if I suck so bad that the tour gets cancelled? What if I suck so bad that [Television Comic Slash Filmic Second Banana Actor] curses me out in front of everybody? What if this stupid bra explodes? What if my face breaks out? What if I'm allergic to whatever perfume Marnie spritzed all over me?*

Jenn started rubbing my shoulders. 'Are you melting down, honey?'

'Me? Never. No way. Nope. No siree. Yes. Absolutely. Completely.'

'Cool,' she said. 'It'll be a hoot watching you lose your shit on stage.'

I spun around. 'I am so *not* going to lose my shit on stage.'

She winked at me. 'I know you won't. I just wanted to hear you say it out loud.'

I stood up and pulled her into an embrace. I was drowning and she was my lifeboat. 'I really do love you, Jennifer Bradford.'

'I love you too, Nay Nay Braver.'

'Hey, I thought I said don't call me—'

Just then, the door burst open. It was Gib. I looked at my watch – exactly 9.32. 'Female Bradford, unhand Braver right now. It's showtime. Rhythm section, get prepared for deployment. Braver, stay put.'

'Nope,' I said. 'No way. I'm coming with everybody else. I don't wanna be here all by myself.'

Gib gave me an appraising look. 'Maybe you're not a diva, after all.'

Travis said, 'She's *definitely* not.'

'Not yet, at least,' Frank whispered.

Gib roared, 'I HEARD THAT, CRAFT!'

The next two-plus hours were a blank. Jenn later told me

that I hit notes she'd never heard me hit before, and that I did my tiger-pacing on stage at warp speed, and that during the instrumental break of 'And Then', I took the hand of some guy who was standing right by the stage, and he swooned. Apparently it went pretty well.

I came to when we were back in the dressing room – which was filled with celeb types, and record industry types, and other alleged VIP types. My parents were there, Sara Rogers was there, the Intrepid Trio was there, Marnie was there, and, of course, Simon was there.

It felt like the entire room was bearing down on me. People were asking questions, and throwing compliments, and touching my bare arms. Simon held my hand and wouldn't let it go. It was all, *Naomi* this and *Naomi* that. It was too much. Not *too* too much, mind you, just a little bit too much, definitely too much to the point that I needed to get the hell out of there. I excused myself from the throng and snuck out the door. Gib stood in the hallway, arms folded, seemingly on high alert. 'Braver. Superb performance. What can I do for you?'

It might not be so bad having my own personal security guard, I thought. 'I want to go outside. Can you come with me?'

'Absolutely. I got your back.'

He led me though the backstage maze and out the stage door. There were a few people straggling in the alley, but Gib shooed them away. 'Would you like me to stand *here* –' he pointed to the ground right beside me – 'or *there*?' He pointed at the street.

'*There* would be great. Thank you.'

Finally I was alone. I stared up at the purple, star-dotted Manhattan sky. The highlights and lowlights of my musical career flashed through my head like a slideshow: me and Jenn in her childhood bedroom, in our jammies, listening to

Ella Fitzgerald. Me and Jenn fumbling our way through one of her amazing new tunes in our apartment. Me and Jenn performing for Bonnie – and hardly anybody else – at Beaned. Travis and Frank joining the band and making us whole. The four of us in the studio with Simon behind the mixing board. Simon and I making love on the studio floor.

Not a bad life so far, I thought, tears cascading down my cheeks. *Not a bad life at all.*

Part Three

On the Road Again, For the First Time

Simon was right about one thing: models and actors hit on me. A lot. In every city. Before every show. And after every show. And, if the circumstances were right, on the way to and from every show. Jenn thought it was hilarious. Gib didn't like it. Travis really didn't like it. And Simon *really* didn't like it. Frank never weighed in on the subject.

Me, I didn't mind it so much, especially since Gib was always within shouting distance, and that made me feel safe and protected. Our road manager/security guy had the remarkable ability to sense exactly when the throngs were making me uncomfortable. Check that: he had the remarkable ability to sense exactly when the crowds were *about* to make me uncomfortable. In other words, he psychically gauged when I was close to my breaking point. Thanks to him, I never broke. This meant I could sit back and bask in everything there was to bask in.

Like after our first show in Los Angeles, when [Galactically Gorgeous Film Hunk] and [Galactically Gorgeous Film Hunk's Unhinged Wife] asked me to autograph their copy of our CD.

Or like before our second show in Los Angeles, when [Younger Than You'd Think It Boy] asked me out to lunch. I had to turn him down because we were leaving town first thing in the morning. And when Gib said first thing in the morning, dammit, he meant first thing in the morning.

Or like after that second show in Los Angeles, when [Sobered-Up Fortysomething Chick Singer/Songwriter] let it be known she'd like to co-write a song with me. Naturally, I directed her to Jenn. I was more than happy to handle vocal detail and leave the composing duties to Ms Bradford.

Or like after our show in Austin, Texas, where the hottest guy I'd ever seen – and remember, I'd met [Galactically Gorgeous Film Hunk] the previous week – asked me to kiss him on the cheek. I did. Jenn saw it, cracked up, then kissed his other cheek. The guy looked like you'd be able to knock him over with a feather.

Or like after our show in Atlanta, where a shy teenaged girl mumbled to me, 'I was gonna quit singing until I heard your record. It inspired me to keep trying. Thank you.' That night on the bus, Jenn said the girl reminded her of a fourteen-year-old version of yours truly.

Or like after our show in Tampa, where our dressing room was filled top to bottom with flowers, courtesy of, well, we never found out who they were courtesy of. I hoped it wasn't some stalker guy – just an anonymous fan.

The shows themselves were terrific, an absolute delight. And Marnie was on target about how good it was to have Simon along as a monitor man. Night after night, thanks to his mixing-board wizardry, I was able to hear everything that was happening on stage, and that meant *everything*: Jenn's increasingly intricate pianisms and always superb vocal harmonies; Travis's rock-solid grooves; Frank's funky backbeats. Their enthusiasm and consistency – along with our audiences' collective positive energy, which was most often directed right at me, Jenn's piano licks and licking notwithstanding – made me sing better than I ever imagined possible. After each show, I saw a little more respect in everybody's eyes, and by 'everybody', I mean the rest of the band, and Gib, and yes, even Simon. There was something about the way my associates were looking at me that said, *wow*. It was pretty cool.

Simon was great to all of us onstage, but he saved his offstage greatness for me. Even though everybody knew about NaomiandSimon, everybody pretended that there wasn't a NaomiandSimon to know about. Whenever we checked into a hotel, Gib gave everybody in the band their individual room keys, after which Simon and I made a show of going our separate ways. A few minutes later, when the theoretical coast was theoretically clear, Simon would gently knock on my door. I'd let him in, and he'd do *stuff* to me.

But it wasn't always *stuff* that involved nudity and aroused private parts. Sometimes it was just a long back rub with scented massage oil. Sometimes it was a foot rub with yummy peppermint lotion from the Body Shop. Sometimes he'd just play with my hair until I fell asleep.

After the first of our three shows at Slim's in San Francisco, Simon and I curled up into bed, as usual. Simon whispered, 'Naomi, are you still up?' It was 2.00 a.m., and we'd had a particularly grueling show that night. Slim's was a neat club, but it had horrid acoustics, and despite Simon's best efforts, the sound onstage never settled down. I wasn't able to hear myself over the rhythm section, so I overcompensated by singing too loudly. My throat was fine – after all the shows and recording sessions, my vocal cords were like leather – but the rest of me was kinda pooped. All I wanted to do was sleep, sleep, sleep.

After Simon gave me a couple more 'are you awakes', I finally grunted, 'Mglzpajlk' just to shut him up.

'I'm sorry about tonight,' Simon said. 'That place is a sonic disaster.'

Apparently 'Mglzpajlk' didn't work, so I grunted, 'Ysoasdojwe.'

'I'll suss it out for tomorrow. It'll be way better. I promise.'

Apparently 'Ysoasdojwe' didn't work either, so I grunted, 'Shut up, Simon. I need sleep. Desperately. Right now.' Then I turned my back on him and put a pillow over my head.

He chuckled, rubbed my shoulder, and said, 'No problem. Sleep, beautiful Naomi. Sleep.' He paused, then whispered, 'I think I love you, Naomi Braver.'

My eyes exploded open. Only Jenn and several of my relatives had told me they loved me. I mean, let's get real, here: logistically speaking, aside from Douchebag, what other boy had gotten so close to me that they would've even considered dropping the 'L' word? Nobody, that's who. So you'd think that when a guy like Simon – a hot, talented, intelligent, seemingly decent guy like Simon – professed his love, I'd turn into a puddle of goo.

But I didn't. That San Francisco bed was a goo-free zone.

I don't know exactly why. Maybe it had to do with the Tony/porno connection. I mean, what if all boys taped their lovemaking sessions? Based on my limited experience, it was possible. I almost got out of bed to look for a hidden camera.

Nonetheless, six months before, if Simon No-Last-Name told me he loved me, I'd have melted like strawberry sorbet during a Brooklyn summer afternoon. He was a hottie, and eminently lust-able, and I thought about him all the time – way too much, honestly – and he made me forget about Tony. Now, well, the melt factor was a big, fat zero. Why? It may have been because I was in a good place emotionally – I was happier, and more confident, and more successful than I'd been in my entire life – so it's possible that I wasn't craving love or validation, and maybe realized at some level that it wouldn't be a good idea to put my happiness in the hands of an apparent catch like Simon.

On the other hand, Billie Holiday once sang, 'You don't know what love is', and maybe that was the case with me. Did mere contentment and good sex and back rubs equal love? I may not have known what love was, but I felt that what Simon and I had wasn't enough. The irony was that he had this habit of pushing for more. I kept saying, *We're fine, we're fine, we're fine*. Then he'd say, *More, more more*. Then I would say, *It's enough, it's enough, it's enough*. Then he'd say, *More, more more* again, and I'd find myself saying, *Okay, okay, okay*, whether I thought it was okay or not. It felt twisted to me, but maybe that's the way these things went.

It was fortuitous that I was buried under my pillow. That meant I could pretend to ignore Simon's declaration right then. But that didn't mean I could ignore it forever. It would have to be dealt with eventually.

A Fairly Long One-Act Play Starring Naomi, Jenn, Travis, Frank, Gib, Simon & Marnie

The scene: *our heroine Naomi and her band are in their tour bus following a raging show in Phoenix.*

GIB: Excellent performance, plebs, excellent indeed. Now prepare for roll-call.
FRANK: I don't really see why you need to do this every night. I mean, we're all sitting right here in front of you. Nobody's missing.
GIB: This is the way Aaron Gibson does business. So sound off. Craft?'
FRANK: I'm here. Duh. [*Even though he's a mild-mannered man, Frank seems to like needling Gib.*]
GIB: Can it, Craft. Braver?
NAOMI: Check.
GIB: Female Bradford?
JENN: Right here, handsome.
GIB: Male Bradford?
TRAVIS: Yo.
GIB: Lake? Lake? Lake? [*He snaps his fingers in front of Marnie's face.*] Lake, get those headphones off and answer me!

MARNIE: Hunh? Oh, yeah, here.
GIB: Simon?
SIMON: Check.
GIB: Thank you, troops. You're free to go. But first, Simon, answer me this: what's your last name? I prefer to address my troops by their last names.
SIMON: Why?
GIB: Because this is the way Aaron Gibson does business.
SIMON: But because why?
GIB: Just because. Now give it up!
SIMON: Um, I'd really rather not discuss it.
TRAVIS: C'mon, Simon. He calls me 'Male Bradford', for cryin' out loud. If I can deal with that, then you should be able to deal with whatever it is you need to deal with. I mean, to paraphrase Brad Pitt as Tyler Durden in *Fight Club*: 'Once you lose everything, you can do anything.'
SIMON: And how does that apply to my last name?
TRAVIS: It doesn't. I just like saying it. I think I'll even say it again. 'Once you lose—'
JENN: Pipe down, Travis.
TRAVIS: You pipe down, Jenn.
JENN: Screw off, baby brother.
TRAVIS: You know, this baby brother shit is getting—
GIB: *Female* Bradford! *Male* Bradford! Quit bickering right this second! I swear, you two act like you're five. Now Simon, please reveal your last name, before I bust out my new Jiu-Jitsu move on your cartoid. It's called the Kimura. Male Bradford, you'll love it.'
TRAVIS [*smiling broadly*]: I bet I will.
GIB: Thank you, Male Bradford. Simon?
SIMON: Okay, fine. Simon is my last name.
GIB: Is that the truth? Because I have sources. Two phone calls, and that information's mine, along with your Social Security number, your checking account number, and your mother's

checking account number. I could even erase your identity if I wanted to.
SIMON: Yes, Gib, it's the truth.
JENN: Then your first name is . . . what?
SIMON: Nobody knows it. Nobody except my relatives and the IRS, and that's the way it's gonna stay.
GIB: Wrong. These are your co-workers. You're stuck with them in close confines for many months. You have nothing to be ashamed of. And besides, if you don't tell me, I'll crush your larynx with my pinky.
NAOMI, JENN, TRAVIS, AND FRANK: Ooooooooh!
SIMON: Fine. Fine. *Fine.* Here you go. It's Seymour. Are you guys happy? It's Seymour. I'm Seymour Simon.
JENN: SEYMOUR?! *SEYMOUR* SIMON?! *Bwah ha ha ha ha ha!*
SIMON: Fuck off, Jennifer.
JENN: Hey Trav. Knock knock.
TRAVIS: Who's there?
JENN: Seymour.
TRAVIS: Seymour who?
JENN: Seymour Butts.
SIMON: Jennifer, fucking zip it—
JENN: Ooh, ooh, Trav, better one, better one. Knock knock.
TRAVIS: Who's there?
JENN: Seymour.
TRAVIS: Seymour who?
JENN: Seymour Ass. Ooh, ooh, better than that. Knock knock.
TRAVIS: Who's there?
JENN: Seymour.
TRAVIS: Seymour who?
JENN: Seymour Ass Boy. [*Singing*] Ass Boy, Ass Boy, Simon's new name is Ass Boy—
GIB: Female Bradford, Simon here revealed some difficult information. I order you to cease teasing him.
JENN: Okay, handsome, but only because it was you that

asked. Ass Boy, as of right now, I'll quit calling you 'Ass Boy'. Ass Boy.
SIMON: Wonderful.
JENN: But only on one condition.
SIMON: What?
JENN: Gimme some free studio time when we get home. And you have to engineer, not Scott.
SIMON: Oh, c'mon, Jenn. I'm insanely busy.
JENN: I don't need that much time. Just a few hours. I have a couple things of my own I'd like to lay down.
SIMON: Just you? Nobody else?
JENN: Yeah. Just me.
SIMON: Fine, if it's just you. But if I do that, no more 'Ass Boy', or 'Seymour', or any derivation thereof.
JENN: Promise.
SIMON: Okay. Done deal. A free four-hour session at Simon's House of Sounds is yours.
JENN: Cool. Thanks, Ass Boy.
SIMON: Fuck off.
TRAVIS: Ass Boy. Nice one, Jenn. Okay, let's play the color game.
NAOMI: What, pray-tell, baby brother, is the color game?
TRAVIS [yelling in such a sudden, out-of-character fashion that Naomi practically jumps out of her seat]: *Jesus, Naomi, I'm not your baby brother.*
JENN: Whoa, Trav, down boy. She was just kidding. Right, Nay Nay? Tell Travis you were just kidding.
NAOMI [*speechless and unsure what to say*]: Travis . . . What the . . . I was just kidding. And don't call me Nay Nay. So what's the color game?
TRAVIS [*calming down somewhat*]: Okay, we go in a circle and name a band or musical artist who has a color in their name. There are no winners or losers. A good time will be had by all. Everybody in?

Everybody except for Simon offers up some version of 'yeah'.
JENN: What's the problem, Ass Boy?
SIMON: You guys are idiots. I'm out.
JENN: Fine. Stay out. Okay, me first. Al Green.
NAOMI: Green Day.
FRANK: Grant Green.
EVERYBODY: WHO?
FRANK: Jazz guy.
GIB: White Snake.
TRAVIS: Jack White.
JENN: The Moody Blues.
NAOMI: Jon Spencer's Blues Explosion.
FRANK: Freddie Redd.
EVERYBODY: WHO?
FRANK: Jazz guy.
GIB: Black Sabbath.
TRAVIS: Jack Black. From Tenacious D.
JENN: Jack White. From The White Stripes.
TRAVIS: I said him already.
JENN: Tough titties. Naomi, go.
NAOMI: Fiona Apple.
EVERYBODY: WHAT?
NAOMI: Apples are red. Get it?
SIMON: Not funny, Naomi. Stick to the singing. Christ, I hate touring. What're you guys gonna do when it gets to be morning and it's bright outside? Play Punch Buggy?
JENN: Punch buggy red!
Jenn then punches Simon in the bicep. Hard. Maybe a bit too hard.
SIMON [*rubbing his arm*]: It's always amazes me that the bigger a band gets, the smaller their maturity level becomes. I swear to God, someday I'm getting out of this business and going to an island in the South Pacific. All you bands are interchangeable. The guys are drunks, the girls are ditzes, and everybody's a fucking child . . .

Simon goes on in this vein for a while. The rest of the Naomi posse gets bored with his rant, so they trudge off to their respective bunks. Except for Naomi, who – much to her chagrin at that particular moment – is kind of stuck with the Artist Formerly Known as Simon, and the Artist Currently Known as Ass Boy. She hopes he'll chill out soon – because frankly he is *acting like a bit of an Ass Boy – but right at this moment, she's worried he won't.* Very *worried.*

THE END

Solo Project

We were given a twelve-day break in between our first American tour and our first European tour, and boy did we need it. Touring may seem glamorous, but trust me, it's hard work. During my tenure at Beaned, I once pulled a seventy-plus-hour week when Bonnie went off to follow the Grateful Dead. That's seven straight ten-hour days of hawking hot beverages, during which I was on my feet for all but, like, six seconds. That was a breeze compared to being on the road. I will admit that the road was way more fun, though.

Jenn and I slept more or less non-stop for two days after our return. On the third day, Jenn said to me over breakfast, 'I'm gonna ring up Seymour.'

'By *Seymour* you mean *Simon*, right?' I asked.

'Yup. *Seymour*.'

'So what're you calling *Simon* about?'

'Remember when *Seymour* said he'd give me some free studio time?'

'Yeah, I remember when *Simon* mentioned that.'

'Well it's time I took *Seymour* up on it.'

I didn't know what Jenn was planning to do with her free studio time. I *did* know she'd written a whole bunch of songs while we were out on the road – you have a lot of dead time in the tour bus on the way to and from your gigs, and many bands write entire albums while traveling the world. While Jenn had been impressively prolific on the bus, none of her new tunes had made it into the Naomi repertoire. As a matter of fact, she never even played them for me. For that matter, she never even mentioned to me that she'd been writing regularly. The only reason I knew these new tunes existed is because once in a while, she'd casually announce to nobody in particular, 'Well, kiddies, your pal Jenn just banged out another hit.' It seemed like she was holding out on us, but I didn't think it would be right to tell her I felt that way.

In all our years of making music together, we'd never discussed our individual artistic goals, just our dreams as a team. Thus far, we'd accomplished more than we ever imagined. Sure, back when we were at Beaned, we'd joke about how we were going to dominate the music industry, and sell a bajillion records, and become huge rock stars, but those were just jokes. Stuff like that never happened to people like us. Check that: stuff like that never happened to people like *me*. Stuff like that, when it happened, generally happened to people like Jenn.

That's because Jenn is gorgeous, and I'm okay looking. Jenn oozes sensuality, and I ooze . . . something, but not sensuality. Jenn is creative and original, and I'm a decent musical interpreter. Jenn is charismatic, and I don't repel people. Jenn has star quality, and I'm just along for the ride. *She should be the star*, I often thought, *and I should be her sidekick*. Not that I ever looked at her as my sidekick, but it seemed to be the general consensus of the world-at-large that she was my right-hand woman, rather than my equal partner. But if you pay close attention to our live shows, you can tell it's Jenn's band. She's the one who calls the shots:

she picks what songs we play, and in what order; she counts off each tune; she makes sure that Travis and Frank always do what they're supposed to do. Apart from our cover of 'Knocks Me Off My Feet', each and every song we play is a Jenn Bradford composition. *Her* sound is *our* sound.

At least that's how I felt about the whole thing. The rest of the listening public didn't necessarily agree. Like in most of the articles about our band, she rarely got a mention. Critics had been heaping accolades upon Naomi *the band* since the day our album hit the streets, but awkwardly for me, most of the articles and reviews centered on me, Naomi *the singer*. Like for example, *Spin* raved about our album, saying, 'Naomi ain't Sarah Vaughan. Naomi ain't Janis Joplin. Naomi ain't Madonna. But Naomi *is* Naomi, and Naomi ain't bad. A devastating, and – let's tell the truth, here, chilluns – totally arousing voice.' Or like *Entertainment Weekly* gave our album a grade of A-, and said that, 'Naomi is the anti-pop-tart: no posing allowed.' And even *Rolling Stone* liked us: 'If Liz Phair married Sheryl Crow, and they had a child who was midwifed by Ani DiFranco, and babysat by Tori Amos, it'd probably be Naomi. Either that, or it'd be one confused kid.' Once in a rare while, ya gotta love *Rolling Stone*.

But none of these journalists had any clue that Jenn was by far the most irreplaceable member of our little ensemble. I personally thought there were a bajillion singers who were better than me, and I'd guesstimate that at least fifty per cent of them were hotter than me, high-tech bra or no high-tech bra. All of which meant that if one day I was walking down the street and a safe fell on my vocal cords – not my entire body, just my vocal cords – and I wasn't able to ever sing again, Jenn would easily be able to find a new, improved version of yours truly. But take Jenn away from Naomi *the band*, and Naomi *the singer* would be screwed, and it would be a public screwing, because I'd be contractually obligated to record an album that would most likely be loaded with compositions by some of Mitch Busey's songwriting friends. And I'd bet good money that without Jenn's songs, her vocal harmonies, and her compositions, that album wouldn't be all that.

But on the other hand, considering the way we were marketed, and my heightened profile and all, there's still a better-than-average chance I'd probably still succeed, regardless of the quality of my Jenn-less record. But it would be a hollow success, because for me, making music without Jenn would be like not making music at all. Nobody will ever write for me the way she writes for me. Okay, that's a bit of a misnomer: Jenn doesn't write for me *per se* – she writes for herself, first and foremost. But her songs fit in my mouth better than any Double Stuf Oreo ever could. The lyrics, the melodies, and the harmonies all say, *Naomi! Naomi! Naomi!* I don't know if that was her intent – we never discussed it – but it sure felt that way.

It was the proverbial eight-hundred-pound gorilla in the living room, but we'd yet to discuss how she felt about the way the public perceived us. I had no desire to initiate that conversation. It'd be like, *So, Jenn, does it bother you that nobody's acknowledging your brilliant work? Does it bother you that after each show, I get macked on by a bunch of starry-eyed boys, while you only get chatted up by a guy or two, even though everybody in the world knows you're way more beautiful than me? Do you care that every article about us is all Naomi, all the time? Is it freaking you out that I'm with Simon?* That'd be an icky chat, right?

Which finally brings us back to Jenn's trip to the studio. Because of the aforementioned eight-hundred-pound gorilla, I was hesitant to ask her what she'd planned to do with Simon. But she must've not even noticed the gorilla, because she cheerfully volunteered the information.

'This is gonna be *totally* weird,' she said as she rushed around the apartment, gathering up various lyric sheets. 'I've never done anything like this before. I'll be all by myself. Just me and Simon. Just me and my songs and a piano.'

'Sounds cool,' I said, wanting to appear neutral and nonchalant. 'So you're gonna be there for what, four hours?'

'He told me he's not doing anything in particular today, so we could go as long as I want. I don't know how long any of this'll take, really. But it's good to know that I don't have to stare at the clock, you know?'

'Yeah. I know.'

'I'd ask you to come, but you look fried, and you need to get some rest. So you stay here and chill out, and I'll tell you all about it when I get home. Don't wait up, though.'

'I won't.'

I tried to wait up. Unfortunately, despite the insane amount of sleep I'd gotten over the past two days, I couldn't. Jenn was right. I was exhausted. So I fell asleep before 9.00 p.m. And I didn't hear Jenn come in.

A Random Knight in Shining Armour

The next week, we flew to Europe for a few shows in England, Italy, France and Germany. Apparently both our album and single had sold so well in the UK and points west that they were virtually impossible to find in stores or on the European internet outlets. So the overseas Naomi fans had been buying our CDs online from American vendors, which was both impressive and flattering, because the Euro-buyers had to pay a *huge* overseas shipping fee. Why anybody would want to pay so much extra for me and my German boobs was beyond me. And speaking of German boobs, Otto and Ernst were going to be at all of our performances in their home country. Marnie said they were very excited to see their product in action.

Our European touring party was minus one key figure: Simon. Marnie and Gib were the only non-band members traveling with us. Mitch hooked us up with some sound guys in London that he said were really good, so Simon got stuck in Brooklyn. I was in two minds about Simon not being there. I knew that part of me would miss him terribly – even for just those brief couple of weeks – but I also knew another part would be happy for some alone time. There was a third part that was clearly concerned about the impending lack of sex, but I ignored that part as much as I could. I was in Europe to do a job, not to get laid.

I was seated in the same row as Travis on the British Airways jet that would zoom us over the Atlantic, me next to the window, him on the aisle. Thankfully, the middle seat was empty, which gave me more room to stretch out and nap. I'd been looking forward to the plane ride for a while, as it would be the first time I'd have some veg time in, like, forever. No cell phones to answer, no photo sessions or interviews, no wardrobe fittings, no nothing. Just seven-or-so hours of semi-solitude.

Unfortunately, Travis wanted to talk. I didn't. So I ignored him. Didn't work. He kept blabbing.

'I can't wait to get there, Naomi, I mean, I went to Nice when I was in elementary school, as I'm sure you remember, because Jenn came too, and it was super fun, and I always vowed that I'd make it back, but I never thought it would be as a member of a band that has a gold record, or for that matter that I'd ever be part of a band, I mean, you guys know how much I used to love sitting by Jenn's bedroom door, listening to you guys play, and now in a sense I get to sit by that door almost every night.'

That seemed like a rhetorical run-on, so I didn't feel the need to respond with anything more than a grunt. Travis didn't seem to mind, though.

'I can't wait to see you in front of a Euro-audience,' he continued, 'I mean, they're going to flip, *totally* flip, because hearing the record and seeing you live are two very different things, you know, on record, you can't see your eyes and mouth, and you can't hear your voice crack on the high notes, and when you crack on the high notes, you come across as so human, and vulnerable, and *real*, and even though the record is really intimate, it still doesn't capture the true Naomi Braver experience, but what's going to be most amazing is playing at the Glastonbury Festival, in front of, like, a hundred thousand people.'

'Don't remind me,' I groaned. He was acting like a puppy dog – a cute, floppy-eared, floppy-haired puppy dog – and I couldn't bring myself to completely blow him off, no matter how tired I was. 'Remember your first rehearsal?'

As was his habit, he ran those long fingers through his hair. 'Yeah. When I was screwing up my solo on "You're Not Done Until I'm Done" at Irving Plaza, whoda thought that we'd ever be all first-classing it up?'

'Not me. And whoda thought when I was *totally* freaking out before the Irving Plaza gig that I'd only be *partially* freaking out before Glastonbury.'

'I guess you're all grown up now, Naomi. You're a woman. A real woman.'

I couldn't tell if he was being serious, but him saying that still made me feel good, because sometimes I didn't think I was a real woman. Sometimes I thought I was twelve.

'Thanks, Trav. That's sweet. Now I don't want to be rude, but I'm going to sleep.'

For a second, he looked taken aback, annoyed and saddened all at once. But then he recovered, and said, 'Remember the movie *Outbreak*? There's one scene in there where Kevin Spacey says to Dustin Hoffman, "Why don't you try to get some sleep?" Then Dustin says, "Why don't *you* try to get some sleep?" Then Kevin says, "I slept back in July!" That's what touring feels like, doesn't it?'

I laughed. 'It kind of does, Trav. I'm gonna crash now, okay? Because I *didn't* sleep back in July.'

He gave my hair a playful tousle. 'Crash away. See you in London.'

*

We were scheduled to play a 'VIPs Only' show at Ronnie Scott's Jazz Club in Soho a mere two days after we touched down at Heathrow – and I say 'mere', because by the time I de-jet-lagged forty-some-hours later, it was just about time to soundcheck.

Soundchecks are mostly for the instrumentalists. Us vocalist types do our stuff once the sound guys are happy with the band's mix in the front of the house, and the band guys are happy with the mix onstage. The singer saunters to the microphone at the end of the whole process, which means the singer has an hour or two to kill at the club while the musicians and the techies do their thing.

Generally, I'd spend that downtime with Marnie. We'd go over business, or solidify schedules, or talk about boys, or gossip about celebrities, or – and this was the best of all – she'd give me a massage. And that day at Ronnie Scott's, what with all the jet lag and the crappy English food, boy, was I was in serious need of a rub-down.

Marnie always had her fold-out massage table within shouting distance for emergency situations such as this. We went into the small dressing room in the back of the club, she set up the table, I stripped, she pulled out her massage oil, and got rubbing. And she was an *excellent* rubber. She worked on my shoulders for about fifteen minutes, my lower back for about ten, and my arms for five. She was just about to get busy on my legs when there was a sharp knock at the door.

It was Gib. 'Braver, be on-stage in six minutes. And no dilly-dallying.'

I groaned to Marnie, 'Just when I was getting comfy. Can't he go away?'

Marnie hollered, 'Gib, our girl is chilling out, here. So *you* need to chill out.'

'Lake,' Gib said, 'I'm in charge of this operation, and it's my job to make certain that Braver is where she needs to be when she needs to be there. And she needs to be on-stage in six minutes, no, now *five* minutes!'

'Fine, Gib,' I said. 'I'll be there. Right on time.'

'Thank you, Braver,' Gib said. 'Good to know that *someone* around here has some respect for authority.'

Marnie gave the door her middle finger, then said, 'I'm gonna go kick him in the balls. You cool here?'

'I'm fine. I'm gonna lay here for another minute or two. Or maybe three. Or possibly four. Maybe even five. Possibly six.'

'Insubordination from the star! I love it. You work that diva thing.'

'Hey, I'm not a diva! I'm just Naomi from the block.'

'Baby, like it or not, you're on a different block now. Deal with it. Enjoy it. *Revel* in it. You go ahead and lay here as long as you need to. Jenn and the crew'll be happy to jam without you for a while.'

'Okay. I'll be a diva for a while. How long should I diva for?'

'I'd say ten minutes.'

'Ten minutes it is.'

'Excellent. Happy diva-ing.' Then she left.

Marnie did such an excellent job of cooling me out that three seconds after she was out of the dressing room, I almost crashed. Fortunately, somebody – I assumed it was Gib – banged on the door right before I drifted off. 'I'm coming, Gib,' I said blearily. 'I'll be out in a second. Calm down already.'

'Is that you, Naomi?' an unfamiliar male voice asked.

'Um, yeah. Who's that?'

The door flew open. I couldn't make out who it was, because I was blinded by a series of flashes. Then a few seconds later, the flashes stopped. 'Sit up, Naomi,' said the man. 'Let the world see those tits.' He then kneeled down on the floor and shot a few more pictures of me with what I could now see was a digital camera. I covered my eyes and sat up so I could wrap a towel around myself – which was a bad idea, because he sprinted around the table and got a full-on shot of me topless, *sans* Ernst and Otto's masterwork. 'Okay, I'm done here,' the English-accented photographer cheerfully said. 'Thanks for everything.' He ran off, leaving the door wide open.

I covered myself with a towel and screamed at the top of my lungs, 'GIIIIIIIB! HELLLLLLP!'

In a blink, my security man was in the doorway, a concerned look on his normally grouchy face. 'Tell me what you need, Braver.'

'ThisGuyCameIntoTheRoomAfterMarnieFinishedGivingMeAMassageAndHeTookPicturesOfMeNakedWithADigitalCameraAndThenHeRanAwayAndIThinkHeWentToTheLeftOrMaybeToTheRightAndYouHaveToFindHimBecauseIDon'tWannaSeeMyBoobsOnPageThreeOfTheSunSoGetHimGetHimGetHim!'

'Done and done.' Then he sprinted off to the left.

Marnie, Jenn, Travis and Frank showed up a minute later. 'Which way did he go?' Travis asked.

'IDon'tKnowButGibWentToTheLeftSoYouShouldGoToTheRightAndYouHaveToFindHimBecauseIDon'tWannaSeeMyBoobsOnPageThreeOfTheSunSoGetHimGetHimGetHim!'

'Got it,' Travis said. Then he and Frank sprinted off to the right.

Jenn and Marnie sat down on the massage table on either side of me. 'Honey,' Jenn said as she gently rubbed my lower back, 'if you want to postpone the show tonight, we'll do it. Those limeys will just have to deal with it.'

'Absolutely,' Marnie agreed. 'I'll go tell the promoter right now.'

She headed towards the door, but I grabbed her elbow and said, 'We're going on. We're starting on time. We're gonna kick ass. That's all there is to it.' I was talking tough, but I sure didn't feel tough. I knew the best way to shake off the sleaze would be to get onstage and sing, sing, sing. 'I'm gonna put on my clothes, then we'll soundcheck.'

Jenn said, 'There's nobody to soundcheck with. The entire band and all the sound guys went to find the photographer. They'll dial in the sound when the show starts. You'll be fine. I mean, this isn't as bad as Tony Esposito's videotape.'

I glared at her. 'That doesn't make me feel any better. Let's go get some drinks.' I hadn't eaten all day, and when I'm on an empty stomach, I'm a total lightweight: one beer, and I'm done. But in this case, Jenn fed me three beers from Ronnie Scott's well-stocked bar, so I was *really* done. I was actually kind of curious to see how I'd perform with a solid buzz on.

Turns out I did okay. Sometimes alcohol can be your best friend.

When I got back to my hotel room after the gig, I threw myself on to the bed and landed on something small and square and hard – it was a box. It just said 'TO NAOMI' in magic marker. No 'from'. No return address. No store name or logo. No nothing. The only thing I could figure was that it was a trinket from Simon. He wasn't one for romantic gestures, but maybe the thought of me being gone for a while lit a fire under his butt.

Well, it turned out it wasn't from Simon. It was a digital camera. It wasn't in a manufacturer's box, and it was scratched and dented, clearly well used. I picked it up and scrolled through the pictures housed in its memory. There were some shots of [Pretentious Actor Who Always Plays the Heavy] looking really pissed off. There were some shots of [Charming Actor Who Wishes He Was Cary Grant] with a cocked fist. There were some shots of [Really Bad Rapper Turned Really Good Actor] naked, save for a pair of sunglasses.

And there were a bunch of shots of me with a shocked look plastered on my face. There were also a bunch of shots featuring me covering my eyes. There were also a bunch of shots featuring me sitting up, my real, honest-to-goodness, non German-manufactured, tiny little boobs visible to the world.

Horrified, I threw the camera on to the floor. I paced back and forth, back and forth, trying to stave off a well-earned panic attack. After five or so trips around the room, I noticed a note at the bottom of the box:

THERE'S A CERTAIN ENGLISH PAPARAZZI PERSON WHO, SHALL WE SAY, UNWILLINGLY DONATED HIS CAMERA TO YOU. HE HAS NO DIGITAL VERSIONS OF THESE PICTURES, SO THEY CANNOT AND WILL NOT EVER SEE THE LIGHT OF DAY. I'M SURE YOU HAD A TERRIFIC SHOW TONIGHT.

A One Act-Play Starring Naomi & Jenn

The scene: our heroine Naomi is clad in her favorite light blue flannel jammies, buried under the covers on a king-sized bed in a king-sized hotel room in London. That night, Naomi's band gave what she considered to be their best performance in their brief history, but in spite of that, Naomi is in a weird space, because some English photographer/ sleazemonger did some sleazy stuff during the band's soundcheck – which is why Naomi is clad in her favorite light blue flannel jammies, buried under the covers. The girl needs some comforting, and there's nothing more comforting than your favorite jammies. There's a knock at the door.

NAOMI: Go away!
JENN: It's me, honey.
NAOMI: Go away!
JENN: No way!
NAOMI: Yes way!
They go on in this vein for a while, until Naomi finally realizes Jenn isn't going away, so she throws the covers on to the floor and stomps to the door with a proposition.

NAOMI: I'll let you in when you come back with some Double Stuf Oreos.
JENN: I already have some.
NAOMI: Prove it. Slide one under the door.
Jenn slides a cookie under the door. Naomi picks it up and examines it. It looks vaguely like an Oreo, but it sure as hell wasn't an Oreo. Naomi is displeased.
NAOMI: This is not a Double Stuff, Jenn.
JENN: It's the best I could do. We're in fucking England, and it's after fucking midnight. Gimme a fucking break.
Naomi takes a small bite of the cookie. Then another. Then she shoves the rest of the thing into her mouth. Then she relents and opens the door.
NAOMI: Hey.
JENN: Hey. You okay? You disappeared right after we were done. We were all concerned. Travis was freaking. He thought you got kidnapped by some West London toughs.
NAOMI: West London toughs?
JENN: Yeah. Must be from a movie.
NAOMI: It's nice that he was concerned, but I'm fine.
JENN: Right. Are you *really* fine?
NAOMI [*after a deep, shuddering sigh*]: I guess. [*Motioning to a digital camera on the nightstand.*] Wanna see the pictures?
JENN: Nah. I've seen you naked more than enough times. Kind of tired of it, actually.
NAOMI [*laughing*]: Thanks tons.
JENN: Listen, do you want me to stay with you tonight?
NAOMI: Yeah. That'd be great. We'll have a pajama party.
JENN: I guess that means I should get my pajamas.
Jenn quickly leaves the room, then even more quickly returns clad in a green-plaid flannel nightshirt.
JENN: Okay, let's get into bed.
The two girls crawl under the covers. Naomi rests her head on

Jenn's shoulder.
NAOMI: Tell me a story.
JENN: What, like 'The Three Bears'?
NAOMI: No. Something about you.
JENN: Hmmm. Hey, d'you wanna know what I did in the studio that day with Simon?
NAOMI: Absolutely.
JENN: Okay. I recorded ten songs.
NAOMI: Ten songs? Which ones?
JENN: I did six of mine that you haven't heard before, and four covers.
NAOMI [*a tad jealous that Simon heard Jenn's new songs before she did, but curious despite herself*]: What were the covers?
JENN: All old soul songs. 'Ooh Child', 'Rock the Boat', 'Never Gonna Say Goodbye', and 'On the Radio.'
NAOMI: And you sang them?
JENN: Yup.
NAOMI: Just you singing and playing piano?
JENN: Yup.
NAOMI: Hunh. What'd Simon say about it?
JENN [*after a thoughtful pause*]: Simon's an interesting guy. I don't quite get what goes on in his little head. He said some weird shit. Anyhow, he loved it. That's why I ended up getting home so late that night. He wanted me to overdub some background vocal harmonies.
NAOMI [*a bit unenthusiastically*]: When do I get to hear it?
JENN: Well, I kinda want to let it sit for a while before I play it for people.
NAOMI: 'Play it for people'? Like what kind of people?
JENN: Oh, you know, you, and Travis, and Frank, and some other friends. And Mitchie-boy.
NAOMI: Why're you gonna play it for Mitch?

JENN [*after a deep breath*]: I want to make a record of my own someday.
NAOMI: What do you mean, just you doing your songs solo with a piano?
JENN: Maybe. Or maybe with another group. I haven't really thought it through.
NAOMI [*trying to keep her unjustified anger and fear under wraps*]: Nice timing to tell me this. What's wrong with the group you're in now?
JENN: That's just it. It's just a group *I'm in*. I sometimes feel like a hired hand. It's not your fault. I'm not blaming you at all – it is what it is. And it's not a bad thing. I love what we're doing, and I'm proud as can be. But I'm kind of itching to do some other stuff.
NAOMI: You couldn't have let me hear your original songs first? You always play them for me before anybody.
JENN: Yeah, I thought about that.
NAOMI: But?
JENN: I didn't.
NAOMI [*suddenly super tired*]: Let's talk about this another time, okay? Like I said, it probably isn't the best time to bring it up.
JENN: You're right, it isn't the best time. But I haven't hung out with you alone in, like, forever. You're always with Marnie, or doing an interview, or getting a massage, or getting mobbed by fans, or sleeping. Who knows when the next time I'll be alone with you is?
NAOMI: I get it. But I'm tired. We'll set up a time to talk at some point before Glastonbury.
JENN: Should I make an appointment with your secretary?
NAOMI: Whatever. Let's just go to sleep. Thanks for the cookies.
JENN: Whatever.

The two retire to separate sides of the bed. And thank

goodness it was a king-sized, because neither of them had any urge to speak with the other.

THE END

Glastonbury

I'm going to assume the vast majority of you have already read about our oh-so-wonderful performance at the Glastonbury Festival, if not in one of the unauthorized Naomi books, then in *Entertainment Weekly*, or *People*, or *Us*, or maybe even in your local daily newspaper. Or maybe you saw the clips on MTV or VH-1. Then again, maybe you were living under a rock that week, and you missed the whole thing. On the other hand, it did blow over relatively quickly – the music-buying world sometimes has a very short memory – so it's probably not a bad thing for me to recount exactly what happened.

First off, a little bit about the Glastonbury Festival. The Festival's official website says, 'The Glastonbury Festival of Contemporary Performing Arts, to give it its full title, is a three-day festival held most years on a seven-hundred-acre site in Somerset.' (Somerset is a rural area in the middle of nowhere; it's sort of the UK's answer to Scranton, Pennsylvania.) 'The Glastonbury Festival is unique,' the site continues. 'It's the largest greenfield music and performing arts festival in the world. The entertainment consists of rock and pop on two stages, an acoustic stage, a jazz stage, a theater/cabaret/comedy stage, a cinema stage, a dance tent, juggling, and just about anything else anybody considers entertaining.' Jenn summed it up best when she said, 'It's a limey version of Woodstock, only bigger, and without the crap acid.'

Like I said, they loved us in England, and the Glastonbury Festival programmers all but begged us to perform there. It was on short notice, but the fine folks at Éclat Records scrambled around and made it happen. Another cool thing was they wanted us to play not on the acoustic stage, or on the jazz stage, but on the main stage. Or should I say Main Stage. The reason for the capital letters? Because a hundred thousand or so people converged there to check out the more popular acts. And we were one of the more popular acts.

There weren't any dressing rooms at the festival – with over a hundred different groups, how could there be? – so before the show, just like every other band there, we hung out in our tour bus. 'You nervous, Trav?' Jenn asked.

'Hell, no. I feel good. No, I feel *great*! My fingers are in phenomenal shape. And I'm not talking just my right index and middle finger, I'm talking *all* my fingers, all ten of 'em! Those fingers are ready to entertain a hundred thousand people like they've never been entertained before, and—'

Jenn interrupted, 'You're petrified, aren't you?'

'Sis, I'm pooping my pants.'

'Yeah. Me too.' She turned to our drummer. 'How're you doing, Frank?'

'I'm cool.' Nothing fazed Frank. (A note to all you people putting together a band: try to find an unfazeable drummer. And when you do, hold on to him tight, because they are few and far between.)

'And you, Naomi?' Jenn asked curtly. 'How's the star of our show?'

'Fine,' I said with equal curtness. 'Just swell.' The vibe

between Jenn and I had been kind of weird for the last three days. This was to be our first gig since she told me about her Naomi-less career aspirations, and I hoped that the weird vibes wouldn't carry over on to the stage. My plan was to take the high road and apologize before the show. But, well, I didn't.

Marnie decided we should wear super-casual clothes, rather than our usual expensive designer gear. For Travis and Frank, that meant jeans and T-shirts, and Marnie was feeling so generous, she let them choose their own. 'Let the boys have their fun,' she joked. 'Let them show Europe they're fashion savvy.' Frank wore all black, and Travis's red T-shirt had a picture of Al Pacino on the front, and the phrase, 'SAY HELLO TO MY LITTLE FRIEND' on the back. Ya gotta love that movie-loving goofball.

An hour before we were to take the stage, Marnie and I huddled in our bus's back lounge to discuss my wardrobe. For Jenn and I, super-casual also equaled jeans and T-shirts – except our T-shirts were of the teeny-tiny type, and our jeans were of the low-riding variety. When she showed me the postage stamp-sized top I was supposed to wear in front of a hundred thousand people, I said, 'No way. Nope. No siree. Not gonna happen. Never.' Our ensembles came straight from The Gap, and they looked great, proving that it was completely unnecessary to spend $200 on a six-ounce piece of cotton. Not that that would stop Marnie, though.

'Naomi, the closest audience member is two hundred yards away. Nobody'll see nothin'.' She was right. The stage was probably a good two stories high, and the barriers were set at least fifty yards back. But she didn't take into account the football-field-sized video screen at the other end of the field.

'Did you forget about that screen?' I asked. '*Everybody* will see *everything*.'

Marnie sighed. 'Naomi, this is more or less the same shirt you wore in the video.'

I peered at the tiny piece of cotton. 'I'd say it's less.'

'Just try it on. You'll look hot. Sexy.'

'And sleazy,' I added.

'Nope. Just sexy.'

'But what about the bra? It'll be totally visible.'

Marnie shook her head. 'No it won't. Trust me on that one.' Then she mentioned a certain female pop goddess who wore the bra to a certain award show wearing a certain outfit that, for all practical purposes, was non-existent – and her boobs looked astonishing. I'm sworn to secrecy on that one, but if you think about it really hard, you might remember who it was.

'*No way*. There's absolutely no way she was wearing this thing under that thing.'

'She was. It was Ernst and Otto's finest moment.'

'Ah hah!' I said. 'That's why you want me to dress like that. Ernst and Otto are here, aren't they?'

'Maybe.'

'And they want to see if I can pull it off in front of a hundred thousand people, don't they?'

'Maybe.'

I groaned. 'Come on, Marnie.'

'Just try it on. If you despise it even just a little bit, you can do what you want. But it'd be nice if you could wear it for me.'

'Great. Lay on the guilt trip. Help me on with this stupid thing.' I was at the point where I could more or less put on the bra by myself, but it saved a ton of time – and it always got done perfectly – when Marnie lent a hand. At that point, we were only thirty minutes from showtime, and I needed a hand badly.

All dressed up, I walked into the middle part of the bus,

where I promptly crushed Travis's foot with my thick-soled Steve Madden platform sneakers. I nailed him but good, and he screamed, '*Ow, fuck*', then, holding his foot and grimacing, he checked me out big time. 'Damn, Naomi, you look crazy hot. New outfit? Amazing. Best one yet. Sexy but not sleazy.'

Marnie whispered, 'Toldja so.'

'Well I'm glad you all like it. Gotta please the masses. And those wacky Germans.'

And who should poke their heads on to the bus right at that moment? That's right, those wacky Germans.

'*Guten Abend*, Naomi,' Otto said.

'Congratulations on your success,' Ernst said.

'We are very happy for you.'

'Very happy, indeed.'

'We are proud of the part that we have played in your success.'

'Your success is one of our greatest successes.'

'Breasts make the woman.'

'And women make the breasts.'

'But we help with the breasts.'

'Thus we help with the women.'

Gib, as was often his modus operandi, then appeared out of nowhere.

'*Stand to attention, all of you!*' he roared. He sounded like he was in an exceptionally scary mood, so we stood to attention, even Ernst and Otto. He gave the Buestenhalter Gesellschaft team an impassive stare and said, 'State your business.'

'We are the inventors of the bra,' Ernst said.

'The brilliant bra,' Otto said.

'The bra of the stars.'

'Or at least the bra of this star.'

'And she's become quite the star.'

'Partly because of the bra.'

Gib asked, 'What the hell are you two talking about?'

'Do you like Naomi's breasts?' Ernst said.

'Because they're not really Naomi's breasts,' Otto said.

'They sort of are.'

'But not really.'

Gib said, '*Silence*. Were you planning to leave, or should I escort you off the bus?'

'We would like to stay,' Otto said.

'Naomi is one of our favorite clients,' Ernst said.

'We enjoy her singing very much.'

'So we will stay.'

'Nobody gives me orders, pal,' Gib said.

I wished I could've hung around for a while – a lengthy conversation between Gib, Ernst, and Otto could've made for some high comedy – but the masses were waiting.

Finally, it was showtime.

It started out great. Frank was his usual reliable, remarkable self. Travis was also in exceptional form; in fact, I'd never seen him so dynamic. He was a human kangaroo, pogo-ing around the stage without missing a note, or dropping a beat. Say hello to my little friend, indeed.

On the other hand, Jenn – looking utterly gorgeous in her little girly-girl outfit, way cuter than I did in mine – was kind of aloof. Her piano playing was fine, but she was emotionally distant, and wouldn't make eye contact with me. That made me not want to make eye contact with her. By the second to last song, we were all but ignoring each other.

And then it was time for 'And Then'. I said to the audience, 'Here's a song written by our piano player, Jennifer Bradford. She writes lots of wonderful songs. Some of which she even lets me hear.'

Jenn took her wireless vocal mic from its stand and wandered towards center stage – something she never did. Come to think of it, aside from our final night at Beaned, she'd never previously left the piano during a performance, so I was properly disconcerted. She positioned herself right beside me and said, 'Thank you for the lovely compliment, Naomi. It makes me proud to be in your band. That's right, I'm just little old Jenn in big Naomi's band. It's not like it's *our* band, or anything.' For some reason, the crowd found this hilarious.

'I'm glad you like being in *my* band,' I said. 'I'm glad to have you in *my* band.'

'Wait a minute. So now you're agreeing that it's *your* band?'

'You just said it yourself.'

'I'm allowed to. You're not. Anyhow, maybe I won't be in your band someday . . .'

'Is that right?'

'. . . or maybe I'll be in your band forever. I can do anything I want.'

'Oh, don't go all Helen Reddy on me.'

'Oh, I'll go Helen Reddy on your ass. Hardcore.'

'Yeah, well, maybe I'll go Carole King on your ass, and make you feel the earth move under your feet. Or under my feet. Whatever.'

'Yeah, well, maybe I'll go Rolling Stones on your ass, and put you under my thumb, and you'll become the girl that I once pushed around. Or something like that.'

'Oh, yeah? Well, maybe I'll go Elton John on your ass, and be the bitch that came back.'

'Oh, yeah? Well, maybe I'll go . . .'

Before Jenn and I could butcher any more classic rock songs, Travis crept up behind us, grabbed us both by the waist, and calmly said, 'Guys, over there.' Then he pointed to the crowd. A crowd, if you'll recall, which numbered over a hundred thousand.

Oopsie.

Just like that, we remembered where we were, and who we were, and what we were supposed to be doing. Jenn turned to me and said, 'We'll finish this discussion later. It's time for some damage control. Follow my lead.' She then jogged back to the piano, knelt down, and proceeded to fellate the entire keyboard – and not just the black keys, like in the video. The camera zoomed in on her mouth, and the crowd went wild.

We managed to successfully rock our way through 'And Then'. As the tune wound down, Jenn took an impromptu extended piano solo that sent the crowd into paroxysms of joy. With the final note still ringing through the massive sound system, the four of us converged at the front of the stage, held hands, and bowed in unison, Jenn's and my embarrassingly timed 'discussion' momentarily forgotten.

Forgotten, that is, until every journalist within a fifty-mile radius got all up into our faces and reminded us about it. Over and over again.

39

My Dinner With Simon

On the plane ride home, Jenn and I had a heart-to-heart, and we decided to take some time apart. It wasn't a divorce, mind you, it was just a trial separation. It was her idea, and even though it felt she was kicking me to the proverbial curb, I was on board with it right away. It was the pragmatic, practical thing to do – Jenn was always the pragmatic, practical one – and as much as it stung – and it did sting – it was the right thing to do, if only because the less we were in each other's presence, the less likely it was that one of us would strangle the other with some piano wire. And if one of us were to get arrested for attempted murder, well, there would go our careers. And I was kind of liking having a career. Or at least *this* career.

Logistically speaking, the timing was perfect, because we didn't have any concerts scheduled for the next month. The only things on our docket were the second video shoot – 'Hearts Ablaze' was the unanimous choice to be the second single – and an appearance on *Saturday Night Live*. And we desperately needed the chill time, because after our mini-vacation, we would embark on a three-month shed tour. That tour would be particularly important for two reasons: visibility and money. At that point, the visibility issue was more about maintenance – 'And Then' peaked at number three in *Billboard*, but was still on the chart, plus the video was still in heavy rotation on MTV and VH-1, so we were *out there* – but money was becoming a problem, in that we personally hadn't seen much of it yet.

The lack of funds wasn't a tragedy, but I didn't have enough in my bank account to afford a three-month security deposit on a new apartment *and* professional movers. Plus I wasn't going to be home much in the following months, so it would've been silly to rent a place anyhow. This meant that during Jenn's and my trial separation, I could either stay with my parents, or with Simon. Being that I was a grown-up – and a pseudo rock star at that – crashing with my mom and dad would be unhealthy and depressing. So I opted for Plan B. Or I guess, Plan S.

Simon was thrilled. 'I've never lived with a girl before. The longest relationship I've ever had was a year, but we didn't even consider moving in together. I couldn't imagine living with her. She was far too clingy and needy.' Interesting that Simon would say that, considering he was proving to be pretty damn clingy and needy himself. Mr Pot, meet Mr Kettle. 'But I feel totally at ease with you, totally comfortable with our relationship.'

'Slow down there, cowboy,' I said. 'I'm *not* moving in with you. This is *temporary*. As soon as our little shed tour is over, I'm getting my own place.'

Simon gave me an indulgent smile. 'We'll see about that,' he said.

That night I packed up my essential stuff – clothes, CDs, books, make-up, coffee grinder – then Simon came to pick me up. After I dumped everything on to the floor of the chill-out room, we went to celebrate at that cute little Italian restaurant right by his place. We downed our appetizers and most of a full carafe of wine, then Simon took my hand and said, 'Naomi, I have a question for you.'

Uh-oh. This sounded semi-serious. 'Um, okay. Shoot.'

He put down my hand and fiddled with a breadstick. 'Will you be my girlfriend?'

Ah, this again, I thought. I still didn't want to be Simon's girlfriend; no way, no how. Wrong place, wrong time, you know? Plus there was that needy/clingy thing. All that being the case, the question of the moment was, *How do I drop the bomb without totally destroying or alienating him?* I snatched up a breadstick, and spoke slowly, choosing my words carefully.

'Simon, Simon, Simon.' After that, I promptly ran out of words.

Sixty silent seconds later, Simon asked, 'Well?'

'Okay, you're a wonderful man, and I can't tell you enough how much you've meant to me both personally and professionally.' I'm sure those words sounded a bit too formal and carefully chosen to him, but it was the best I could do, given the lack of preparation. 'But this *needs* to be casual right now. I can't give you the proper time or energy. Actually, it's more like I don't have the time or energy to give.' And then came the big lie, the infamous cliché that I never imagined saying to a guy as cute as Seymour Simon: 'It's not you, it's me.'

He swallowed, took a deep breath, and said, 'I'm surprised to hear something as trite as "It's not you, it's me" come out of your mouth.'

I gave him points for perceptiveness. 'Well, it did. But that's the way it has to be. I like you, and I like being with you, but I'd like to keep things casual. Come on, we have fun together. Isn't that enough?'

'Naomi, I'm almost forty years old. At some point, I have to at least try to be a grown-up, and one part of trying to be a grown-up, I think, is to attempt a mature relationship.'

'Okay, I understand, but, well, in some ways, we have a mature relationship.' What the hell was I saying?

'And how do you figure that?'

'Well, let's see. I guess because of my career, it'd be *impossible* to have an honest-to-goodness mature relationship. I'm too busy. So if you realize and accept that, you're being mature.' Boy, I was slinging it now.

'Hunh. I sorta see your point.'

'You do?' I was impressed, because I didn't really see my point.

'Yeah. I do.'

Out of curiosity, I asked, 'Then what is my point?'

'You want to *pretend* we're girlfriend and boyfriend for a while. Part of the reason you want to stay with me is so you can see how we interact in our normal lives. I mean, it's one thing for us to share a hotel room in Oklahoma City, but it's another thing entirely to be together in one house on our home turf.'

I nodded and clucked my tongue. 'Interesting theory. But it's wrong. Not even close. Don't try to analyze too much. It's all very simple. We keep it informal, or I stay with my parents.'

He blanched. 'Oh. I see. Well, if that's the way it has to be, so be it. I'll take whatever Naomi I can get.'

'That's *exactly* what I want to hear you say.' I leaned across the table and gave him a nice, lingering kiss. He was sometimes infuriating, but I really did like the guy – plus he was an excellent kisser. But no matter how much I liked him, NaomiandSimon couldn't be a priority in my life right now. I mean, even if The One showed up on my doorstep, I couldn't prioritize him. Us young rock star types shouldn't be tied down, anyhow.

After I broke the kiss, I said, 'Oh, not for nothin', Simon, but we never played Oklahoma City. You must've been thinking about some other chick singer.'

He nodded. 'Oops. Maybe I was.'

You see why I wanted to keep it casual?

My Lunch with Travis

A couple of days after I took up temporary residence at Simon's place, I walked over to the neighborhood bodega so I could find a ripe mango to cut up into a fruit salad. In the midst of my fruitless fruit search, I felt a tap on my shoulder. I was wearing a baseball cap and sunglasses, so as not to get recognized, but apparently somebody had seen through my lame disguise. Without turning around, I said, 'I'll be glad to sign your autograph. But let me finish picking out a mango, okay?'

A very familiar male voice said, 'Bitch, I wouldn't take your autograph if you paid me.'

I perked up. 'Is that you, Travis?'

He cracked up. 'The one and only.'

I squealed happily, then gave him a huge hug and a kiss on the cheek. But he kind of turned his face towards me, and it ended up being one of those half-cheek-half-lip kisses that are so damn weird for a boy and a girl who aren't boyfriend and girlfriend. 'Hey there, bass player. Long time no see, right?'

He hugged me back, letting his big bass player hands linger around my waist. 'It's only been a week.'

'Well it feels like it's been forever. I kinda missed you, you big goofball.'

'Yeah, I missed you too.' We just looked at each other for a moment, just looked. He was giving me a cockeyed smile. I couldn't stop looking at it. His hair was in extra-floppy mode, and I wanted to push it out of his eyes, but that would have been strange. But I still wanted to. But I still didn't. And I wanted to look away. But I couldn't. He finally broke the silence. 'Have you eaten yet? I was over at my parents, and I was getting bored, so I was gonna go and grab some brunch at this cool diner over in Flatbush.'

'How'd you recognize me?' I asked. 'I thought my costume was pretty good.'

'Do you want the honest answer?'

'Sure.'

'Being that I've played dozens and dozens of concerts with you, and being that I stand almost directly behind you at all of those concerts, I could pick your ass out of a line-up.'

I put my hand on my butt and said, 'There isn't much of an ass there.'

'What there is, to me, is eminently recognizable. C'mon, let's go get some pancakes.'

We went to the greasiest greasy spoon diner in Brooklyn. You walk in there, and you immediately put on three pounds from all the butter particles floating around. 'Stools or booth?' I asked Travis.

'Booth. No question. I've had a thing for diner booths ever since I saw *Boogie Nights*. There's this scene where Burt Reynolds as Jack Horner, Marky Mark as Dirk Diggler, Julianne Moore as Amber Waves, and Heather Graham as Rollergirl, go to this diner, and sit in a booth, and just talk about . . . stuff. Then of course, there was the best move about diners ever, and it was called, of course, *Diner*, and if you'll recall, that was back when Mickey Rourke was cool, not that he was *really* cool or anything –'

Just then, the waitress came over, which was fortunate, because Travis looked like he was close to asphyxiation. After we ordered our pancakes, I asked, 'You seem a little tense there, kiddo.' I tapped his forehead. 'What's going on up there?'

He blushed, then said, 'I dunno. It's kind of hard to talk about.'

'The only way to talk about it is to talk about it. Spit it out.'

'It's just . . . I'm just . . . it's just that this whole thing with you and my sister is a drag.'

I nodded. 'For now, this is the way it has to be. We need some time away from each other. We've seen each other virtually every day since elementary school. It's break time.' This felt almost exactly like my 'let's keep it casual' talk with Simon. Different topic, same vibe.

Travis said, 'Yeah, I understand. That's the exact same thing Jenn said. But it's weird for me, because I feel like I'm in the middle.'

'That's totally not the case. This has nothing to do with you at all, and besides, you should be siding with your sister anyhow. Blood is thicker than, um, other stuff.'

'Yeah, well, that's the thing.'

'What's the thing?'

Right then, the waitress brought over our pancakes, thank goodness, as I was suddenly ravenous. I told Travis I needed to get a few bites down before I'd be able to continue chatting. We nibbled in silence for a while, then he said, 'So, that thing.'

'What thing?'

'The thing where I said *that's the thing* a couple minutes ago.'

'Oh, *that* thing.'

'See, the thing is . . .' He paused. He paused some more. He paused even more than that. Then, finally, 'I'm in love with you.'

I dropped my fork on to my plate, and it landed in a puddle of syrup, which splattered all over both of our shirts. 'Shit,' I grunted, then I grabbed a pile of napkins and wiped off the sticky goo.

Travis's shirt didn't sustain as much damage as mine, so it took me a good long while to clean myself up. When I looked up, Travis was staring at me with an intense look that practically set my hair on fire. 'So,' he said, 'what do you think about that?'

'You're Jenn's little brother,' I said. 'You *can't* be in love with me.'

'Naomi, I've been in love with you since I was, like, eleven.' He stared down at his plate for a bit, then continued. 'It was the way you sang that did it at first, but then I started paying attention to how you interacted with Jenn, and how you were always so sweet, and so cool, and so pure, and so vulnerable, and so funny. How could I *not* fall in love with you? How could *any* guy not fall in love with you?'

I felt like I'd been smacked on the head with an anesthesia-soaked pillow. 'Travis, I don't know what to say.'

'I know what you should say. You should say, *I'm gonna dump Simon*. You should say *I'll give you a chance*. You should say, *Let's take it slow and see where it goes*. You should say, *It doesn't make any difference that we're in a band together*. You should say, *It doesn't make any difference to you that I'm your best friend's nerdy little brother—*'

'You're not nerdy.'

'Maybe I am a little bit, but all cool people have some nerd in them.'

'I have a *lot* of nerd in me.'

'Which is part of the reason you're so cool, and why I care about you so much, and why I want us to be together.'

I stared at the syrup stain on my shirt. 'I had no idea.'

'Yeah, well, this is the kind of thing you don't exactly advertise.'

'Does Jenn know?'

'Oh, yeah. She's known for years.'

'Man, you Bradfords are excellent secret keepers.'

'Thanks. So you still didn't answer me. How do you feel about what I just said?'

If I didn't want to hurt Simon at dinner, I *really* didn't want to hurt Travis at lunch. But in the long run, I knew it would be way better to be honest. 'Travis, you're one of my favorite people in the world.'

'Shit,' he whispered. 'Here comes the big kiss-off.'

'This isn't a kiss-off.'

'Well it sure isn't a kiss-on.'

'Travis, it's the wrong time, and the wrong place, and honestly, I'm the wrong person.'

'No you're not. You're the right person. The rightest person.'

'I'm a neurotic freak.'

'No you're not.'

'I'm skinny and weird-looking.'

'No you're not.'

'I'm a perfume whore.'

'No you're . . . oh . . . wait . . . maybe you are.'

'I'm too old for you.'

'No, you're totally not. But that wouldn't matter, because I dig older chicks. Not that you're old, or anything.'

'And frankly, Travis, you can do way better than me.'

'No, Naomi, frankly I can't. I've tried. Seriously, you've always been my ideal. If you'd met most of the girls I've dated over the last few years, you'd laugh. They're Naomi clones.'

' "Naomi clones"?'

'They've all got your big eyes, and your long neck, and your slender body. That's how Jenn figured out that I liked you.'

'What, she saw your girlfriends and said, "Gee, they all look like Naomi. You must worship her"?'

Travis gave me a sad chuckle. 'Almost verbatim.'

'And I'm sure she tried to talk you out of it.'

'Nope. She's been pestering me to tell you for months now. Ever since I joined the band, for that matter.'

'But why now?'

Chewing on his thumbnail, he said, 'I guess because you moved in with Simon.'

'I haven't moved in. I'm staying with him until I find an apartment.'

He brightened. 'Really? That's great!'

'Yeah, it *is* great. Great for *me*. I've never lived alone. I've never really *been* alone. It's either been my family, or Jenn. Never just me.'

He nodded. 'Yeah, that's great, really great. You should be alone. Totally. You don't need Simon.'

'You're right. I don't need Simon. But I like Simon. And I kind of want to be with Simon right now, I suppose. So Travis, this portion of our conversation has to end. I can't be with you. It won't work. You're my best friend's little brother. You're my friend. You're my *dear* friend. You're my bass player—'

'I'm your bass player? I thought I was a bass player in *our* band.'

'Semantics. The point is, your friendship and musicianship is vital to me. *Vital*. You can't let how you feel about me mess up our relationship.'

He gave me a frustrated snort. 'No, we wouldn't want that, would we.'

He looked despondent. I wanted to see at least a glimmer of that cockeyed smile, so I tried to be funny. 'But you'd better keep being my friend. If not, I'll kick your ass.' Hey, I didn't say I was actually *being* funny. I just tried.

It didn't work. Another snort. 'Yeah. I will. You know I will. I've been able to do it all these years.'

'Phew. Thank goodness.'

'Yeah. Sure. Thank goodness.'

We finished our brunch in virtual silence. The only things we discussed were the pancakes and the weather. I paid the bill, then said, 'Don't hate me, okay?'

'I could never hate you in a million years, Naomi. I probably shouldn't have said anything. I should've just kept looking for another Naomi clone.'

'Maybe it was best you got it off your chest.'

'Maybe.'

I stood up and said, 'Let me walk out of here alone.'

'Boy, you're all about being alone these days, aren't you?'

'I guess.'

'Okay,' he said, 'I guess I'll see you at *Saturday Night Live*.'

'Yeah. I guess so.'

'Okay. Bye.'

'Bye.' I could feel his eyes on me as I all but sprinted out of the diner and into the nearest cab. I needed to talk to somebody about this – but who? Simon? Nope. Jenn? Nope. Marnie? Nope.

Travis was right about one thing: right at that moment, I was alone.

Jenn was all but gone, probably hating me for becoming what I'd become. Simon was all but gone, probably hating me because I refused to love him forever and ever. Travis was all but gone, probably hating me because I didn't love him. And I was all but gone, probably altered beyond recognition.

I should warn you now, dear readers, that being a rock star isn't as cool as you'd think. I'm not saying don't do it. I'm just saying prepare yourself to be alone, stuck inside your head, for days at a time.

Live From New York, It's Naomi!

The fine folks at Éclat Records informed us that all the late-night network TV shows – *Saturday Night Live*, *Leno*, *Conan*, *Letterman*, everybody – desperately wanted to book us, but as much as the label wanted us to, we couldn't do all of them. After approximately three minutes of discussion, we chose *SNL*, which was a no-brainer. Why? On the nightly shows, the musical guests only get to perform one song, whereas on *SNL*, they get two.

SNL's guest host that week was [Swarthy Hotshot Big Budget Action Star], which thrilled Travis no end. It was not that he was particularly enamored with [Swarthy Hotshot Big Budget Action Star's] body of work; it was more that [Swarthy Hotshot Big Budget Action Star] had been *there* and done *that*. With our band, Travis had been *here* and done *this*, too, but I suspect that despite the fun he had with us, his ultimate dreams and goals were more filmic than musical.

And speaking of Travis, I have to give that floppy-haired film geek massive credit in that during our preparation for *SNL*, he tried his hardest to make like our relationship was exactly the same as it was before his big declaration. 'I know you told me you didn't want me to stop being your friend,' he said the Friday afternoon before the show.

'True,' I grunted as we stood in the stage wings, waiting for Frank to finish soundchecking. I have to admit that right that second, I was more than a bit distracted. Performing for a hundred thousand people in a foreign country – i.e., Glastonbury – is one thing. Performing for millions of people throughout the world – people you couldn't see – is another. I was way nervous.

'And I'm not gonna stop being your friend,' Travis said.

'Uh huh.'

'I can't lie that it'll be hard. There's a part of me that'll always hold out hope.'

'Yeah.'

'Maybe someday, Naomi. Maybe the time, and the place, and the circumstances will be right. You know?'

'Sure.' Even though I was barely paying attention to Travis, I recognized from his tone that he was saying something that was important to him, but I couldn't focus on anything other than me. Right at that moment, I was the most important person in my life.

The loudspeaker in the studio boomed, 'BASSIST TO THE STAGE. BASSIST TO THE STAGE IMMEDIATELY. THANK YOU.'

'Okay, gotta run,' Travis said. 'But in my mind, our relationship hasn't changed. Got it?' Lost in my own little world, I didn't answer him. He repeated, '*Got it?*'

'Hunh? Oh, yeah. Got it.'

Travis and my relationship ostensibly hadn't changed, but my relationship with Jenn hadn't changed much, either. Okay, maybe it had changed a little; the Cold War was still in effect, but we'd reached an unspoken détente. She was polite to me. I was polite to her. No hissy fits. Just short, non-inflammatory sentences. *Very* short sentences.

'Nervous?' Jenn grunted as Travis did his soundcheck.

'Yeah. You?'

'No. Psyched.'

'Good. Seen [Swarthy Hotshot Big Budget Action Star] yet?'

'Yeah. Hot. You?'

'No. Psyched to, though.'

'He asked for you.'

'Yeah?'

'Yeah.'

'What'd he say?'

'He said, "Where's Naomi?" '

'That's it?'

'That's it.'

'What'd you tell him?'

'Said I didn't know.'

'What'd he say then?'

'Nothing. Nothing about you, that is.'

'Really?'

'Yeah,' she grunted. Then she whispered into my ear, 'He was too distracted by me grinding my thigh into his crotch.'

The loudspeaker in the studio then boomed, 'PLANIST TO THE STAGE. PLANIST TO THE STAGE IMMEDIATELY. THANK YOU.'

'Gotta run,' she said.

A few minutes later, Jenn's mix was sorted out, and it was time for my soundcheck. After they had my mix all nice and tight, the director asked us to run through both of our songs so they could work out the camera angles. There were three floor cams trained right at me, one floor cam strictly on Jenn, a swooping crane camera that wooshed over us time and again, and a camera wedged in between Frank's snare drum and hi-hat. It was all pretty overwhelming, but considering it was my first experience with television, I acquitted myself quite well. Or so I thought.

'Naomi,' the director shouted, 'I need more of you!'

'What do you mean?' I asked.

'Y'know,' she said, 'more of you.'

'But all the cameras are on me the entire time. If there's any more of me, there won't be much of anybody else.'

Jenn mumbled, 'Yeah, you'd like that, wouldn't you?'

I spun around. 'Excuse me?'

She gave me a fake-ish pseudo smile. 'Nothing, Naomi. Everything's fine. Just pay attention to the director. She wants more of you. Just like everybody else in the world.'

I glared at Jenn, then asked the director, 'I'm sorry, but I have no idea what more of me you need.'

Travis sauntered over. 'I think what she's saying is to open yourself up. Look at the camera. Smile. Be yourself. Have fun.'

The director beamed at Travis. 'That's exactly what I mean,' she said. '*Exactly*. Bass player, you should direct.' She was right. He was a talented, perceptive dude, that Travis Bradford.

'Hells yeah, he should.' Jenn smiled.

Travis blushed. 'Yeah, well, maybe someday.'

'Hey, guys,' I said, 'I still don't know what everybody's talking about, but maybe we should try it again.'

'Not right now we won't,' the director said. 'We're done with you for today. I need to work with the cast. Some of them are having, shall we say, a bit of trouble this week – especially [*SNL* Cast Member Whose Crappy Movies Gross Millions Of Dollars].' Then she shrieked, 'Isn't that right, [*SNL* Cast Member Whose Crappy Movies Gross Millions Of Dollars]!'

Naturally, [*SNL* Cast Member Whose Crappy Movies Gross Millions Of Dollars] was standing right behind us. 'Have this woman fired,' he joked.

'Boy, show some respect. Three years from now, I'll still be here on the show, all happy and successful, and you'll be in the straight-to-DVD bin.' She turned to me and said, 'Call time for tomorrow is six p.m. We'll see you then.' A 6.00 p.m. call time might seem early for an 11.30 show, but there was a full-blown dress rehearsal at seven. So in effect, we'd do the show twice, the only difference for us being that we wouldn't wear our matching black retro '80s-era Armani men's suits until the actual telecast.

[Swarthy Hotshot Big Budget Action Star] was waiting for us in front of our dressing room. Actually, as I soon found out, he was waiting for *me*. How did I know that? Because he said, 'Ah, Naomi. I've been waiting for you.'

'Hi,' I said, suddenly feeling shy. Even though I wasn't a big fan of [Swarthy Hotshot Big Budget Action Star], he was charismatic and cute as hell. 'Nice to meet you.'

Jenn shouldered me aside. 'Hey there, [Swarthy Hotshot Big Budget Action Star]. What's going on?'

'Not much,' he told Jenn. Then he asked me, 'Wanna grab some coffee after I'm done with my blocking?'

'Well, I—' And who should walk up right at that moment? None other than Seymour Simon himself.

'Simon,' I said, 'this is a surprise. I thought only band and cast were allowed backstage.'

He wrapped his arm tightly around my waist and gave me a peck on the cheek. 'You'd have been impressed by the way I talked myself back here. I even impressed myself.'

Jenn said, 'You certainly are impressive, Ass Boy.'

'I thought we were done with Ass Boy.'

'Yeah,' she said, 'well think again. I'm outta here.' Then she stomped off.

Simon asked me, 'What's gotten into her?' Then he offered his hand to [Swarthy Hotshot Big Budget Action Star]. 'What's happening? I'm Simon. I produced their album. And I'm Naomi's current flame.'

'Yeah, I know about you,' [Swarthy Hotshot Big Budget Action Star] said. 'You do good work.'

I removed Simon's hand from my waist. 'Simon, you are not my flame.'

'Hey, I didn't say I was your boyfriend. Just your flame. That's right, [Swarthy Hotshot Big Budget Action Star]. Not boyfriend.' He gave [Swarthy Hotshot Big Budget Action Star] an exaggerated eye roll. 'She'll shoot me if I ever say "boyfriend".'

'Simon,' I stage whispered through gritted teeth, 'stop it.' Then, at normal volume, I said to [Swarthy Hotshot Big Budget Action Star], 'I'm sorry about this. Let me finish here, then we'll go grab some coffee, okay?'

[Swarthy Hotshot Big Budget Action Star] said, 'That'd be—'

Simon interrupted, 'Sorry, big fella. Naomi has a meeting right now. No time for coffee.'

'Meeting?' I asked. 'With who?'

'Mitch and Marnie want to talk to you about, um, wardrobe for tomorrow.'

'Why? I thought we were all set with the Armanis.'

'Don't ask me. I'm just the messenger. Anyhow, everybody's over at the Éclat office. We'll hop a cab as soon as you're ready to go.'

'Fine,' I sighed, then I asked [Swarthy Hotshot Big Budget Action Star], 'Can I have a raincheck on that coffee?'

He shrugged. 'We'll see. I'm mostly tied up until show time, and I'm flying back to Cali first thing on Sunday morning. So if I don't see you tomorrow before we get on the stage, have a good show, alright?'

'Thanks. And you have a good show, too.'

Simon took my hand and dragged me towards the elevator. 'Okay, we've gotta bolt. Stay cool, [Swarthy Hotshot Big Budget Action Star].'

We caught a taxi the second we stepped outside the Rockefeller Center, and Simon gave the driver his home address in Brooklyn. 'Wait a minute,' I said. 'What about the meetings?'

'No meetings. It's just that you look stunning, and the second I saw you, I knew I had to have you.' He leaned over and whispered into my ear, 'I'd take you right here in the cab, if you'd let me.' Then he licked my ear just the way I liked to have it licked. His stubble felt so sexy against my cheek that I couldn't help but momentarily forgive him. When he grazed his index finger up my thigh, I remembered why I put up with him – because, dammit, he made me feel good, and pretty, and sexy, and desired, like nobody else ever had. We spent the rest of that day – and night – in bed.

The next morning over breakfast, I said, 'You know what? After that stunt you pulled after our *SNL* rehearsal, I think I'm gonna call you Seymour.'

His eyes widened. 'C'mon, Naomi. That's not cool.'

'It's cooler than Ass Boy. Besides, kidnapping me wasn't cool, either.'

'I didn't *kidnap* you,' he protested. 'I just made sure you got back to our place safe and sound.'

'Back to *your* place, you mean. Not *our* place. *Your* place.'

'I'm not gonna stop trying.'

'Please stop, Seymour.'

'Christ, that name makes my head hurt. Why do you have to go there? What'll it accomplish?' He could barely get out the word 'Seymour' without choking on his Cheerios.

'Well, Seymour, I guess from now on when you hear the word "Seymour" come out of my mouth, it'll be my way of reminding you not to do stupid stuff like kidnap me.'

'But I didn't kidnap you,' he said, 'I just got you a—'

'Yeah, you got me a ride back to your place, whatever. Point is, Seymour, when it comes to our semi-relationship here, you need to pull yourself together. And me calling you Seymour will remind you of that fact.'

He sulked for a minute or two, then said, 'You know, you're lucky I like you so much. You and Jenn are the only people I'd let get away with that kind of bullshit.'

Regarding our *Saturday Night Live* experience itself, if you've read this far, you're a fan, and if you're a fan, you saw it, and even if you didn't see it live, you probably caught one of the many reruns, and even if you didn't catch any of the reruns, you probably saw the bits and pieces of our performance that Sara Rogers cut into the 'Hearts Ablaze' video. But if you didn't see any of it, there's nothing to say other than we kicked ass. Our first tune was, naturally, 'And Then', which we nailed. We then nailed 'Hearts Ablaze' even harder. Travis jogged all over the stage. Jenn dry-humped the piano bench. Frank was Gibraltar. And I stared the camera down, just like Travis and the director said I should.

As all of you who regularly check out *SNL* recall, at the end of the show, the host, the musical act, and the entire cast gathers on the stage for the good nights. [Swarthy Hotshot Big Budget Action Star] took my hand, yanked me to center stage, stared the camera down – which, unlike myself, I'm sure he didn't have to be told to do – and said, 'Thanks to the cast! Thanks to the crew! And special thanks to Naomi!' Then he lifted me up and gave me a kiss. On the lips. With a bit of tobacco-tasting tongue. Wow.

Despite what you might have read in the tabloids, I never saw him again.

In the Opinion of the Blabberingst Blabbermouth known to Mankind, Sara Rogers and I Talk Too Damn Much

Things remained icy on the Naomi and Jenn front after our *SNL* appearance, but in spite of that, the two of us managed to have a civil and productive powwow over lunch later that week regarding the clip for 'Hearts Ablaze'. The civility and productivity might have had something to do with the fact that Travis was at the restaurant with us. You'd think that grown, successful, strong women such as us would've been able to handle that sort of thing without a referee. Well, at that particular moment, you'd have been wrong.

We agreed that Sara Rogers was awesome, and should be hired for a repeat performance; fortunately, the fine folks at Éclat Records were more than happy to accommodate us in any way possible. Considering how much money we'd earned for them, it stood to reason they would cater to our every whim. On the other hand, there was the possibility that Éclat readily agreed to our video concept because – even though Sara's asking fee was up in the stratosphere – our concept was dirt cheap.

The dirt cheapness, mind you, was by design – specifically, *my* design. My favorite videos were the more performance-oriented ones. Sure, a video that tells a story like 'And Then' can be really cool, but when I watch a video, for the most part, I just want to see the band play. That's what I suggested at lunch, and Jenn and Travis agreed. As a matter of fact, they agreed immediately – *too* immediately, even. I wondered if Jenn gave her thumbs-up because she wanted to shut me up. I wondered if Travis gave his thumbs-up because he wanted to jump my bones. I also wondered if I was being paranoid.

But Sara liked my idea, which made me feel a bit better about the whole thing. 'Excellent concept, Naomi,' Sara said during a conference call in Mitch's office. She was in Los Angeles working on a big-money video for [Eternally Youthful Five-Piece Rock 'n' Roll Geezers]. 'I'm thinking a combination of some live concert footage from your first tour, plus a bit of your *SNL* gig, plus some shots of the four of you wandering around near where you and Jenn grew up in Brooklyn would totally work. I've always felt a video that follows up an elaborate monster-success video should focus on the band, not the production. Less is more.'

'Absolutely, babe,' Mitch said, 'I couldn't agree more. D'you guys remember the second vid we did for The Cosmetics?'

I said, 'No, I can't say that I have.'

'Mitch,' Sara groaned, 'I've heard you tell this story a dozen times. I'm sick of it. Do you need me for anything else, or can I go?' It was easy to picture the annoyed look on Sara's face.

'Don't go yet, babe. We're not done here. Just let me preach and teach, okay? Besides, you're the one who comes off as the hero of this little tale.'

Sara's pained sigh was so audible that if I stuck my head

out the window, I might've been able to hear it, even from three thousand miles away. 'Fine, but try to keep it short. My assistant editor has to cut out at five, and I need—'

'That's funny, babe,' Mitch said.

'What's funny?'

'That your assistant editor has to cut out. Get it, babe? Cut out? Cut? Editors cut? Get it?'

Sara groaned, 'I get it, Mitch. Now tell your story so Naomi and I can get on with our lives.'

'You got it, babe.' He glanced at me. 'By the way, babe, where's your piano player? She usually comes to these things.'

'She didn't feel like coming,' I sighed.

'Why not?' Sara asked.

Mitch said, 'I bet the two babes are still pissed about that Glastonbury thing.'

Sara asked, 'Yeah, what exactly happened there, Naomi?'

'Do we really have to talk about this right this second?'

'No, I can wait,' Sara said. 'I'll grill you and Jenn when I get back to town.'

'You can try grilling her, but don't bother with me, because I'm way tired of talking about it.' I said. I was pretty sure Jenn wouldn't touch it, either.

'Hey, can you two babes quit your yakking for a minute?' Mitch asked. 'You both talk too damn much. I can't get a word in edgewise here.'

Sara cracked up. 'Now *that*'s funny . . . *you* not being able to get a word in edgewise.'

Mitch scratched his head. 'Why's that funny, babe?'

I could practically hear Sara's eyes rolling. 'Nothing. Just tell your story so I can get off the phone already.'

'You got it, babe. So, The Cosmetics.'

Sara said, 'Did you ever hear them, Naomi?'

'Nope.'

'You're lucky. They sucked.'

Mitch angrily said, 'They did not suck, babe. They were just . . . limited.'

'Yeah,' Sara said. 'They were limited in that the only thing they could do was suck.'

'Anyhoo,' Mitch continued, 'their first single did okay. Top ten radio, top forty *Billboard* alternative. I gave them *beaucoup* bucks for their first video, which their director pissed away on special effects. The dudes must've been on screen for one minute out of the entire thing.'

Sara said, 'Actually, they were on screen for only fifty-three seconds.'

'Yeah, right. Those boys needed more bang for their buck, so' – he motioned to the speakerphone – 'I brought in babe, here. We came up with a treatment kind of like the one you guys are doing for "Ablaze" – minimalist, sleek, slick. Good shit. But The Cosmetics' management wanted something bigger, better, stronger, faster. So right in the middle of this meeting, my promo babe runs in and says, "MTV wants The Cosmetics to play Spring Break. MTV is in lust with The Cosmetics. They want to bone them up the bung." '

I asked, 'Is that *exactly* what your promo babe said? That they want to "bone them up the bung"?' I still can't believe the phrase 'bone them up the bung' crossed my lips.

'Well maybe not *exactly*, but that was the gist.'

'That's a pretty disgusting promo babe,' Sara said.

'Whatever. Now will you two *please* shut up and let me talk?'

'Sorry, babe,' Sara mocked. 'I just love hearing you get all riled up like this. Don't you, Naomi?'

'Absolutely,' I laughed.

'Eff you both,' he said. 'So once their management heard that, they asked to triple the video budget. How could I refuse? So I called director babe over here and told her the scoop. She came up with that other treatment, and it was effing great. But it tanked because the song was . . . limited.'

Sara said, 'Personally, I thought the video turned out pretty well, too. But Naomi, that band sucked. I could've made something of *Citizen Kane* quality with those morons, but their lameness still would've caught up with them.'

'They weren't lame, just . . . limited,' Mitch reiterated.

'Right,' Sara sighed. 'Limited. Anyhow, I'll be back in town next week. Naomi, coordinate with your band and figure out a day that I can come out to Brooklyn and shoot you guys. I think I'll do it myself. Just you guys, me, and a hand-held. Lo-fi, you know?'

'That sounds awesome,' I said.

Sara asked, 'And speaking of your band, how's Mr Bradford?'

'Travis? He's, y'know, he's good.'

'Glad to hear it. He's a great kid. If I was into boys, I might well make a move on that one.'

Hearing her say that was a bit unnerving. I forced out a laugh, and said, 'Yeah, he'd probably like that. He still has a thing for you.'

She chuckled, 'Oh, he's made that abundantly clear. I haven't heard from him in a few weeks, though. He used to email me a couple of times a week. I kinda miss that skinny man. Tell him I'm looking forward to seeing him.'

More discomfort. 'I will.'

Mitch said, 'Okay, you two babes can blab all you want. I've gotta bolt. Things to see, places to be, people to do, busy, busy, busy.' He stood up, then added, 'I swear, I've never heard so much useless blabbing. Remind me never to have chick bands work with chick directors again. Shit, I don't understand why Simon likes working with chicks so much, I mean hell, the guy even effed [Sassy Underage Soul

Crooner], and [Super Sexy Junk in the Trunk Boob Hanging Out Rapper], and [Mega Mega Super Super Hot Hot Hoochie Shaker], and those are the only ones I know about for sure . . .'

Um, say what?

'. . . but seriously, you babes talk too damn much.'

A One-Act Play Starring Naomi & Jenn

The scene: our heroine Naomi and her band are in Brooklyn, filming a segment for their second video. Naomi and Jenn are annoyed with each other, and since they're both incredibly stubborn, neither one has bothered to initiate a discussion that might lead to them making up, which is why they haven't had an honest-to-goodness multi-syllabic conversation in many, many weeks. During a break in filming, Naomi, feeling jazzed and happy from being in front of the camera, feebly offers Jenn a pseudo-olive branch, although at first, she still can't bring herself to speak in honest-to-goodness multi-syllabic sentences.

NAOMI: Hey.
JENN: Hey.
NAOMI: So.
JENN: So what?
NAOMI: So. Great video.
JENN: Yeah. Swell.
NAOMI: So. You look cute.
JENN [*running her index finger down the insanely expensive Tracy Feith black halter top provided by the record label*]: Thanks.

NAOMI [*after waiting ten seconds for a return compliment*]: Do I look okay?
JENN [*sarcastically – or so the eternally paranoid Naomi thought*]: Sure.
NAOMI: Thanks.
JENN: Sure.
NAOMI [*mumbling*]: Maybe we should try and talk some stuff through.
JENN: You're mumbling. Speak up.
NAOMI: I said, maybe we should try and talk some stuff through.
JENN: I can't hear you. Did you blow your voice out? Did Ass Boy blow your voice out? Or did you blow Ass Boy's voice out? Or did you just blow Ass Boy?
NAOMI [*floodgates opening*]: You know, I'm trying to be nice, here, I mean we're leaving for a long, hard tour next week, and we're gonna be stuck on a bus together, and we're gonna see each other nonstop, and I thought it would be good for everybody if we could try and get along for the band's sake, and our sanity's sake, plus I don't want to be stressed out on stage each night, and I don't want you to have another meltdown like at Glastonbury—
JENN [*floodgates also opening*]: Me have a meltdown? *Me* have a meltdown? Girlfriend, that was your meltdown, and yours alone.
NAOMI: Oh, so you had nothing to do with what went on there.
JENN: I'm not saying I'm blameless. But I *am* saying that according to you, it's your band, and since that's the case, you have more responsibility about what happens on stage than your *underlings* do.
NAOMI: *Underlings?* There're no *underlings* here. I'm not your *overling.*
JENN: You are! You said so yourself!

NAOMI: I'd *never* say something like that!
JENN: You *totally* said that. Okay, not *exactly*, but that's *exactly* what you meant. Do you want me to remind you *exactly* what you said? Because I remember *exactly* what you said.
NAOMI: Fine. Tell me *exactly* what I said.
Jenn then recounts the argument that her and Naomi had onstage at the Glastonbury Festival. But it's not your average recount. No, Jenn recited the heated conversation verbatim.
JENN: Can you imagine what would've happened if I hadn't given the piano a blow job? The crowd would've stormed the stage.
NAOMI [flatly]: Whatever. Sorry.
JENN: Great. Nothing I like better than a sincere, heartfelt, unsolicited apology.
NAOMI: Whatever.
JENN: Yeah. Exactly. *Whatever* is right.
They sit in silence for a moment.
JENN: And by the way, thanks for what you did to my brother. He's miserable. And he's *never* miserable. I blame you.
NAOMI: What do you blame me for? For not being able to feel about him the way he feels about me? You can't manufacture feelings. At least *I* can't.
JENN [*sighing, clearly exhausted*]: Naomi, I can't do this right now. Just try to get over yourself a little bit, okay?
NAOMI: Get over myself? What the hell are you talking about? *You* should get over *yourself.*
JENN [*shaking her head*]: I have to go. See you next week.

Jenn sticks her arm up and hails a taxi in, like, two seconds. Jenn's a bastion of beauty, and never has trouble getting cabs. Naomi, while cuter than she's ever been in her entire life, still isn't as cute as Jenn, so after three minutes of ineffective waving, she walks towards the Manhattan Bridge. The two-

hour walk to her friend Marnie's apartment, she decides, will be good for her. It'll give her time to figure out how to fix the Jenn situation . . . or if she even wants it fixed . . . or if it's her that's supposed to do the fixing. She'll also need to contemplate what kind of effect the Naomi and Jenn war will have on her band. And she might even wonder for a minute or three if she's acting like a diva bitch, and if she is, whether she'll be able to stop.

THE END

The Hoohah Johnson Experience

I don't know why the Kevins named their band The Hoohah Johnson Experience, and when I asked them, White Kevin only gave me a skeevy giggle, and Black Kevin said, 'Trust me, Naomi, you don't wanna know.' The Kevins, for those of you who aren't into the jam band scene, are Kevin McAllister and Kevin Parr, a.k.a. Black Kevin and White Kevin. McAllister is African–American. Parr is Caucasian. Black Kevin plays drums and is cool. White Kevin sings and plays guitar, and is a pain in the ass.

The Hoohah Johnson Experience was the band's fifth name, the previous four being Anti-Auntie, The Jennifer Zone, Down The Up Staircase, and, logically enough, Black 'n' White Kevin. The reason for the constant name changes was that the Kevins and their bandmates were, as Black Kevin so succinctly put it, 'music industry whores', a fair description, because for the decade they'd been together, Kevin and Kevin have changed their style to suit the changing times. Like Anti-Auntie was a straight-up, no-nonsense rock band. And The Jennifer Zone was a semi-original-sounding grunge-pop band. (Jenn had The Jennifer Zone's only record, and liked it quite a bit – and not just because of the group's name.) And Down The Up Staircase was sort of hip-hoppy. And Black 'n' White Kevin was drum 'n' bass.

After the second Black 'n' White Kevin record tanked, they almost gave it all up. They even got real jobs; Black Kevin as a personal assistant for [Constantly Going In and Out of Rehab Girl Singer/Songwriter], and White Kevin as a marketing coordinator for – you guessed it – Éclat Records. One weekend when [Constantly Going In and Out of Rehab Girl Singer/Songwriter] was back in rehab, the Kevins and a couple of their friends spent eight hours in [Constantly Going In and Out of Rehab Girl Singer/Songwriter]'s studio jamming. No agenda, no new band names, no schemes on how to get another record deal – they just played music for the sake of playing music. Hour after hour, they jammed and jammed, and next thing you know, they decided they liked being a jam band.

On the surface, a double bill of Naomi and Hoohah didn't make much sense, but Hoohah had earned themselves a cult following, and jam band audiences tend to be pretty open-minded, so Mitch figured we could reach people we hadn't reached previously. As for our fans, well, our demographic was filled with fourteen-year-old girls who probably wouldn't care for Hoohah. But that didn't really matter, because our fans were only there to see us. To the hardcore Naomi-ites, any other performer was incidental.

As it turned out, the Kevins and the rest of the Hoohahs were thrilled to be offered our opening slot. 'I admire what you've done, and how you've done it, Naomi,' Black Kevin said after the soundcheck for our second show of the tour, a hometown gig at the Jones Beach Theater in Long Island. 'Dig your music. Dig your aura.' He paused, then looked at his shoes. 'Plus I dig Jenn.'

'Yeah, a lot of boys dig Jenn,' I said.

'Nah, man, a lot of boys dig *you*. *I* dig Jenn. I *dig* Jenn.'

'So you're saying you don't dig me? Gee, thanks.'

'You know what I mean, man.'

'I guess I do. And don't call me *man*,' I joked. He mumbled an apology, then I asked, 'Are you crushing on her?'

'Yeah, man. Totally.'

Kevin was *very* good looking. Tall. Ripped. A devastating smile. Wide, expressive eyes. At that point, as far as I knew, Jenn wasn't seeing anybody. Hmmm. 'Would you like me to give you a formal introduction?'

He shrugged, and shot me a small smile. 'Nah, it's cool. I'm sure I'll sit down with her at some point.'

Hooking up this beautiful man with Jenn, I thought, would be an excellent way to start mending our fences. Then again, she might see my matchmaking as a hollow attempt to placate her, so I figured it would be best to let nature take its course. 'Okay, Kevin. Go get her, tiger.'

'Thanks, man.'

Murphy's Law Revisited

'Hearts Ablaze' became a monster hit – not quite as monster as 'And Then', but almost – so Mitch Busey threw a whole bunch more money into the project. 'You gotta spend serious Benjamins to make serious Benjamins,' he explained. (After he said that, Jenn mumbled, 'When do we get some serious Benjamins of our own?' Mitch didn't hear her, but I did, and frankly, I wondered the same thing myself.)

The number of bodies we hauled from city to city grew exponentially. For the first American tour and our trip to Europe, our traveling party consisted of me, Jenn, Travis, Frank, Marnie, Gib and Seymour – although, if you'll recall, we went Seymour-less when we voyaged across the pond. For the shed tour it was me, Jenn, Travis, Frank, Marnie, Gib, Seymour, two sound guys, four boy roadies, one girl roadie, and a rented six-piece string section. And that isn't taking into account the folks who traveled with us for a brief time, like some of the fine folks from Éclat Records or some random journalists. Not only that, but we added another tour bus to our convoy, plus an eighteen-wheel truck loaded with a super-high-end sound system, gaudy stage decorations and special effects, and many, many different outfits for me. We also had an enormous Oriental rug in tow, which was Marnie's idea. I'd taken to performing barefoot, and Ms Lake didn't want me to catch a cold or get a splinter.

Musically and visually, this all translated pretty well. The string section's stringing was so sweet and warm that when they played behind me, I felt like I was surrounded by cotton candy. Jenn, Travis and Frank sounded better than ever. Frankly, my job was pretty easy. If you saw any of the shows, you know that we came off as cool, professional and, best of all, entertaining.

In terms of how we all interacted together offstage, well, as you now know, that wasn't as smooth. And like I said at the beginning of this book, it all came to a head in Chicago. Remember this little tirade, courtesy of one Jennifer Bradford:

> *'I'm quitting,' Jenn yelled, 'because you act like everything is all Naomi, all the time, and yeah, you're the one that the people see and hear first and foremost, fine, I accept that, you've been out front since day one, but it seems like you've conveniently forgotten there're three other people on stage with you, and one of them – namely me – is pretty much the person who makes this band sound the way it sounds, and if we don't sound the way we sound, we're still stuck at Beaned playing for, like, sixty people, and people are gonna realize that when they hear my solo stuff – and they* will *hear my solo stuff, trust me on that one, Naomi – and I'm also outta here because of what you've done to my brother, and I don't care that you didn't mean to, you did it, it's done, it can't be undone, and you know what else, well, I'm almost embarrassed to admit this in front of the entire tour bus, but I will because I'm on*

a roll here, but part of the reason I'm outta here is because I wanted this guy, and you took him, and he macked on me, and I didn't go for it, and I didn't tell you, and I don't know why, and whether you know it or not, honey, these are the kinds of things that tear bands apart, and, for that matter, tear friendships apart!'

After the dust sort of settled, Frank piped up, 'Can we declare this band meeting over? Please say yes.'

Jenn and I screamed at the same time, '*Yes!*'

'Thank God,' Frank said. 'Trav, let's blow.' Frank is much smaller than Travis, but the drummer easily yanked the shell-shocked bass player from his seat, then all but threw him towards the back of the bus. He stopped, gave Jenn a steely look and said, 'If I were you, I wouldn't walk away from this band. I'm sure when your solo record comes out, you'll be huge. But what we have now is . . . is . . . is *precious*.' He pointed one finger at Jenn, and one at me. 'What's going on between you two is big' – he then spread his arms wide apart – 'but what's going on with all of us is bigger. Don't be stupid and blow it for everybody.'

Right after he shut the door, I started crying. 'What'm I gonna do what'm I gonna do what'm I gonna do? I've never been without you—'

'Oh, quit whining. I'm not going anywhere right this minute. I'll finish the tour. I'm a professional. And besides, Travis would kill me if I bailed now.' She'd calmed down and had modulated her voice level by then. From her tone, you'd have thought we were having a regular old conversation, not a conversation about the destruction of both a hugely successful rock band, and a hugely successful friendship. But the fact she spoke so evenly and matter-of-factly made the whole thing more real. Jenn was outta here.

'You'll be fine,' she said. 'Mitchie-boy'll find you a whole new band for the next record. You don't need me.'

For a millisecond, I almost believed her. But only for a millisecond.

My God, What Have I Done?

If Gib hadn't gotten all chatty on us, the bus on our ride to Milwaukee would have been a monosyllabic morgue.

'Braver, Female Bradford, I thought I'd never say this, but it's too damn quiet around here. Where's the bitching? Where's the arguing? Where's the whining?' Gib then raised his voice up an octave. '*Jenn, why don't you blah blah blah! Naomi, why don't you wah wah wah! Jenn, you can blah blah my blah blah! Naomi, you can wah wah my wah wah!*'

Jenn and I then yelled in unison, '*Gib, you can blah blah my wah wah.*' I shot Jenn an ironic, can-you-believe-we-said-that-at-the-exact-same-time look. She shot me an unironic, I-want-you-to-die-like-yesterday look, then stormed off to her bunk, where she stayed until the following night's gig. No breakfast, no lunch, no dinner, no soundcheck. It was just sleep, then solitude, then show.

As it happened, that Milwaukee show was brilliant – at least technically speaking. Nobody made a single mistake. Everything was perfect: the tunes, the transitions, the in-between-song patter, *everything*. It was utterly professional . . . and utterly soulless. That was what we had become. Professional and soulless. Just like so many other thriving bands that spend too much time swimming in a cesspool of offstage negativity.

After the set, I hopped on to the bus, threw on some sweats, hopped off the bus, trudged out to the corner of the parking lot – carefully tiptoeing so as not to cut my bare feet – and plopped my skinny ass down on to the gravel. I stared up at the purple, star-dotted Wisconsin sky. The highlights and lowlights of the last year flashed through my head like a slideshow. Okay, that's not totally accurate – it was only the lowlights: Jenn and I melting down in front of a bajillion people at Glastonbury. The interpersonal deadness of the 'Hearts Ablaze' video shoot. Travis and Frank's constant – and more than justifiable – annoyance with the infantile behavior of our band's female contingent. Simon's increasing crankiness and clinginess. The ice-cold flawlessness of tonight's show.

And worst of all, that brutal, wrenching band meeting last night.

And I asked myself, well, how did I get here?

I didn't sign up for this. I didn't ask to be a single-named so-called diva. I didn't ask for videos, and magazine covers, and television shows, and personal bitches. I just wanted to sing. I wanted to make music with my friends. I maybe wanted a kissable boyfriend. That's all. And I didn't think that was asking anybody too much.

For a second, I saw myself bailing, just jumping off the circus train. But that was just for a second, because I was well aware it was far too late to back out. Contracts had been signed. Gigs had been booked. Travis, Frank, Gib, and who knows how many other people, were depending on me. No, wait – everybody was depending on *us*. That's *us* as in me and Jenn. Or should I say Jenn and me? Because in my heart, she had always come first. I mean, can you blame me? Since high school, she'd given me tons of emotional support, tons of awesome songs, and tons of unconditional love.

If I didn't do something, there wouldn't be an *us*. There would just be a *me*. And even though Mitchie-boy, and the press, and the fans had bought into the Naomi cult of personality, this wasn't ever supposed to be about me alone.

This has to be fixed, I thought, tears of pain cascading down my cheeks. *This has to be fixed now*.

I stood up and sprinted to the bus, ignoring the fact that the gravel was tearing the soles of my feet to shreds. I climbed the stairs, marched right up to Jenn, and asked, 'You wanted what guy?'

For a good minute, she shot me the blankest look in the history of blank looks, but then it dawned on her I was picking up where last night's conversation had more or less left off.

'Simon.'

'Simon?'

'Simon.'

'SIMON?'

'SIMON!!!'

'SIMON???'

She went back to using her normal voice. One of us had to. 'Yes, Naomi, Simon. I wanted him sooo badly, from the second I laid eyes on him, I wanted him, I mean his face, and his lips, and his eyes all drove me insane, *insane*, like the kind of insane that makes it hard to function properly, but I functioned properly, oh yes I did, and I resisted my mind and body's every impulse, which was to jump him, but I didn't, because I didn't want to screw up anything with the record, because playing music is the most important thing to me in my life, more important than sex, more important than boys, more important than *anything*, and for my entire life, you've been next to me while I played music, and even though I wanted him *bad*, the band and the music was my priority, but then when he wanted you, and I couldn't talk you out of it, I started to freak out for a million different reasons, but I saw you were happy, so I kept my mouth shut, but then when I went to his place to record my solo stuff, you were kinda getting on my nerves, and then while he was setting up the microphones, he got all flirty, and I got all flirty back, I couldn't help it, and it started out nothing big, just some little forearm touches, and an accidental boob brush or two, that sort of thing, and then he tried to kiss me, and I kissed him back, and I realized this would've killed you, so I changed my mind and told him, sorry, we can't do this because I don't want to be another picture on your studio wall, and I don't want to hurt Naomi, but he kept trying, and I punched him in the stomach, and he finally stopped, and he told me not to tell you, and I didn't, and the whole thing got me sadder and madder and madder and sadder, and I couldn't get it under control, and next thing you know, we're not talking, and I'm still sad, and I'm still mad, and I can't help it, and I can't stop it.'

Unstuck

Right then, something clicked. No. No. No. I would *not* take a stage without Jennifer Bradford. I would *not* go into a studio without Jennifer Bradford. She's the sister this only child always dreamed of, the other half of my musical heartbeat. I love her. I *lurve* her. Always have, always will. She was *not* quitting the band. Not on my watch.

I reached over and caressed the side of her face. She flinched at my touch, which broke my heart a little bit. I knew this was going to be a rough few minutes – possibly the roughest few minutes of my life – but I plowed ahead, because I *had* to, pain be damned. 'I'm not letting you go anywhere, even if it means I have to handcuff you to Gib's leg,' I whispered. 'This is me, Jenn. A somewhat fucked-up version of me, but still me. We're going to make this work. We're going to make up. Right now. And you have to accept that. You. Are. Not. Leaving. This. Band.'

'I. Am. So. Leaving. This. Band.' But did I see her eyes soften a bit? Or was I projecting?

'You don't want to go anywhere. And you want *us* to be *us* again. I know you do. I know I do. You. Have. To. Let. It. Go.' I was still whispering. I guess I was trying to hypnotize her or something.

But the hypnosis didn't take. 'You can't let stuff go *just like that*, Naomi. Things get stuck.' Tears welled up in her eyes. Jenn never cried out of sadness; her tears were always joyful. I looked deep into those gorgeous eyes of hers, and I saw the love – the *lurve* – buried deep down there. I just had to dig for it.

'Well, get it unstuck,' I said, still whispering, still hypnotizing. 'Because we're gonna make up. Seymour Simon is not important enough to keep you and me apart. A stupid article in *Rolling Stone* is not important enough to keep us apart.'

Jenn gulped, then shakily said, 'You still don't get it, Naomi. You just don't.'

I backed away from her. 'Tell me.'

'It's kind of about Ass Boy, it's kind of about stuff like the *Rolling Stone* articles, it's kind of about you not loving Travis, but what hurt the most is that you didn't give a ripe fuck about my solo project. All you cared about is how it would affect you. That's what put me over the edge.'

I nodded. She knew me too damn well for my own good. 'Maybe that's the truth a little bit. Actually, it's the truth a *lot*. It scared me. And I'll work on that. I promise. Problem identified. It will be fixed. We can't *not* make up. We're the Intrepid Duo.'

I could see her weakening. 'Okay, but what about Travis? You simply cannot treat my baby brother they way you've been treating him.' She gulped again, then her tears began to flow in earnest.

I touched her cheek again; this time she leaned into my hand.

'Jenn, I adore Travis. The last thing I'd ever want to do is hurt him. I haven't treated him any differently since the day he told me that he loved me. Did you know he told me that he loved me?'

She sniffled, then nodded. 'He's loved you forever. And I've known that forever, even before he admitted it to me, probably even before he could admit it to himself. And your thing with Ass Boy is breaking his heart.'

My eyes were teary to the point that I couldn't see Jenn clearly, even though she was standing about two inches in front of me. 'Sweetie, I can't help how he feels about me.'

'Yeah, I know. I know.'

After what felt like six years of awkward silence, I again asked *the* question: 'So are you staying, or what?'

For a while she just looked at me – looked inside of me, really – gave the tiniest of smiles, and quietly sang, '*And then I'm gonna wrap you in my arms. And then I'm gonna keep you safe from harm.*'

I pulled her towards me by her waist, buried my face in her neck, and laugh/cried, 'You are *so* cheesy.' After a couple of minutes of hugging, I had an idea that might help further seal our reformed bond, and restore my sanity. 'You know what? I'm gonna dump Seymour's ass. I'll dump his needy, jealous, whiny, sleazy ass right this second.' Despite herself, she laughed a little, then I said, 'Trust me, you were better off without him.'

Still holding me close, she said, 'Yeah, you're probably right.' She then gently pushed me away, sniffled, and asked, 'I have to know. Was he good in bed?'

I laughed. 'Only you would ask something like that at a time like this.'

'I have to know.'

'Of course you do.' I took a deep breath. 'Truth?'

'Truth.'

'Amazing. Astonishing. Mind boggling.'

She gave me a rueful smile. 'I figured as much. But Nay Nay, you can do better.'

We stared at each other for a hot minute. Nothing was

said. We just *knew* it was okay. It would take work, but as you well know by now, Jenn and I are persistent as hell. If anybody could repair everything that needed to be repaired, it would be us. I said, 'Thanks. And don't call me Nay Nay.'

We laughed, then cried some more, then laughed again, then hugged, like, forever.

The Intrepid Duo was back.

I Dump Seymour Simon's Needy, Jealous, Whiny, Sleazy Ass

I kissed Jenn on the cheek, *finally* disentangled myself from our embrace – an embrace that had gotten tighter and tighter by the second – and said, 'If you'll excuse me, honey, I have some dumping to do.'

She let out a shaky, tear-filled chuckle. 'Thank you, Nay Nay.'

'I told you, don't call me Nay Nay,' I laughed. 'And you're welcome. But I'm not just doing this for you, Jenn. I'm doing it for me. What him and I have is not healthy.' *Except for the sex*, I thought. *That was really healthy*. In the interest of global happiness and harmony, I quickly purged that thought. 'But if it so happens that dumping him will make you happy, well, that's something I'll have to live with.'

Jenn chuckled again, and put her hand on my shoulder. 'Be brave, young lady. Do the Intrepid Duo proud.'

'I'm on my way,' I said. I took two steps, spun around, and asked, 'Were you really gonna quit?'

'Yeah,' she said. 'I dunno. Probably. Maybe. Not really. Possibly. Who knows?' As I headed towards the back of the bus, I thanked my lucky stars that Jenn Bradford was still on board.

Simon was crashed out in his bunk. His headphones were on, which meant that he hadn't heard Jenn and I. Phew. Yes, he had macked on Jenn, and yes, he had probably slept with a bajillion chick singers, but he wasn't evil – just really, really jerky – and we did have some fun. Considering what happened, though, it would be hard to remember that down the line. But I would deal with it, because that's what you do in these situations: deal with it.

I tapped him on the shoulder. 'Rise and shine, Simon.'

His whole body jerked, then he involuntarily sat up and conked his noggin on the top of his bunk. He tore off his headphones and rubbed his head. 'What the hell, Naomi? I was asleep. What time is it? Christ.'

'It's late. We have to talk.'

We have to talk. Those are four words you never want to hear from your boyfriend or girlfriend, from your husband or wife, or, in this case, from your casual lover. Simon, for all his faults, was a bright guy, and he knew immediately that something was up. He eyed me warily, and said, 'Talk about what?'

'About stuff. Get up. Now.' I cocked a thumb at the back lounge. 'I'll be waiting in there. Speed it up.' Who knew I could be such a badass?

Travis and Frank were huddled up in the back lounge multi-tasking, and in this case, multi-tasking meant at once playing video games, listening to *Rubber Soul*, and intensely conversing. And I knew the conversing was intense, because the second I opened the door, they both clammed up, and Travis's face turned beet red. 'Hey, guys,' I said.

'Hey, Naomi,' Frank said.

'Yeah. Hey,' Travis said.

'Sorry about me and Jenn being assholes.'

'No problem, Naomi,' Frank said.

'Yeah. No problem,' Travis said.

'I thought you guys went to bed.'

Travis said, 'I wanted to play some *Grand Theft Auto*.'

Frank said, 'I wanted to be away from you two.'

'Thanks for your honesty, Frank,' I said. 'Now take a hike.'

'No problem, Naomi,' Frank said.

'Yeah. No problem,' Travis said. But then he added, 'Why?'

Just then, Simon threw open the door. 'Okay, what's the deal? Why'd you get me up?' He then noticed Travis and Frank gawking at him. 'What's happening?'

Travis glared at me. 'Oh. I think I know why you want us to leave.' He got up and said, 'Fine. I'm outta here.' Then, much to his credit, he gave Simon a not-insignificant shoulder bump on his way 'outta here'. I had to admire that. It took Travis a bajillion years to confess how he felt about me, so clearly this was a man who had an impressive ability to keep his emotions bottled up inside. It was good to see him vent, even just that little bit.

Frank conscientiously turned off the Playstation and the CD player. 'You two have a good night now, you hear?' For good measure, he also gave Simon a bump, albeit gentler than Travis's.

After the bassist and the drummer were gone, Simon glared at the door. 'What the hell's wrong with those two?' Then he glared at me. 'And what the hell's wrong with you?'

I took a deep breath. This would be harder than I thought – not that I thought it would be easy, but, well, you know. 'We have to talk.'

'Yeah, you mentioned that. About what?'

'About us.'

'What about us?'

I gave him a teeny-tiny kiss on the cheek. 'I don't want there to be an "us" any more.'

The lounge was dimly lit, but I could still see that Simon had paled big time. 'Say what?' he grunted.

Even though it would have been pretty darn cathartic – and, frankly, kind of fun in a perverse sort of way – I couldn't just out and out tell him he was needy, jealous, whiny and sleazy. 'It's not working out. We want different things.'

'What do you mean, we want different things? I disagree. We want the same thing. Don't we?'

Add clueless to needy, jealous, whiny and sleazy. 'Ass Boy, did you ask [Sassy Underage Soul Crooner] to be your little girlie-friend?'

'Um . . .'

'Or how about [Super Sexy Junk in the Trunk Boob Hanging Out Rapper]?'

'Um . . .'

'Or [Mega Mega Super Super Hot Hot Hoochie Shaker]?'

'Um . . .'

His expression morphed into a death mask. I snapped my fingers three times in his face. 'Hello? Anybody home?'

'Why, Naomi?' he whined. 'Why're you breaking up with me? Tell me. Tell me exactly why. I need to know. I need to know what it is that I've done that made you want to hurt me so badly. It'll hurt me even more, but I need to know.' Add *masochistic* to needy, jealous, whiny, sleazy and clueless.

'Why? You want to know why?'

'Yes, Naomi. Yes I do.'

'You know what? It's not even that you macked on Jenn. Because, actually, at this point, I don't even care.'

He started craning his neck from side to side, as if he was searching for something. 'Who told you about that? What did they tell you?'

When he finally calmed down and bothered to look at me again, I said, 'Seymour Ass Boy Simon, we're done because you're needy, you're jealous, you're whiny, you're sleazy, you're clueless, and you're masochistic.'

'You're the first woman who's ever broken up with me,' he said.

I shrugged. 'I'm not trying to make history, here, Simon. I'm just doing what's best for me.'

He glared the front of the bus. 'I can't believe it. The fucking bitch told.' He stood up. 'Fine. Well, I'm about to do what's best for *me*, which is to get the hell off this tour. Find yourself another producer and monitor guy, diva bitch.' He threw open the door, stormed into the bunk area, and roared, 'Gib! Get up!'

Our tour manager rolled out of his bottom bunk on to the floor, and sprung up catlike. 'Simon, I just fell asleep, and I like it when I fall asleep, and I don't like it when I get woken up immediately after I've fallen asleep, so this'd better be good.'

'Oh, it's good, alright. I want out. Right now. Tell the driver to stop at the next rest area. Then when we get there, you get my luggage out, and then I'm gone.'

Gib shoved Simon against the wall. 'Are you giving me orders, pleb?'

'What does it sound like, baldy?'

Gib's neck tensed and his biceps twitched. He cocked a fist and whispered, 'I haven't hit anybody in eight years, six months and fourteen days, Simon, but that doesn't mean I've forgotten how.'

I put a hopefully calming hand on Gib's shoulder. 'If he wants out, Gib, we should let him out.'

Fist still cocked, Gib said, 'Is that what you want, Braver? Because it's your show.'

Again, Simon was not a bad person, just weak and

unstable . . . and needy, and jealous, and whiny, and et cetera. Okay, maybe he was kind of a bad person. I regarded Seymour Ass Boy Simon for a few seconds. I hated to see it end like this, but if he wanted to be a drama queen, who was I to deny him his moment in the spotlight?

'Let him go, Gib. I did.'

My Calm Assessment of the Simon Situation

'I hate boys.'

Simon and Travis Have a Public Discussion About Stuff I Would Rather Have Had Them Discuss in Private. (Actually, Come to Think of it, I Would Rather the Discussion Hadn't Happened at All, But What're You Gonna Do?)

The next stop on our tour was Houston, and the Illinois-to-Texas trip is a long one, just over eighteen hours. At the rest area, our driver told us that he wouldn't stop for at least eight more hours, so if we needed to stretch, or to pick up some munchies, or to use a real, live bathroom, now was the time to do it. We dutifully trudged off the bus, and did whatever it was we respectively had to do. In my case, that meant peeing, then buying a king-sized container of Double Stuf Oreos.

Jenn and I were the first ones back on the bus, and we set up camp in the front lounge. We were both jazzed about our reunion – and I was double jazzed about the fact that Simon was toast – and we knew we wouldn't sleep, so I pulled out a deck of cards, a Scrabble board, and Trivial

Pursuit. I thrust a fist in the air and shouted, 'Let the games begin!'

'Oh, you are *so* going down, Ms Braver.'

'Is that so, Ms Bradford? Well, smarty butt, pick your poison.'

She regarded the games for a few seconds, then pointed at Scrabble. 'That.'

'Bring it on, beeyatch.'

As we picked our Scrabble tiles, the rest of the touring party slowly made their way back on to the bus. Jenn and I were wrapped up in the game, so we weren't paying any attention to who'd returned from the rest stop. Gib hadn't paid any attention, either. 'Troops, I was distracted dealing with Simon,' he said, 'and I have no idea about anybody's comings and goings. So let's do a roll-call. Braver?'

'Gib, I'm two inches in front of you.'

'Check. Female Bradford?'

'Gib, I'm four inches in front of you.'

'Check. Lake?' Marnie, as usual, was holed up in her bunk, so her muffled cry of 'here' was barely heard.

'Craft?'

Right then, Frank hopped back on to the bus and gave Gib a playful smack on his backside. 'Right here, homeboy.'

'Touch me again, Craft, and you'll be holding your drumsticks with your teeth. Simon?' Gib sang. 'Oh, Simon? Where arrrrrrre you, Siiiiiiimon?'

Jenn asked, 'Gib, did you just make a joke?'

'You know I don't joke, Female Bradford.'

'Yeah,' Jenn said, 'I know.' Then she reached out and gave his crotch a playful, lingering squeeze. 'Maybe you should play around a bit more.'

Gib gently removed Jenn's hand. 'Maybe I should, Female Bradford. But not right now.' See what I missed when I was fighting with Jenn? Maybe she'd tried to seduce

Gib, and it didn't work. Maybe she'd tried to seduce Gib, and it *did* work. I'd have to grill her on that one later.

Frank said, 'Hey, how come she gets to touch you without being threatened bodily harm?'

'Because, Craft, you're a very, very ugly man, and Female Bradford isn't. Now where's that brother of yours, Female Bradford? Male Bradford?' No response. 'Male Bradford!' Still no response. 'MALE BRADFORD!'

'Travis,' Jenn yelled, 'where you at? We've gotta boogie!' No response.

Gib gave an annoyed sigh, then popped open the window and yelled, 'Male Bradford! I request that you let your voice be heard!'

Travis's voice was heard, alright, but it had nothing to do with Gib's request.

'Ironically,' we heard Travis growl, 'if you hadn't have left, I probably would've thrown your ass out of the bus myself.'

'You would've?' Simon asked skeptically. 'All 175 pounds of you? Oooh, I'm quaking. How would you've gone about it, beanpole?' Jenn and I peeked out the bus window, but there was no sign of Simon or Travis anywhere. It was a deadly quiet night – no cars, no people, no nothing – so Travis and Simon could've been anywhere within a hundred-yard radius, and still be heard without being seen. I wondered how long their talk had been going on, and what had already been discussed.

'I have a love in my life,' Travis all but whispered, 'and it makes me stronger than you can imagine.'

'Say what?'

'That's Adam Sandler as Barry Egan in *Punch-Drunk Love*.'

'Great. But what does this "love in my life" crap have to do with me? Why should I care?'

'Because I love Naomi.'

'Oh, give it up, kid. You're a child. She'd never have you. Don't bother. You know nothing about love. *Nothing*.'

' "I might be the only person on the face of the earth who knows she's the greatest woman on the earth. I might be the only one who appreciates every single thing she does." '

I could practically hear Simon's eyes roll. 'Another movie quote?'

'Jack Nicholson as Melvin Udall in *As Good As it Gets*.'

Jenn whispered, 'Damn, that was a good one. You go, Travis.'

I gave her a not-so-gentle shove. 'Take a hike. You shouldn't be hearing this. *I* probably shouldn't be hearing this, but you *definitely* shouldn't be hearing this.'

'Take a hike?' she asked. 'Are you serious? This is can't-miss stuff. You couldn't pay me enough to take a hike.'

'Okay, whatever,' I said. 'Just keep quiet, then.'

Simon said, 'Travis, you're a mediocre bass player, and a child, and you'd make a shitty boyfriend for Naomi. I know what she needs. I know what she wants. I know what she likes. I know where she likes it. I know how to make her like things that she didn't even know she liked in the first place.'

Jenn purred, 'Ooh, what's that one about, Nay Nay?'

'None of your damn business,' I hissed, remembering that night in Miami where we committed an act far too vulgar to be discussed in these pages.

'And if she doesn't want *me* right now, that means she doesn't want *anybody* right now. Especially the likes of you.' I guess you could add *condescending* and *arrogant* to needy, jealous, whiny, sleazy, clueless, in denial and masochistic. Actually, how about let's forget all the extraneous adjectives and just think of Seymour Simon as a douchebag.

Travis broke the silence a few seconds later. 'Poetry will be in my life. So will love. And adventure. Not posturing of love, not playful of poetic games of love for the amusement of a night, but a love that takes over your life. It's like an explosion in your heart that can't be changed, ever.'

'Who said that, champ?' Simon asked.

'Gwyneth Paltrow's character in *Shakespeare In Love*. Paraphrased.'

'You're pathetic,' Simon scoffed. 'You can't even come up with your own words. You have to hide behind other people's, because you're a fucking child.'

'You want to hear my own words, Simon?'

'Not particularly.'

'Too bad, because here they are: I love Naomi, and I always have, and I always will, and she doesn't love me back, but I don't care, because if she's happy, that's cool, and you weren't making her happy, and if you'd kept making her unhappy, that's when I would've somehow, some way, gotten you off this tour, and off that bus, and out of Naomi's life, and I know you think I couldn't have made that happen, because you're a big-fucking-shot producer and I'm just a skinny little bass player, but I could've, I definitely could've, because when it comes to Naomi, I can do *anything*, and that's *anything* as in chasing down some scumbag paparazzi guy who had the balls to take a picture of her naked, and I ran him down even though he roared off on a Vespa, but I ran fast – and I'm not a runner – and I caught up with him at a stoplight, and I punched his nose – I think I broke it, even – then I ran back to the hotel, but on the way there, some cops caught up with me, and when I told them what had happened, they were so disgusted with the paparazzi guy that they gave me a ride back, and I didn't even tell Naomi about it, because I did it just to do it, to protect her, not to win some kind of award, so Mr Seymour Simon Simon Seymour Banana Dingleberry Jingleheimer Schmidt Whatever the Fuck Your Name Is, *you* are the one who has no idea what love is, because you would *never* sacrifice your time, or your heart, or your body to make anybody happy except yourself, because let's be honest here, you just wanted Naomi because she's pretty and talented and a big star, but I want her because she's kind, and intelligent, and funny, and my entire being tingles whenever she's in my personal space, and when she sings, I get dizzy, and some nights when we're on stage, if she's close to me, and she's pouring her heart into every song, it's almost impossible for me to keep playing, but I do, because I don't want to let her down – I'd *never* let her down, no matter what – and you can never understand any of this, because I've known her forever, I've known her since before the make-over, and before the bra, and before the stylists, and I don't care how big her boobs are, or how perfect her skin is, or how many records she's sold, or what magazine covers she's on, all I know is that she makes me happy, and I just care that she's happy, and that's all I care about, and that's something *you* will never, ever, *ever* understand.'

That had to be one of the best – if not *the* best – run-on sentences I'd ever heard.

After a while, Simon said, 'I thought it was the promoter who caught the paparazzi guy.'

'No,' Travis sighed. 'It was me.'

Jenn whispered, 'I thought it was Gib.'

'I thought it was you,' I whispered to Jenn.

Gib – who, as I hadn't previously noticed, was *also* peeking out the window – whispered, 'I thought it was Lake.'

'No,' I said, 'Marnie was with me the whole—' I then realized Gib had been listening in on the entire discussion. 'Oh, great,' I groaned. 'You're hearing all this, too.'

'Braver,' Gib said, 'I'm not hearing anything I didn't already know. *Everybody* knows Male Bradford wants you.

Craft knows. Busey knows. Lake knows. Those idiotic German bra freaks know. The string section knows. Our crew knows. Your opening band knows. The audience even knows.'

Jenn asked, 'What do you mean, the audience knows?'

'Haven't you ever seen the way Male Bradford looks at Braver when she's singing? Those puppy dog eyes? Even *I* couldn't miss it, and I'm a dolt about those sorts of things.'

'You sure are,' Jenn mumbled.

'Zip it, Female Bradford.'

Just then, Travis lumbered on to the bus. He regarded the three of us hanging out the window and tiredly said, 'You guys heard every word of that, didn't you?'

Jenn said, 'You want an honest answer on that one, baby brother?'

'Not really. But give it to me anyhow.'

'We came in right before you busted out the line from *Punch-Drunk Love*.'

He chuckled despite himself. 'Too bad. You missed some really good ones before that. I got on a roll. I pulled out stuff from *Say Anything*, and *Annie Hall*, and *Casablanca*.' He looked down at his shoes, his floppy hair momentarily hiding his face. 'But I'm out of quotes now. I'm fried. I'm done.' He gazed at me, took a deep breath, and said, 'Sweet dreams, sweet Naomi.' Then he walked slowly to his bunk.

Twelve months ago, if you'd have put together a police line-up with the smooth Tony Esposito, the macho Seymour Simon, and the skinny, floppy-haired Travis Bradford, then asked me, 'Which one of these men is the truest *man*?' I most definitely wouldn't have pointed to Bachelor Number Three. The reason for that, of course, is because I was an idiot.

Watching my protector shamble off, I could have laughed. I could have cried. But what I did whisper so only

I could hear, was, 'Sweet dreams to you, too, sweet Travis.' Then I inhaled eight Double Stuf Oreos.

Jenn 'N' Someone, Sittin' In A Tree, K-i-s-s-i-n-g

The Kevins descended upon me not more than six seconds after our tour bus pulled into the 'Restricted Access' area behind the stage at the Woodlands Pavilion just outside of Houston.

'Is it true?' White Kevin ranted. 'Tell me it's true. If it's true, it's classic, a moment that'll go down in modern music history. Did you guys get photographic documentation on it? Or did you record it? Ohmigawd, dude, that'd be awesome. If you did, I swear, I'm stealing the tape and posting it online.'

Black Kevin – who I was starting to think of as 'Sane Kevin' – restrained his partner. 'Chill, man.' Then he asked me, 'What happened?'

What with the Simon thing, the Travis thing, and the Oreo overdose thing, I'd gotten zero sleep the previous night, so I was a tad out of it. 'What happened what?'

White Kevin asked, 'What happened with Simon? We heard he, ahem, left the tour.'

I ran my hand through the tangled mop formerly known as my hair. 'And how, perchance, did you hear that?'

'We have our sources.' White Kevin grinned.

'There're only, like, six people who know about Simon,

ahem, leaving the tour. Who spilled the beans?'

White Kevin cocked a thumb at Black Kevin. 'His girlfriend.'

Black Kevin grabbed White Kevin's thumb and twisted it into what looked like a pretty painful position. 'Dude, can't you keep your trap shut for, like, two minutes?'

'Okay, okay, okay, ouch, ouch, ouch, let go, let go, let go.'

Black Kevin reluctantly released White Kevin's thumb and said, 'Suffice it to say that a cute little birdie happened to mention that Simon took his leave. Me and Moron Boy over here are big fans of Simon's work, and we were curious as to why he moved on.'

I thought for a second about whether I should spill the Simon beans to the Hoohah boys. When the press found out about it, they'd have a field day. The article in *Rolling Stone* would probably read something like this:

> *Fresh from their onstage meltdown at the Glastonbury Festival, Naomi broke ties with Simon. Word is, the band's eponymous frontwoman threw the super-producer out of a tour bus in the middle of Bumfuck, Iowa – and it should be noted that at the time of the throw-off, the bus was cruising along at just under 100 m.p.h. The band's drummer Frank Craft said, 'It was all Naomi. She smacked Simon on his head with her finely German-engineered bra, then literally kicked him on to the street – all while she was in her jammies. Not that Simon didn't deserve it, but it was still pretty ugly.' Naomi herself could not be reached for comment.*

I figured it'd be wise to get my side of the story out there, and White Kevin was a blabbermouth, so if anybody could spread the word, and spread it quickly, it'd be him. He'd probably post it on the Hoohah website that very afternoon. 'Before I tell you anything,' I said, 'you have to answer me one question.'

White Kevin pseudo-seductively put his hand on my waist, and purred, 'I'll answer anything for you, Naomi. Anything at all.'

I flicked his arm. 'Touch me again, and you'll lose that hand.' Black Kevin cracked up.

White Kevin yelled, 'Hey, cut it out! That hurt! Okay, ask me your stupid question.'

'Who told you about Simon?' I had a hunch I knew who the culprit was, but I wanted official confirmation.

Right then, Jenn slinked out of the bus. 'Hey, Naomi. And good morning, boys. You're both looking quite dapper today. Especially you, Mr McAllister.' Then she walked right up to Black Kevin, and kissed him. On the mouth. For a really long time. With lots of tongue. And lots of teeth. Then she reached behind him and cupped his butt.

Both White Kevin and I gawked at the kissing couple. He turned to me and said, 'Does that answer your question?'

After they broke their embrace, I grabbed Jenn by the upper arm, said, 'Excuse me, Kevins, I'll be talking to the both of you later. Jenn, you and me, we're talking now.' I hauled her back on to the bus, and said, 'Details.'

'What, right this second?'

'Yeah, right this second.'

'Intimate details?'

'Absolutely.'

'About me and Kevin fucking like weasels?'

'Damn straight.'

'Even with them around?'

I hadn't noticed that Frank, Marnie and Gib were staring at us. 'Um, hey guys,' I said.

Frank said, 'Please, Jenn, let's have some intimate details.'

'Piss off, Frank,' she said. 'Marnie, where's Travis?'

Marnie said, 'He ran off the bus the second he saw you and Kevin going at it. I think you grossed him out.'

Jenn nodded. 'I can understand that. I'd probably get grossed out if I saw him kissing anybody the way I just kissed Kevin. I wouldn't want to see my brother doing all that tonguing and ass grabbing, and—'

'Oh-*kayyyy*, on that note, everybody, get outta here,' I said. 'Jenn and I need some girl time.'

'Girl time?' Frank said. 'Well, aren't you two just the rock star divas?'

Gib growled, 'Craft, Braver requested girl time with Female Bradford, and it's my job to grant her requests. Out.'

When we finally had the bus to ourselves, I said, 'TellMeTellMeTellMe!'

Jenn took my hands and said, 'Okay. First of all, isn't he hot?'

'Insanely hot.'

'He's got the *best* ass.'

'Uh huh.'

'And his hands are amazing. It's a drummer thing, I guess.'

'Uh huh.'

'And his skin is so smooth.'

'Uh huh.'

'And his cock is—'

'Whoa, time out, that wasn't the kind of detail I'm looking for here. Just tell me how and when you hooked up.'

She gave me a huge grin. 'Honey, we hooked up the day after we met. The third day of the tour.'

'*Excuse me*?' Kevin told me at Jones Beach that he had a crush on you. And that was the second day of the tour.'

'Yeah, that boy moves quickly, doesn't he? What happened was, I'm watching them do their soundcheck, and I'm watching Kevin play drums, and it's like three million degrees on stage, and he has his shirt off, and he's sweating, and he looks amazing, and I'm in a bad mood as you well know, and I thought maybe some attention from a guy would cheer me up, so I walk up to him and I'm like, *You're a great drummer, blah blah blah*, and I'm wearing my little white ribbed sleeveless T-shirt, and my nipples are totally hard, and I totally expected him to stare at them – every guy does when I wear that shirt – but he totally didn't, and when he didn't stare, I *wanted* him to stare, because I thought he didn't think I was cute, but then we start talking, and he's asking me all these questions, and listening to all my answers, and we get into this big discussion about The Beatles – and he knows *everything* about The Beatles – and he was so passionate about it, and he still didn't have his shirt on, and after, like, two hours of this, I finally ask him if he has a girlfriend, and he says no and asks me if I have a boyfriend, and I say no, and we just look at each other for, like, a month – we don't say anything, we just look – and he says, *Are you taking applications for the position of boyfriend*, and I'm like, *Hells yeah*.'

She stopped to catch her breath. 'And Naomi?'

'Yeah?'

'This is serious. He might be The One. Capital "T" for "the". Capital "O" for "one". The One.'

'You just met him.'

'Naomi, sometimes you *just know*.'

'How do you know you *just know*? As far as I know, you've never *just known* before, so doesn't that mean there's no way you can know what *just knowing* is?'

'Honey, trust me, you *know* when you *just know*, even if you've never *just known* before. And he's a great guy. He's a gentleman. He's smart. He's funny. And get this: we haven't even slept together yet. He says he wants to wait until the tour is over, so we can do it right.'

'But didn't you say something about his penis?'

'His cock. Not penis. *Cock.*' She shrugged. 'I didn't say we haven't gotten naked. I mean, have you seen him? You think I'm gonna dry hump this guy forever?'

'I suppose not.'

'But he doesn't want to have actual sex until we're back home, because he wants to make me dinner, and light candles, and play Miles Davis records, and stuff.'

For some reason, that made me tear up. 'That's great, Jenn,' I sniffled. 'I'm so happy for you. So happy.' Then I started bawling.

Jenn looked startled. 'What the hell's wrong with you? You okay? Still freaked about Ass Boy, I bet.'

After a bit, I calmed down and said, 'I'm okay. And Ass Boy is absolute history. It's just that I missed you so much, and I'm so happy we're *us* again, and I'm so happy we're making music together, and I'm so happy that you might've found The One, and I want to find The One too, and all I end up with is Douchebag One and Douchebag Two.'

She pulled me into an embrace. 'Shhh, honey. The One is out there. Believe me. He's really out there.'

We held each other for a bit, which felt great. I needed that hug. Badly. Then we pulled apart and went about the business of putting on the final show of our shed tour. And then we went home.

Another Lunch With Travis

The fine folks at Éclat Records saw fit to give us a two-month break, and the timing couldn't have been better. My voice was shot. My bra was broken. My energy level was nil. My hair was unmanageable – even Marnie was frustrated with my mop. My skin was oily and zitty. My body spoke to me so loudly and clearly – *Naomi, for my sake, please unplug* – that I had no choice but to listen.

My first order of business when I got back to New York was to find an apartment. Check that: find an apartment *with Jenn*. Living alone didn't hold as much appeal for me as it had a few months back. Fortunately, at this point we started seeing some of the money we'd earned over the past year – it was a *lot* of money, actually – so we went out and rented ourselves a gorgeous four-bedroom duplex in a certain area of Brooklyn that I won't reveal. The reason for the secrecy is because as of this writing, we're still living there, and we'd like to keep a somewhat low profile. Not that we don't love our fans – to quote my favorite obscure glam rock band Spacehog, 'We love the all of you' – but you understand.

My second order of business was to buy a car. I'd never owned a car. I never thought I'd own a car. I lived in New

York City, and us NYC types can get by perfectly well using public transportation. But our new apartment came with two parking spaces, so who were we to leave then empty? Also, at this point, Jenn and I were so recognizable that a trip on the 'F' train probably would've turned into an autograph-filled free-for-all. So we bought matching BMW X5 SUVs – mine's blue, hers is black. They're functional, cute, not outrageously expensive, and not too ostentatious. We love them, but before we even got them off the lot, Jenn said that if our second album goes double platinum, she's buying a Ferrari. And a Porsche. And a mansion so she can get on *MTV Cribs*.

We went kind of nuts furnishing the place, not necessarily in terms of quality, but in quantity. Sure, we had tons of money – more money than we ever imagined – but we still thought of ourselves as artsy-fartsy chicks who toil away at a coffee shop, and artsy-fartsy chicks who toil away at coffee shops don't spend ten grand on a couch. No, when artsy-fartsy chicks who toil away at coffee shops buy furniture, they go to Ikea. We had four bedrooms to fill up, plus a living room, and a den, and a huge kitchen, and two-and-a-half bathrooms. We bought so much stuff that we needed three trips each to get everything home.

The day Jenn and I deemed our apartment fit for human consumption, we decided to throw an impromptu housewarming party. Jenn put me in charge of food, so I drove – that's right, *drove* – to the grocery store, where I had quite the déjà vu: I was wandering through the produce section, trying to find a dozen ripe mangos to cut up into an enormous fruit salad, when I felt a tap on my shoulder. I was wearing a baseball cap and sunglasses, so as not to get recognized, but apparently, somebody saw through it. Without turning around, I said, 'I'll be glad to sign your autograph. But let me finish picking out my mangos, okay?'

A very familiar male voice said, 'Bitch, I wouldn't take your autograph if you paid me.'

I perked up. 'Is that you, Travis?'

He cracked up. 'The one and only.'

I gave him a huge hug and a kiss on the cheek. But I kind of turned my face towards him, and it ended up being one of those half-cheek-half-lip kisses that are so damn weird for a boy and a girl who aren't boyfriend and girlfriend.

His slender body felt great against mine. 'Hey there, bass player. Long time no see, right?'

He hugged me back, letting his big bass-player hands linger around my waist. 'It's only been a month.'

This is where the déjà vu stopped and real-time reality took over. 'Well, it feels like it's been forever,' I said. 'I kinda missed you, you big goofball.' Actually, I'd *really* missed him, and had been thinking about him. A lot. But Jenn and I had been so wrapped up with settling back into our lives that neither of us had seen Travis since the tour ended. Come to think of, neither of us had seen *anybody* since the tour ended except for our new landlord, a bunch of car salesmen, and a handful of Ikea employees.

'Yeah, I missed you too,' he said. We just kind of looked at each other for a moment, then he said, 'Have you eaten yet?'

'I had a big brunch . . .'

He looked crestfallen. 'Oh.'

'. . . but if you want to go to Starbucks or wherever, that be nice.'

He looked un-crestfallen. 'Oh! I mean, yeah!'

'Okay. Let me finish up shopping here.'

'You're buying stuff for the party, right?'

'Yeah.'

'I'm on chip and dip detail. And speaking of the party, I

didn't ask Jenn this on the phone, but would it be cool if I brought a date tonight?'

I gulped. Was I jealous? No way. 'Who're you planning on bringing?'

He shrugged. 'Just some girl.'

I gulped again. Maybe I was jealous. No. Couldn't be. 'Yeah, that's fine. That'd be nice. That'd be swell. Where'd you meet her?'

He shrugged again. 'Around.'

I gulped again. 'Around?'

'Yeah. Around.'

I sighed deeply and said, 'Okay. Let's get our shopping done so we can get that coffee.'

We didn't say much to one another at the grocery store, and made *very* small talk during the drive to Starbucks. The place was a zoo, and the only open table was a tiny two-top in the corner. After we scrunched ourselves into our seats, I said, 'So.' Brilliant conversational opener, right?

'Yeah,' he agreed. 'So.'

'So tell me about this girl you're bringing by tonight.' *I'm not asking out of jealousy*, I thought. *How can I be jealous? This is Travis. He's Jenn's little brother. He's the bass player in our band. I know he's in love with me, but I can't be crushing on him.*

'Well,' he said, 'she's gorgeous. A knockout. She's actually a model.'

I'm not jealous, I'm not jealous, I'm not jealous. 'A model? Interesting. Is she really that pretty?'

'Absolutely. I met her at Mercury Lounge last week. You wouldn't recognize her name, but you'd definitely recognize her face. She's been in Victoria's Secret, and she's gonna be in the next *Sports Illustrated* swimsuit issue.'

I gulped again. This gulping has to stop *immediately*. 'Wow. Does she have a brain, or is she a ditz?'

'Be nice, Naomi. Yes, she has a brain. She made Dean's list at Brown.'

'Did you mack on her, or did she mack on you?'

'Oh, she *totally* macked on me. She said she recognized me from *Saturday Night Live*. She's a huge fan of the band. She's way looking forward to meeting you, for that matter.'

'That's great, Travis. Just great.' Actually, I didn't feel so great. Even after traveling the world on our tour, I thought Travis was still a pretty innocent guy, and I felt a Victoria's Secret model might eat him alive. But was that really why I didn't feel so great? It certainly couldn't have been because I was jealous.

Or maybe it could've been, because when he said, 'I'm just playing with you, Naomi. There's no model. There's no date. There's just you', all of a sudden, I felt *great*.

I kicked him in the shin under the table. 'Why'd you tell me you landed a model, you little shit?'

'I wanted to see if you were jealous. And you were most definitely jealous.'

'I most definitely was *not* jealous.' At that point, I finally accepted the fact that I was indeed most definitely jealous. But he didn't have to know that. 'I was just glad to hear that you'd landed a model.' As noted, I wasn't, but my head was spinning, and that was the best I could come up with.

We gazed at each other for a moment, then Travis cleared his throat, and said, 'You want me. You desperately want me. You just don't know it yet. But you will in time. I know it, I feel it. And let's be honest here: you know it, and you feel it, too. One day you'll be walking down the street, and you'll think to yourself, *I have to kiss him, I have to*, then you'll run to my door, you'll ring my doorbell, you'll fall into my arms, and we'll kiss, we'll kiss for hours, we'll kiss for days. It'll be just like you dreamed it would be, even though you didn't know that that's what you were dreaming for.'

A single drip of sweat crawled down my side, and I'm pretty sure my face was fire-engine red. 'What movie is that from?' I asked.

'It's from a film that's still in development. The working title is *Naomi Braver Wises the Hell Up and Falls in Love With Travis Bradford*. I know the studio's still hammering out the casting details, but the director's in place.'

'Yeah? Who's directing this thing?'

'Some guy. He studied with Sara Rogers. You know Sara, right? She's that girl who directed a couple videos by that group Naomi? Remember Sara?'

I chuckled. 'Of course I do.'

'Yeah, it's this guy's first film,' Travis continued. 'No, let me rephrase that: it's his first *full-length* film. He starred in and directed a bunch of short films. None of them were particularly satisfying, though, and the critics trashed them. One review said, "While still quite young, the mature-beyond-his-years director clearly has skills in dealing with women, but he's using said skills in a haphazard, meandering fashion. He needs to focus on what – and who – he truly cares about. He should be honest with himself and everybody else. Above all, he shouldn't give up. He should chase his dream, even if it seems like he'll never catch it." '

'That's one heck of an incisive review,' I said.

'Isn't it, though?'

'So when's this guy's movie gonna open up?'

'Well, like I said, the casting's still up in the air, and, well, the script isn't finished yet, so production hasn't even started.'

'How much of the screenplay is done, so far?'

'The beginning and the middle are totally written.'

'Yeah? Tell me about the beginning and the middle.'

'It's pretty simple, really. Boy meets girl. Boy falls for

girl. Boy tells girl he loves her. Girl tells boy she cares for him, but not in *that* way. Meanwhile, girl goes out with lame dude. Boy gets bummed, but concludes that he and the girl are meant to be together, so he treats the girl the same way he's always treated her – with respect, admiration, and sweetness. Girl finally dumps lame dude. Boy waits for her to get over the lame guy so she'll finally realize he's The One, that her and him are meant to be together.

'Nice beginning and middle,' I said. 'And what kind of ending are we looking at?'

Travis thoughtfully rubbed his chin. 'If it were up to me, I'd go for a happy ending.'

'Yeah? What kind of happy ending?'

'I dunno. I'm sure the screenwriter would be open to suggestions. You have any?' He gulped – this gulping thing was contagious, apparently – and said, 'Like I said, I have a certain idea of how it should play out, but if you have ideas of your own, I'd love to hear them.'

'Okay, how about this. How about we make the *ending* a *beginning*.'

'Um, exactly what does that mean?'

'It means that maybe the boy shouldn't exactly get the girl at the end.'

'No?'

'No. The audience should have the theater knowing that the girl likes the boy – she likes him *a lot* – but before she can completely let herself fall for the guy, she'll need to figure out why she's so hesitant to fall for him in the first place.'

'Oh. That's an . . . *interesting* way to end it, I guess. In some ways, that's not very satisfying, but I suppose you have to take what you can get.'

'No, no, no, that's not the ending – that's just what the audience is supposed to feel. The actual last shot could be the boy and the girl scrunched at a corner table at a coffee shop, maybe a Starbucks, just looking at each other for a few seconds. Then the boy could lean over the table and give the girl the lightest possible kiss on the lips. Then the credits could roll. That way, the audience will know the girl is finally gonna get over herself. They don't know exactly what'll happen to the boy and the girl, but they know it'll probably be pretty great.'

He nodded. 'That's not a bad ending at all. I kind of like that, actually. Leaves a lot to the imagination. And I think the guy that's directing this thing has a *very* good imagination.' Then Travis Bradford just looked at me for a few seconds, leaned over the table, and gave me the lightest possible kiss on the lips.

Finally. The right kissable boy.

He cleared his throat, then, his voice massively cracking, said, 'Yeah, I like that ending. A lot.'

I cleared my throat, then, my voice also massively cracking, said, 'Yeah. It's not a bad ending at all.'

Roll credits.

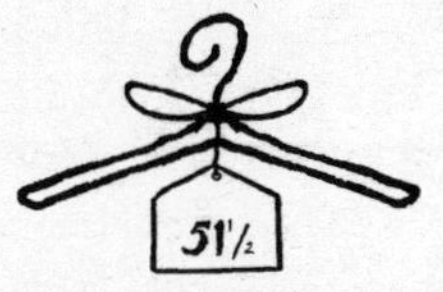

My Calm Assessment of the Travis Situation

'I love boys.'

Epilogue, Part 1

[The 'Where Are They Now' Portion of Our Program]

Travis loves those movies where, while the credits are rolling, they tell you what all the characters are up to – he cited *Animal House* as his favorite example. I don't care for that sort of thing, myself, but he insisted I do it here:

MITCH BUSEY, Mr Éclat himself, finally acknowledged that he's not as young as he used to be, so the new musicians on the Éclat roster are the kind of musicians he listens to in his own time, i.e., torch balladeers and jazz instrumentalists. Not for nothin', but most of the new Éclat artists are female, twentysomething, and hot. He still calls everybody 'Babe'.

I heard through the grapevine that right after our dust-up, **SEYMOUR SIMON** took some time away from the music industry. Simon – who, by the way, earned a ton of money from our album – moved to an infinitesimally small island in the South Pacific for about six months. When he returned to the States, he went right back to work, and, as you probably know, produced a record for a certain Irish alternative band that sold over six million records worldwide. Not that I care, or anything.

BONNIE GRAHAM got fed up slinging java, and made a killing when she sold Beaned to three coffee-addicted dot.com bajillionaire chicks. She and her husband moved to Austin, Texas, partly because, as she explained, 'It's too hot in Texas to even consider drinking coffee, and I swear if I see, or smell, or taste another cup of coffee in my lifetime, I am going to hurt somebody. Badly.' She also told me that since she retired, her sex life has never been better. I told her that that was too much information, thank you very much.

TORI HOLT, BELINDA DAVIES, AND ERICA EINSTEIN made a bajillion dollars with their web design firm called – you guessed it – Intrepid-3 Dot Com. Then they took a chunk of their fortune and bought out their favorite coffee shop, Beaned, which they turned into the coolest Internet/coffee café in the history of mankind.

AARON GIBSON is still our tour manager. It bears mentioning that he grew his hair out. It also bears mentioning that he looked much better without it. It also bears mentioning that no matter how hard I grill Jenn, she still refuses to tell me whether she and Gib slept together. But it doesn't really make much difference now, because Jenn is in love with . . .

KEVIN McALLISTER. The sane half of The Hoohah Johnson Experience has proven himself to be a phenomenal boyfriend. He's all about roses, and candy, and mix CDs, and 'just because' gifts. Plus he's ripped, and it's fun to watch him walk around the apartment shirtless. At least it is for Jenn and I. Travis, not so much.

As for **THE HOOHAH JOHNSON EXPERIENCE**, things stayed status quo with them in the sense that there's *never* any status quo with them. To wit, that means they got tired of being a jam band, and since they toured with us, they've twice changed their name, and musical style, and record label. But Jenn's boyfriend is so dazed by love, that he doesn't care about **WHITE KEVIN'S** inability to make a decision.

The amazing **SARA ROGERS** directed each of our next three videos, and will direct each and every one of our videos for as long as we keep making videos. She also recently finished her first feature film, which starred [Overly Skinny Indie Film Chick], [Hot Older Character-Actor Guy Whose Name Everybody Always Forgets], [Ageless Rock Star's Super Cute Daughter], and [Seventies-Era Sitcom Star In The Midst Of A Remarkable Comeback]. Her and her girlfriend adopted a gorgeous baby boy.

No idea what **TONY DOUCHEBAG ESPOSITO** is up to. Hopefully it involves lots of dental tools and no Novocain.

ERNST AND OTTO repaired **THE BRA** a few months after that magical night at the Tweeter Center. I haven't had any contact with the Buestenhalter Gesellschaft wonder twins since then. The Bra, on the other hand, remains part of the Naomi package.

Tired of the travel, **MARNIE LAKE** shockingly walked away from the music biz. Even more shockingly, she got a nine-to-five gig as a make-up artist for the local NBC affiliate. Even *more* shockingly, she loves it. She still listens to ungodly amounts of music – she now owns twelve, count 'em, *twelve* iPods, ten of which are filled to overflowing – and she still gives excellent massages, and she still alphabetizes her perfume.

Drummer extraordinaire **FRANK CRAFT** left our group just before we hit the studio for our second record. Like the rest of us, he'd earned a heap of money from our little project, and he used his mini-fortune to buy himself *a chance*. A chance, that is, to make it as a full-time jazz drummer. He's not quite there yet, but he plays regularly around town. Jenn and I check him out as often as we can. It's fun to go see him, because we never get recognized in jazz clubs – most jazz fans don't listen to our sort of music – and we love to go places where we don't get recognized. Thanks to Frank's departure, our drum chair is a revolving door. We've been through three different guys since he left, and while all of them were excellent, none of them were Frank.

TRAVIS BRADFORD is my baby. What can I say? I love that movie-quoting, bass-playing goofball. He chased me and he got me, thus demonstrating excellent taste in women.

NAOMI – not Naomi the *person*, Naomi the *group* – recorded its second album for Éclat Records, which was called *Naomi Too*. Both Jenn and I hated the name, but Mitch loved it – it was his idea, so of course he loved it. The best things, to me, about that album were that we produced it ourselves, and it featured a song that I wrote the lyrics for. Granted, my lyrics weren't particularly good – they paled alongside Jenn's miniature pop opuses – but I was still way proud. *Naomi Too* went double platinum, so Jenn, as promised, bought herself a Ferrari. And a Porsche. She's still working on the mansion.

And as for Jenn and me . . .

Epilogue, Part 2

A One-Act Play Starring Naomi & Jenn

The scene: our heroine Naomi stands nervously backstage at Irving Plaza, a dumpy-but-hip-and-happening club in the Greenwich Village section of Manhattan, eagerly awaiting the start of the performance. Her pre-show jitters are as bad as they've ever been, so she's shoving down Double Stuf Oreo after Double Stuf Oreo. Call time is three minutes away. Naomi's partner Jenn sneaks up behind her and gooses her breast while biting her neck.

NAOMI: Hey, cut it out!
JENN: Oh, quiet, you. You love it. You love being kissed and mauled by Bradfords of all shapes, sizes and genders.
NAOMI [*blushing*]: Can't some things be a little private?
JENN: Hey, how do you think I feel, having to listen to you two jerks go at it every night?
NAOMI [*blushing even more*]: My bedroom is, like, a mile away from yours. You can't possibly hear us. Can you?
JENN: Hells no, I can't. And if I could, I'd shove cotton in my ears and hide in the closet under a pile of sweaters. You think I wanna hear my best friend and my baby brother going at it? Yuck.
NAOMI [*almost to herself*]: Maybe we should start staying at Travis's place.

JENN: Oh, shut up. His place is disgusting. Our place rocks. I can't hear you guys. Let it go.
NAOMI: Okay. [*She takes a deep breath*] I've officially let it go. So are you nervous?
JENN: Me? Nah.
NAOMI: I am. I'm freaking out.
JENN: How can you possibly be freaking out? You've performed in front of a hundred thousand people at the Glastonbury Festival – two years in a row, for that matter.
NAOMI: The second time was way better than the first, wasn't it?
JENN: Hells yeah, it was. You've also been on *Saturday Night Live*, *The Tonight Show*, *The Late Show*, *MTV Spring Break*, *Top Of The Pops*, and some TV show in Japan I couldn't pronounce if you put a gun to my head.
NAOMI: It's pretty fun being on television, isn't it?
JENN: Hells yeah, it is. Not only that, but we performed on the Grammy Awards – where, if I remember correctly, our little group won not one, not two, but *three* Grammies.
NAOMI: The one Grammy we kept looks pretty great on our mantle, doesn't it?
JENN: Hells yeah, it does. The ones we gave our parents look pretty great on their respective mantles, too. So taking all that into account, I ask you again: how can you possibly be nervous?
NAOMI: Jenn, this is new. So it's kind of scary. You know?
JENN: Yeah. I do know.
NAOMI: This is like being back at Beaned. This is like being back at the Upper East. This is like being back in your bedroom.
JENN [*nodding, and smiling broadly*]: All of which were great places to be. Okay, gotta run. See ya after the show.
Jenn takes to the stage, a completely bare stage – bare, that is, except for a grand piano, a piano bench, and a single microphone. The crowd goes nuts as Jenn plops on to the

bench and, without preamble, immediately tears into the opening tune of her self-titled debut solo album, an album, it so happens, that Naomi produced. Naomi watches the show from the wings, awed as always by her partner's astounding piano playing, her clever, quirky, and distinctly non-commercial compositions, and her ever-improving voice. Seventy minutes and two encores later, Jenn grabs the mic and yells . . .

JENN: Ladies and gentlemen, I'd like to bring to the stage my best friend, my muse, the love of my life – actually, the love of my *brother*'s life – *NAOMI*!

The crowd goes nuts. Naomi doesn't want to go out there – after all, it's Jenn's night. She emphatically shakes her head. Over and over and over again.

JENN: Honey, if you don't get your ass out here, I'm gonna tell these nice people a little story about some fine German engineering.

Naomi sprints from the wings to center stage. After she catches her breath, Naomi and Jenn launch into a little ditty called 'And Then'. They've performed this song a bajillion times for a bajillion people, but this time, the audience – even though they're screaming and yelling and yelling and screaming – melts away, and it's just the two of them alone with their music. There's nobody else in the world.

THE END

Acknowledgements

Thanks to Hillary Goldsher, Debbie Schore and Lesley Abi Hanna, my chick posse, for their most excellent chick notes.

Thanks to the awesome Little Black Dress crew: Celine Kelly, Sarah Kellard, Jo Wheatley, Emily Furniss, Sarah Thompson and Joanna Kaliszewska. A special shout out to Claire Baldwin for her thorough and awesome *Naomi* dissection.

Mega super special thanks to editrix extraordinaire Catherine Cobain, who, in one of our earliest communiqués, told me, 'You won't regret signing with Little Black Dress. I promise I'll do right by you.' She was right on both counts.

And finally, mega-mega super-super special-special thanks to Natty Boo. Without your love, support and insight *The True Naomi Story* might well have turned into *The Sorta Kinda True But Could've Been Truer Naomi Story*. Ex, oh, ex, oh, heart, smiley face.

Pick up a *little black dress* – it's a girl thing.

978 0 7553 3533 6

ACCIDENTALLY ENGAGED
Mary Carter
PB £4.99

Clair Ivars' flair for reading tarot cards deserts her when predicting her own future, and somehow she finds herself accidentally engaged to a stranger. What else have the cards forgotten to mention?

Mary Carter's crazily romantic novel will ensure you'll never dare doubt a fortune-teller again...

I TAKE THIS MAN
Valerie Frankel
PB £4.99

When Penny Bracket is jilted at the altar by Bram Shiraz, her mother decides to help out by locking him up in the attic. And Penny has some serious questions for her fugitive groom . . .

'Glib and funny, Frankel's always wickedly entertaining' *People* magazine

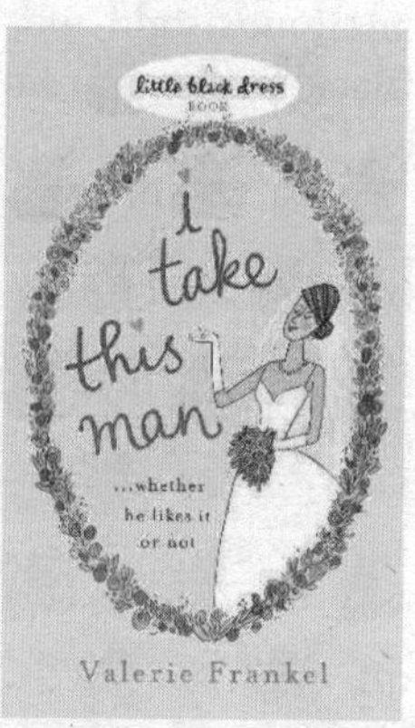

978 0 7553 3675 3